KILL THE WITCH

KILL THE WITCH

Judith Cook

HEADLINE

First published in 1999
by HEADLINE BOOK PUBLISHING

10 9 8 7 6 5 4 3 2 1

British Library Cataloguing in Publication Data

Cook, Judith, 1933–
Kill the witch
1. Detective and mystery stories
I. Title
823.9'14 [F]

ISBN 0 7472 2312 2

Typeset by Avon Dataset Ltd, Bidford-on-Avon, Warks

Printed and bound in Great Britain by
Clays Ltd, St Ives plc

HEADLINE BOOK PUBLISHING
A division of Hodder Headline PLC
338 Euston Road
London NW1 3BH

To Jill and James of the Queen's Head,
Pinner – the Crown Inn of this book.

Acknowledgements

In the book ...

Acknowledgements

To the late Dr A. L. Rowse for drawing my attention to the real Dr Simon Forman with his edited *Casebooks*. Other sources used include the play *The Witch of Edmonton* by Dekker, Ford and Rowley (a sixteenth-century drama documentary!); *The Wonderful Discovery of Elizabeth Sawyer, a Witch, late of Edmonton* by Henry Goodcole, Minister of the Word of God and her constant visitor in the Gaol of Newgate (1621); *Dr John Hall and his Patients*, ed. Joan Lane (Shakespeare Birthplace Trust, 1996), *Culpeper's Complete Herbal* and *Walks Around Pinner* (The Pinner Association).

Prologue

The young couple stood together looking out over the gently rolling parkland. The sun had not yet burned away the mist and it still lay in pools in the hollows. Under the trees, red deer were grazing: a tranquil scene.

'You're quite certain?' he asked her.

She nodded. 'Last month I was unsure but now . . . oh!' Her eyes filled and she began to cry.

Her lover put his arm round her and hugged her to him. 'Come now, dry your eyes – there's no need for tears. It's not as if we're not already promised to each other. At worst there will be a little talk hereabouts but it will soon pass.'

'So you *will* wed me?'

'Of course,' he soothed. 'After all, I've no wish to stand at the church altar in a white sheet holding a candle for three weeks labelled as a seducer or, worse still, pay the price of the yokel who will not acknowledge his child, by spending a similar period in the stocks,' he continued with an attempt at humour. 'I remember young Jack Daws some years back having to sit there with a notice around his neck proclaiming *Jack Daws has got Alys Brent with child*. It brought about a speedy wedding – especially when her three brothers intervened!'

'You're making a joke of it,' she complained.

'Not at all. I was merely trying to cheer you. I love you and we'll wed. What more can I say?'

1

She sighed with relief. 'What shall we do, then? How soon will it be?'

'Leave all to me,' he replied. 'There will be arrangements to be made, of course, if we are to marry in Pinner. I must see to the calling of the banns.' He put his finger under her chin and lifted her face up to his. 'Now,' he told her, 'let me see you smile again. All will be well, I promise you. And now I'll ride over to my father and tell him the news.' He snatched up his hat. 'I'd best say where I'm going, then you can come out and bid me farewell.'

A little while later she watched from the gate as he rode away then turned, almost colliding with the dark-haired man who had come quietly up behind her. She made as if to avoid him but he caught her by the arm. 'So,' he said, 'the outcome is satisfactory, I take it? He came to me just now to say he was off to see his father on what he described as "a delicate matter".' He laughed. 'I took much pleasure in persuading him to tell me what it was about. You should have heard me when he confessed, it would have amused you greatly.

' "I'm so sorry for bringing this upon her", he bleated, to which I responded, sternly, that he should have thought of that before being swayed by his unruly lust! I then demanded what he, as a gentleman, intended to do to make amends to a young maid much approved for her modest life and who he had now put in so shameful a position – under my roof as well, and this a decent household.'

She pulled away from him and rubbed her arm. 'Very well then, we are to wed. He didn't cavil at it – indeed, he seems quite happy.'

The man smiled broadly. 'Well, that would seem to settle that. It is by far the best solution. He did not question but that the child is his?'

'It's not fair, it's not right,' she burst out. 'He's a good and simple young man who loves me dearly. And will he still believe me when the child's born? He thinks me but

2

two months forward, when I know I was already with child when he first took me to bed. What will he say when the child is born so early?'

'Many are, and not all of them small and weakly. I've every confidence in your being able to carry it off. And afterwards . . .' He picked up a tress of her hair and coiled it round his finger. 'Afterwards all will be as before. I always thought you a clever wench and now have no doubt of it, for look how easily you've beguiled him.' He caressed her breast.

She thrust him away with all her strength. 'Have you run mad? How can that possibly be? I shall be a wife soon and, I pray, a good wife too.'

'What's this?' he demanded. 'Why now so coy? I didn't force you, remember; you were willing enough.'

'Aye, and the more shame to me,' she responded, 'though I thought I loved you after a fashion. And now see how far I'm steeped in deception! No,' she continued, 'there must be no "afterwards" for you and me, no matter what we once were to each other.'

He took her by the arms and shook her. 'And that is final?'

'Quite final,' she asserted.

He stepped back and gave her a cynical smile. 'Then I must come dance at your wedding. But your lover had best look to himself, for he has served his purpose. I've no intention of letting you go so lightly.'

There is a charming widow who has recently moved to Pinner and she seems not unaverse to my suit. She is pleasant and amusing, runs her household well and has plenty of common sense: an ideal physician's wife, in fact. And still young enough to bear me a child.'

'You're fortunate,' Simon responded. 'Here's to your success in wooing. I envy you.'

'Surely you aren't saying that there's no woman in the whole of London fit to be your wife,' Hugh marvelled. 'Not a single one to take your fancy?'

'Oh, there's many who take my *fancy*,' the other man assured him, 'including those female patients who brazenly offer to pay me in kind!'

'And do they?'

'Sometimes – when I'm feeling moved that way and the offer is too tempting to decline. No, Hugh, it's not that there is no woman I would wish to make my wife. There's one I love above all things, but she's already married and was when we first met.' He sighed. 'Of late we have been lovers, but that in itself provokes as many problems as it solves, for obviously it must be secret and for days I'm unable to see her at all. When we do meet,' he added, somewhat bitterly, 'it can end in tears or a falling out over the situation we find ourselves in.'

The two men continued talking over their wine for a while longer and then went out into the early autumn evening. The drizzle had stopped and a chilly wind blew upriver with the tide. Dusk was falling rapidly now and the last of the watermen were clustered round the bottom of the steps hoping for a late fare. Simon led Hugh into the warren of narrow streets which made up the Bankside, pointing out some of the landmarks as they strolled along.

'What's that?' enquired Hugh as they passed a forbidding-looking building with small, barred windows.

'The Clink gaol. We're well served for gaols here. The Counter is just over there, but that's mostly used for debtors. The building to our right now is the Bear Pit.

7

Philip Henslowe has finally become the Queen's Bearward – he's been trying for the post for years and now runs it with his leading actor, the great Edward Alleyn. Next to that, as you can see, is our famous Rose Theatre, which also belongs to Henslowe. There's to be a fine wedding some time soon, for his stepdaughter Joan and Ned Alleyn are to wed.'

'Very convenient for the actor,' remarked Hugh.

'Certainly, but it seems it's a genuine love-match. They are most fond, though the young woman is exceedingly plain and Ned Alleyn is much pursued by comely merchants' wives who fancy going to bed with Tamburlaine the Great.'

'Lucky Ned Alleyn!'

'Lucky Ned Alleyn indeed, but uncommonly for a player, he's most respectable and circumspect, and remains true to his promised bride.' The two men went over to the Rose and looked at the playbills affixed to the large oak door: they announced that the next performance would be of *Doctor Faustus*, a new play by Master Christopher Marlowe. 'Now *that* is something I think we should definitely see,' said Simon, 'for I've heard much of it from the poet himself.'

Hugh looked over his shoulder and regarded the notice. ' "The story of how Dr. Faustus, scholar and alchemist, sold his soul to the Devil",' he read out, ' "in exchange for Power and Forbidden Knowledge. See how he becomes the lover of Helen of Troy and indulges in the Seven Deadly Sins! And mark how, in the end, Satan claims his Dreadful Bargain and drags him screaming down to Hell!" Well, that certainly seems to cover everything,' he chuckled as they turned away. 'Where are we bound now?'

'To the nearby Anchor Tavern, much patronised by the players and poets, where I hope we may find my friend Tom Pope, who is a member of the company at the Rose.'

'Speaking of weddings,' said Hugh, 'if we can be in Pinner by noon on Saturday then I'm invited to one and you would certainly be welcome too. It's likely to be a lavish and boisterous affair.'

Simon's friend Tom was indeed in the Anchor, and after a pleasant hour over a quart or so of ale he invited both men back to his own house, assuring them that his longsuffering wife Jenny would be happy to find them some supper. Of all his married friends, Simon envied the Popes the most, for theirs was obviously a close and fulfilling partnership in spite of the uncertainty of Tom's chosen vocation.

The next couple of days passed busily enough. Where a patient was amenable, Hugh was interested in sitting in on Simon's consultations, and when there was a wish for a horoscope to be cast, he joined his colleague in poring over the necessary charts and documents with him to see if they agreed on the result. They also, as planned, went to the Rose to see *Doctor Faustus*. It was clear that the groundlings were unsure what to make of it at first, wordy as the play was, though they applauded the thunderclap and smoke which heralded the arrival of Mephostophilis (played by Tom Pope) through the trapdoor in the centre of the stage. However, by the time the scenes featuring Helen of Troy and the Seven Deadly Sins were reached, the crowd had settled down and they particularly enjoyed the ending when a huge Hell Mouth was revealed, belching red smoke (vigorously pumped out by stagehands), from which came a troop of small red demons, played by the apprentices, who proceeded to drag Faustus shrieking down to Hell.

'A strange piece,' commented Hugh as they stood in the pit of the theatre waiting to congratulate Tom Pope, 'though the verse was very fine indeed. Your friend Marlowe is certainly a poet of stature. But the whole was, I think, uneven.'

'And what did you think of Ned Alleyn as Faustus?'

'Also very fine, though different in style, I think, to your Richard Burbage. Your playhouses are lucky to have so many fine actors.'

9

At this point Tom appeared among a crowd of actors and came over to receive their warm congratulations. Traces of the ghastly greenish-white make-up he had worn in his role as Satan's emissary still lingered around his eyes and nose. He thanked them for their compliments, adding, 'Though I don't know if the authorities are likely to be so pleased. I understand that Marlowe's causing mutterings in high places. *Tamburlaine the Great* was well enough, but kings who lust after young men and scholar alchemists who challenge God – well, that's altogether different, especially when "peddled" to the ignorant and uneducated! Or so I've been told.'

'And you?' enquired Hugh. 'Do *you* believe in all this selling of souls and witchcraft and Black Magic?'

Tom thought for a moment. 'I think that people can persuade themselves of such things. I keep an open mind. Do you know,' he went on as they left the Rose, 'that there are already legends about the play? Folk tell each other in hushed tones that when we took it to Exeter – which we did – and played it outside the Cathedral, that when the demons came to carry Faustus off to Hell, there was one among us who was unknown to the company, a *real* demon, who frightened us so much that we ran at once into the Cathedral and spent the whole night on our knees.'

Simon laughed. 'I take it the story is somewhat exaggerated.'

Tom smiled. 'So far as I recall, the play ran late that day and we did all rush off afterwards – to the nearest tavern!'

They parted on friendly terms and the two doctors returned to Simon's house. Their plan was to leave the city the next afternoon and spend the night mid-way between London and Pinner; this would enable them to arrive at their destination refreshed and in good time for the wedding. In spite of having sworn, following a recent disastrous trip to Scotland, that he would never leave London again, Simon had found it very hard to settle back into his old life; as he had told Hugh, his frustrating

10

relationship with his mistress, Avisa Allen, was not helping matters. Her husband was suffering at present from some minor ailment which kept him at home all day, making it impossible for Avisa to visit the Bankside for any length of time without risking gossip.

As Simon came through his door, he was greeted at once by Anna who had obviously been anxiously awaiting his return. 'There's someone here to see you urgently, doctor,' she said. Behind her stood a young woman with a worn face, dressed in a red gown all the shabbier-looking for being much decorated with tarnished gold ribbons.

'Is it Robin, Emma?' asked Simon, guessing the situation.

'He really is dying this time, Simon,' she said with a break in her voice. 'I know he's said it often enough before, but this time I'm sure it's true.'

Simon turned to Hugh. 'She speaks of her lover. If you will excuse me, I must go at once even though I don't imagine there's anything I can do except possibly ease his passing. But the old rogue and I have been acquaintances for a good while.' He went into his study, returning almost at once with his bag and ushered Emma out, promising to be back as soon as he could.

He returned some hours later looking tired and depressed, and in answer to Hugh's enquiring look, shook his head. 'Poor Robin is past all human aid, and it still makes me sad even though he dug his own grave with the tools of drink and wenching and refused all advice or help. He would live his life *his* way – and now he's dying his way as well. A poet and a man of the theatre to the end, he's even staged his own deathbed! He lay there, propped on pillows, and inscribed in front of all of us a letter to his estranged wife in Norwich demanding she send money for his funeral expenses. This after having married her, run through her fortune, left her with child and never returning!

'Then he gave each of us a homily on how we should behave to avoid his fate. Kit Marlowe was there – they

11

were old drinking mates – and he had the worst of it. Robin beseeched him to turn from his evil life, his search after forbidden knowledge and witchery, ending with the spine-chilling warning he had given him once before: that he amend his life before it is too late "for little do you know how, in the end, you will be visited"! They do say dying men can prophesy. All I know is that it made me shudder.'

'What of the young woman? I must say from her appearance I took her for a whore.'

'Emma Ball? So she is, but she loves him dearly and he was quite happy to let her whore for him to keep him in funds for drink and gambling. They were estranged after she bore a son, for he refused to recognise it as his.'

'Is it?' asked Hugh.

'Oh, I think so. He looks so very much like Robin. She called the child Fortunatus – can you imagine a less appropriate name? The boy is too sickly ever to see out infancy, and his father has adamantly refused to give him his family name.'

The next morning, having dealt with his business commitments, Simon was changing his clothes preparatory to their journey to Pinner when Hugh came into his chamber. Seeing him half-undressed, he apologised but Simon beckoned him in saying he was nearly done. As he reached for a clean shirt, Hugh looked in surprise at the great scar which curled over his shoulders. 'Heavens, man, how did you come by that?' he exclaimed.

'On a visit to Scotland. I'll tell you about it over the next few days if you have time. This souvenir was given me by a Scots soldier in Edinburgh when I was trying to escape from the city, having been unjustly accused of murder.'

Hugh was astonished. 'God's Blood, Simon! And all the while I've been taking you for a simple physician like myself. Now *that* I'd certainly like to hear. Can I look at it?' He peered at the scar and ran his finger along it. 'It healed well. You had good treatment.' Then he bent over and frowned. 'But what are these tiny pinpoints along both sides of it?'

'Stitch marks,' Simon informed him. 'I was near dead from blood loss when I reached safety, and the woman of the house took needle and thread and sewed up the wound. She told me it was a practice not unknown on the Scottish Borders.'

'And was she beautiful, this lady of the house with such neat stitchery?' teased Hugh.

'She was well into her middle years, though handsome with it. There was a younger woman, however . . .' He stopped.

'I thought there might be,' smiled Hugh.

'It's not as you think,' returned Simon abruptly, 'though she was indeed fair and witty and most brave.'

'And where is she now?'

'In her grave on a wild hillside. Of that too, I will speak when time allows.'

After an overnight stay in a pleasant inn the two men were up betimes to ride the rest of the way to Pinner. When they had been travelling for half an hour or so, Hugh turned off from the main road into a ride which led through woodland, explaining that it was a short cut. 'It should be safe enough at this time of day,' he said as they rode easily, side by side, 'though it has something of a reputation for harbouring highway robbers and cutpurses. I wouldn't risk it at night.'

They had been riding for another quarter of an hour or so when angry voices could be heard from the track ahead, causing them to rein in. 'Your highway robbers, perhaps?' suggested Simon.

Hugh looked thoughtful. 'Possibly – though I doubt it. But we'd best go forward and see what's to do.'

A further five minutes brought them into a glade where the source of the noise was immediately apparent. A group of young men stood in a circle brandishing long staves

13

while facing them, with her back to a tree, was an elderly woman. Her purpose for being in the wood was obvious, for at her feet was a loose heap of sticks which she had presumably been gathering for her fire. The soft leaves and ground had muffled the sound of the horses so that the jeering youths reacted with surprise when Hugh shouted at them to leave the old woman alone.

'So it's you, is it, Cuddy Banks?' he continued, riding into the midst of them. 'I might have known. Whenever there's a to do or trouble, there you are in the forefront. Determined as ever to secure your reputation as a roaring boy, are you? What are you about now?'

The snub-nosed unappealing youth in the forefront of the group turned at this and regarded Hugh with a mutinous expression. ' "Thou shalt not suffer a witch to live". That's what the Bible says, Dr Brett, I've heard it often enough in church. And Old Mother Saxton here's a witch all right, everyone knows it.'

'And what do you say to that, Mother?' Hugh asked her quietly.

She shrugged. 'What do you want me to say? Whatever it is I won't be believed. All I was doing was gathering a few poor sticks to take home to make a fire when these curmudgeons set on me.'

'Get off with you, hag,' Banks burst out, 'or I'll make your bones rattle in your skin.' He put his arm back again, but this time Hugh was ready. Leaning down, he wrenched the stave out of the bully's hand.

'Would you strike me again?' Mother Saxton cried out. 'Well, may your bones ache, your joints cramp, and pains stretch and crack your sinews!'

This provoked an immediate noisy reaction from the youths. Cuddy Banks turned on Hugh. 'Now are you satisfied?' he demanded in an aggrieved manner. 'You heard her lay a curse on me yourself.'

Hugh dismounted and went over to him, regarding him face to face. 'I heard a terrified old woman say the first

14

thing that came into her head – and you brought that on yourself. What are you all doing here anyway?'

'We came to practise our morris,' returned one. 'Japhet there plays our hobby horse, though that's presently being repaired, but we all have with us our bells . . .'

'And a tabor and pipe,' broke in another. 'You see, there's to be a grand contest next month among the towns and villages, and we are determined to win. We wanted to practise secretly so none should know what we do.'

'Well, this is scarcely the way to go about it,' said Hugh. 'We could hear you miles away, couldn't we, Simon?' The other man nodded. 'So be off with you now,' he told them firmly. 'There are plenty of other places in the wood where you can practise in private.' Most of the young men appeared to accept this with good grace and began to pick up the bags and rings of bells they had brought with them; Cuddy alone made no move.

Looking down from his increasingly restive horse, Simon noticed a printed book of some kind lying on the ground. Intrigued, he dismounted and picked it up. 'I thought so,' he said, turning the pages. 'It's an almanac, Hugh. I'm surprised to find so fine a one in such a place.'

'It's mine,' said one of the lads, hurriedly putting his hand out for it. 'My father's the local schoolmaster and it belongs to him. He'd punish me for certain if he knew I'd taken it out of the house. I brought it here for us to see if we could discover if we might have good luck on the day of the contest.'

'When is that?' enquired Simon.

'The fifteenth of next month.' The lad opened the book at the right page and handed it back to Simon. 'Perhaps you can read its meaning better than me. See, it's full moon,' he said, peering over Simon's shoulder.

Simon laughed, handed the book to him then turned to Cuddy. 'I have little trust in such things unless other matters are taken into account, but you may do well enough. Though you know what they say about full moon

15

– "when the moon's in the full, the wit's on the wane". Best you note that – Cuddy, is it?'

Cuddy scowled. 'Who are you?'

'This is my friend and colleague Dr Simon Forman,' Hugh informed him. 'Now get along and we'll also be on our way. We've a wedding to go to at noon.'

'I'll tell my father of you,' said Cuddy, pouting like a spoiled child. 'He's well regarded, is Dad. He'll not have his son spoke to like this, doctors or no doctors. And when I tell him how that old witch cursed me, he'll see *her* off and all.' Then, realising this made little impression on his audience, he glowered, picked up his stave, brandished it once more at the old woman and loped off after his friends. Hugh and Simon watched them go, then Hugh turned to Mother Saxton.

'And you?' he asked her. 'Did they hurt you?'

She shook her head wearily. 'Nay. But they would have done, had you not come by, sir.'

'Have they grounds for accusing you of witchcraft?'

'I make up potions from herbs though not for harm, live on my own, have more wit than most, though you might not think it, and look as I do – a wall eye and a withered arm. I'm shunned and hated like a sickness.'

'The eye no doubt you were born with,' remarked Simon, 'but the arm . . . May I look?' Mother Saxton held it out towards him and he took it gently in his hand, pulling back the sleeve. 'This is the result of some dire injury. How did it happen?'

'The man my mother called her husband at that time pushed me on the fire when I didn't bring him his broth fast enough. I was but eight. There was no money for an apothecary and they bound it up as best they could, and when it healed it was as you see.'

'No doubt the sinews were damaged beyond aid, but a poultice of hound's tongue would have helped. Even now such a one made from burdock might ease it, don't you think, Hugh?' His friend agreed, adding that if she cared

16

to visit him the next day he would show her how to make up such a thing, then she would be able to do it for herself; after this he remounted his horse, calling to Simon to do likewise. They must be on their way if they were to reach Pinner before noon.

'Take your bundle of wood and go home, Mother Saxton,' he said to her, 'and come to me tomorrow. I'll see no harm befalls you.'

At that they rode briskly away down the ride. Mother Saxton watched until they disappeared out of sight then turned to go, but after a few paces she stopped, still convulsed with fury against Cuddy Banks and his friends. 'Why not?' she muttered to herself. 'Why not? I've heard the old wives tell of those who conjure up familiars in the shape of ferrets and weasels, owls and black cats – though by what means I know not.' Once again she began walking away. 'Vexation, shame, ruin light on them all! Satan damn them to Hell!'

It was at this point that the black dog appeared. It was an unprepossessing-looking animal, its bones sticking out from its dull fur. On seeing Mother Saxton it stopped in its tracks, looked at her, then came across and of a sudden licked her hand.

'Bless me!' she exclaimed, somewhat taken aback. 'Has my cursing raised you?' The dog whined and rubbed its head against her. The woman regarded it thoughtfully. 'Are you indeed some emissary come from the Devil to catch my soul?' The dog whined again and looked up at her out of soulful brown eyes.

'Well,' said Mother Saxton, 'whatever you are and wherever you're from, you're welcome to come home with me.' She smiled suddenly as an idea came to her. ' 'Tis all one to be a witch as to be counted one! Since they cry me as a witch then a witch they shall have.'

17

Chapter 2

Wedding Day

Simon and Hugh rode into Pinner a little before half-past eleven and went at once to Hugh's house, a handsome timbered dwelling next to an inn and near to a fine, square-towered church, the gate of which was decorated with love knots of white and yellow ribbon. A small crowd was already gathering outside the main church door.

The two men received refreshment from Hugh's elderly housekeeper then made themselves presentable for the wedding.

'Whose is the marriage?' Simon asked as they were about to set off.

'It's between a local couple, Harry Thornton and Susan Carter – a somewhat sudden affair, arranged in haste.'

Simon smiled broadly. 'Such a thing is hardly unknown when both bride and bridegroom are young and lusty!'

Hugh looked thoughtful. 'That might well be the case, and she certainly gives every appearance of doting on him, but . . .'

'But what?'

'Well, it had long been expected hereabouts that she'd marry Guy Somerton, a local man of good substance. They were very close and there's no doubt it would've been the better match. Young Harry's a nice enough young fellow, and years back the family were the most important in the neighbourhood – they still live at the Manor – but his father is now no more than an impoverished squire whereas Somerton has both land *and* wealth. Harry even had to take a post elsewhere for some time to earn his bread.

'As to the girl, her father's a well-to-do farmer and she'll bring Harry a substantial dowry; indeed, it may be the saving of old Adam Thornton, for it's said he's up to his ears in debt. Even the roof of the Manor leaks!'

'If what you say is true, then one would have thought her father would have chosen the wealthier suitor for her,' returned Simon.

Hugh agreed but added that the couple's fathers had been lifelong friends, 'And I can only suppose that, combined with the lure of an old name, brought about the decision.'

'Not to mention the fact that if our original surmise is correct, he would have had little choice in the matter. It makes one wonder if young Harry had some encouragement to pick the cherry! And if, as you say, she seems to dote on her young bridegroom, no doubt she didn't take much persuading to anticipate matters.'

By the time they reached the church, people were already going in and as they did so the bride's procession arrived, walking alongside an open carriage which was decked with ribbons and flowers, even the horse wearing a garland. The two doctors stood and watched her father hand the bride down. Obviously no expense had been spared, for Susan Carter wore an elaborate gown of pale yellow silk, richly embroidered with sprays of flowers and seed pearls, stretched over a substantial farthingale which could either have demonstrated her father's wealth or concealed what might be thought better hidden; possibly both. Her long, light-brown hair hung down almost to her waist and was crowned with a wreath of flowers.

She was certainly a pretty girl, Simon reflected, but with the kind of youthful bloom that soon fades with time and childbearing. Stepping down behind her was another young woman with stronger features, darker hair, but with a pronounced resemblance. 'Her sister Phillipa,' Hugh informed Simon. 'She's a year or so older but not yet affianced – and has much the greater wit of the two. I've sometimes thought she secretly favoured Guy Somerton. Well, perhaps after all she may be in luck. Certainly a match there would be a happy outcome.'

They went inside the church and found themselves a place near the back from which they had a good view of the congregation and all the comings and goings. Simon took this opportunity to observe the groom. Harry Thornton was also well dressed for the occasion, looking handsome in a dark-blue velvet doublet, much slashed, and decorated with more of the white and yellow love knots. He stood quietly chatting to his companions who, from the looks on their faces and his reaction, were subjecting him to no little raillery.

'That's Somerton over there,' whispered Hugh, motioning towards a tall man standing at the side of the church near to the front. The spurned lover was somewhat older than Harry and his friends, and most personable – or would have been, had his expression not been one of discontent and irritation. There were certainly many undercurrents here, thought Simon, but before he could dwell on this the bride came into church on her father's arm and the ceremony began.

The vows and rings were exchanged, the blessing pronounced and a group of musicians in the gallery struck up a lively air on their viols and flutes as the newly married couple came down through the church to the congratulations of their friends and families. 'What happens now?' asked Simon.

'We go to the Manor for feasting and dancing,' said Hugh. 'It's not worth riding there for it is only on the outskirts of the town and within easy walking distance, back along the lane on which we came into town this morning.'

Outside the church gate the congregation had been

joined by interested onlookers; bride and groom were having trouble making their way through the crowd to their carriage as first one, then another, pressed forward to wish them well. Two more carts had arrived, also decorated for the occasion, to take the groom's men and bride's maids to the Manor while a more sober vehicle waited near by for Harry and Susan's widowed fathers.

It was then that there came the sound of a vehicle being driven in no small haste, and around the corner came a cart pulled by a panting horse whose hoofs clattered noisily on the cobbles. The driver reined in, and Simon saw that beside him sat the young man who had dropped the almanac in the woods.

'Welcome, sluggard,' called out one of the groom's men. 'Did you forget to rise this morning?'

'Yes, Jack, where were you?' demanded an older man, pushing his way through the crowd. 'Am I to be shamed before all the town because my own son forgot where he should be this day?'

The young man leapt down from the box. 'No, Father, I did not forget, but perhaps it was foolish to have spent time practising the morris in the wood, although I thought I had plenty of time. Indeed, I was just on my way back with my companions when we found a man lying beside the path. He'd obviously been set on, for he was far gone with knife-wounds. While we wondered what was best to do, most fortunately this carter came by. The poor wounded fellow lies even now in the cart, and I came with the carter to guide him to the doctor's house, though I fear there's little hope.'

There was a buzz of noisy conversation as both Hugh and Simon made their way to the cart, one worthy intoning that it was time and more those cut-throats were brought to book. 'Aye, and hanged at the crossroads for all to see as a lesson to any such evildoers,' concurred another, wagging his head sagely.

Hugh climbed into the back of the cart, motioning

22

Simon to join him. Both bent over the man lying there. Blood oozed from the back of his head, and the soaked straw told its own tale. Hugh knelt down and gently lifted the man's head, and it was soon clear that he had received a great blow across the base of the skull from some heavy weapon such as a cudgel. Grazes across his knuckles argued that he had tried to fight off his aggressor or aggressors when first attacked. Even as Hugh shook his head at Simon to show the case was hopeless, the man gave a sigh, almost as if he were about to awake, then died.

'There's nothing to be done here,' said Hugh, rising to his feet. 'Can someone show this good carter where the man can decently be laid until tomorrow?' He and Simon got down from the cart and Simon gave the driver a coin for his trouble. It was then that a girl's voice was raised in great distress: the bride was now at the forefront of the crowd, white-faced and trembling.

'It's a bad omen,' she cried. 'Surely it will bring us all ill luck?' She looked at Hugh and shrieked: 'See! He has blood on his hands.'

Hugh looked down and saw that she was right. 'I'm sorry, but it comes only from tending the poor fellow. I'll return home at once and wash before we join you for the wedding feast.' He smiled reassuringly at the tearful young woman. 'I'm sorry you've been subjected to this, Susan, but it is an unfortunate mischance, no more, and you mustn't let it spoil your happiness. There is no bad omen in this. There are cut-throats and thieves abroad every day of the year, and this unlucky traveller merely happened to be waylaid by some such.' Then he turned to Harry. 'It would surely be best if you take your bride away now and prepare for the festivities. Meanwhile perhaps some of your guests will take a look at the victim and see if they recognise him. He means nothing to me, but then I've only lived here these last four years.'

Several men including the schoolmaster came forward, shouldering aside the usual ghouls who love to gawp at such things, and the victim was soon identified as a distant cousin of the bridegroom who lived some miles away and had a small farm. 'The poor soul must have been on his way to the wedding,' said the schoolmaster, 'possibly even bearing a gift which might well have been why he was set on.'

'And also for his purse,' added another grimly. 'For see, the strings of it are still fixed to his belt.'

The schoolmaster sighed. 'Time was when you could have sent a child or a man with a bag of gold in safety through the woods, but now there are so many masterless men, sturdy beggars and discharged soldiers abroad that nowhere is safe any longer. Here, Jack,' he called to his son, 'go with the carter to the inn yard and see if they will take the body in an outhouse until tomorrow. I agree you had good reason for being late, my boy, but you and I will speak later of why you were from home in the first place. You know my views on the pagan morris, not to mention that scoundrel, Cuddy Banks. He was an ill-behaved brat at school – and he has changed not a jot since he left!'

It was many hours later and, after much feasting, the large room was being cleared for the dancing which would go on until it was time to prepare bride and groom for the nuptial chamber. There had been plenty of good food and unlimited wine and ale – paid for, so Simon had been informed, by Saul Carter, the bride's father, who had agreed that the Manor, in spite of its obviously rundown appearance, was a more suitable place for such an event than his farm.

Simon, pleasantly uninvolved with the throng of family and guests, and mellowed by wine, sat in a corner where he could observe all that was going on. He was pleased to see that the bride had overcome her earlier fright, for she looked flushed and happy, and was chatting animatedly to the girls who had attended her. Strangely, it was the groom who seemed more distracted. Several times Simon noticed him gazing unseeingly into the distance as if he were oblivious to what was being said to him. Well, he reflected, if Harry Thornton was having second thoughts it was too late now.

Simon was joined shortly afterwards by young Jack, who offered to replenish his wine cup. When he returned with the brimming beaker Simon commented on the morning's misfortune.

'Aye, my father will have much to say to me tomorrow, I fear. You heard his views on the subject of the morris and Cuddy. But it is true, we were on our way home. We'd somewhat lost heart for practice after . . . after the business with Mother Saxton and anyway, I was expected at the church.'

'So you were all together when you found the dying man?'

'All of us but Cuddy.'

Simon was startled. 'But I saw him follow after you myself.'

Jack shrugged. 'Well, we never saw him again. We assumed he must have gone straight home to complain to his father as he had threatened. He doesn't take kindly to chiding.' They chatted a while longer but then the musicians struck up a lively air and Jack left to solicit the hand of one of the bride's maids.

Hugh, meanwhile, was talking privately with the widow on whom, he had told Simon, he had designs. A comely woman of about the same age as Avisa Allen, Mistress Jessica Morrell had a sprightly turn of conversation. It certainly had the makings of a match, Simon thought. He sighed and for the hundredth time wondered why he, always so susceptible to the charms of women, had set his heart on someone who, unless death intervened, would be forever unobtainable except for snatched meetings and the rare night.

Considering this, his eyes roamed around the room as the dancers took their places. Given the pick of the young women present – which, alas, he did not have – he decided the bride's sister, Phillipa, would offer the most sport. The young woman in question, aware that she was being watched, looked across and gave him a broad and provocative smile. Time passed and the fashionable galliards and more formal measures gave place to the old country dances which proved so enticing that even Simon found himself wanting to join in. Seeing that Phillipa was for once standing alone, he went over and asked her if she would dance with him.

'I'm surprised a fine London physician like you feels brave enough to venture to try our barbarous country capers,' she commented as 'Strip the Willow' was announced.

'I grew up with them,' he told her, 'and make no secret of the fact that I'm but a poor farm labourer's son from a village near to Salisbury. How I came to be where I am and by what means is another matter.'

She gave him a lively look. 'Then perhaps you will tell me of it sometime.' They joined the line of dancers and for the next half hour, Simon had no time to think or talk as dance followed dance until Phillipa was claimed by someone else. It was a very long time since he had taken to the floor in such a fashion and, mopping his brow, he went in search of refreshment.

Almost all but the old or infirm had now joined the dance – even Hugh and his widow, who showed a pretty ankle in green clocked stockings when her skirt spun out around her. But from an open doorway behind him, Simon heard the sound of raised voices and turning in that direction, he noticed that the bride had withdrawn into a small side chamber and was deep in heated conversation with Guy Somerton. Unable to quell his interest, Simon stepped quietly to one side in the shadows from where he could see without being seen. The altercation was obviously coming to an end, for Susan kept looking anxiously over her shoulder to see if they were being overheard.

'Look, Guy, all this is quite useless,' she said, as if to end the matter. 'I am now married to Harry at my own wish, and that is final. Whatever was once between us is in the past. You must know that.'

'All I know, Susan, is that you were as good as promised to *me*, which is why . . .' He stopped short. 'I never thought this marriage to be more than one of convenience.'

'Even if that were so – and it is not, for I truly love Harry – I told you weeks ago and will say it again now: I will not break my marriage vows and put myself, body and soul, in such jeopardy and wonder that you can even hint at such a thing.'

He took her by the arms, his face contorted with emotion. 'I will not let you go. I can't, I won't!'

She pulled away from him. 'I must go back to the dance. To my *husband*.'

'Very well then,' he said, stepping back, 'but I give you fair warning. You'll both rue the day.'

It was an unpleasant little scene and Simon did not wonder the bride looked distressed when she passed close by to him. However, after pausing a moment to compose herself, she straightened her gown, tidied her hair and went over to her husband to hang on his arm with every appearance of a doting bride. Somerton, after standing looking after her a few minutes, strode out of the room, crossed the floor to where Saul Carter was sitting with Adam Thornton, made his farewells and left the party, banging the door behind him. If anyone noticed, no comment was made.

Finally it was time to see bride and groom to bed. First the girls disappeared with Susan, then, after a little while, the young men with Harry. Watching Susan's departure Simon had to admit that if she had already anticipated the pleasures to come, then she was making a very good show of maidenly modesty. Women were such excellent deceivers!

Once in the bridal chamber the girls unlaced Susan's

27

silk gown and removed her stays and farthingale. Then
came the petticoats, one trimmed with fine lace. Susan sat
on the side of the bed in her shift and yellow silk stockings,
then she untied the garter with the rosette from one leg
and stood up on the bed.

'Who'll be the next bride?' she called out. Hands shot
up in the air as she tossed the garter high. There was a
scramble for it from which Phillipa emerged the victor, to
cries that it was unfair!

'Not at all,' she announced, stowing it carefully away in
the bosom of her gown, 'for am I not the oldest of all of
you? Already the good wives are warning me of permanent
spinsterhood and so leading apes in Hell.'

Susan sat down again and removed her stockings, and
one of the girls combed out her hair. Then suddenly she
clutched her sister's hand. 'Surely you're not feared of
what's to come?' asked Phillipa. Susan said nothing. 'There
are many here would envy you the coming night's sport.
Go to it and make a fine boy!'

A noisy chorus of song and the determined sound of
feet came along the landing as the groom's party arrived
at the bedroom door, which was flung open to many bawdy
jests. Harry, looking somewhat sheepish, stood among
them, a loose gown over his nightshirt. Ceremonially, his
friends marched him into the room and all watched as he
took his place on the bed beside his bride.

'Get off with you now,' he said. 'God's Breath, will you
leave us in peace!'

'You're sure you don't want any help or advice?'
enquired one wag.

Harry picked up a pillow and hurled it at him. Slowly,
amid much laughter, the young men and women departed.
Once he was sure they had all gone, Harry went over to
the door and firmly bolted it against any joker who might
have further designs on their privacy.

Downstairs in the room below, clearing up had begun
and the guests were leaving. Hugh was saying a tender

farewell to the widow who had offered him and Simon a place in her carriage, but they declined as both felt a walk in the fresh air would help clear their heads.

There were a number of people with the same idea and they all chatted together as they made their way back into the town. Simon found himself beside the schoolmaster, whose name he had learned was Andrew Page.

Andrew and his son were still arguing about Jack's involvement in the coming morris dance contest, his father's view being that it was pagan nonsense best forgotten in these enlightened times. 'They say it comes from the Moors – the Moriscos,' he grumbled to Simon, 'which speaks for itself. Where in Ovid or the Greeks do you hear of such a pastime for young men?'

'But we are told both Romans and Greeks danced, and surely they were pagans too?'

'What is one to do, Dr Forman?' asked the schoolmaster. 'I try my best to instil into them some notions of logic and the new science, and what do I get for my pains? My own son jaunting off to the wood to dance in a circle to twangling bells and the banging of staves on the very day he should have been at the altar steps with young Harry! Not to mention the fact that he is shortly bound for the Inns of Court to train for the law and so should be at his books.'

'Your son explained to me this morning that they were rehearsing for a contest,' replied Simon, without thinking, 'when we came across him and his friends in the woods.'

The schoolmaster stopped. 'This morning? You met Jack this morning?'

'Dr Brett and I were riding through the wood when we came on . . .' he stopped suddenly, wondering what best to say next. 'When we came upon a group of young men in dispute with an elderly woman.'

'Old Mother Saxton,' Jack put in shamefacedly. 'You know, they say she's a witch.'

By this time they had almost reached the town and

Hugh had halted, waiting for Simon. 'What dispute?' Page enquired.

'She was gathering firewood and Cuddy told her she was stealing it, and then she cursed us and the next thing we were all shouting at her and—'

'And we heard them bellowing from down the ride,' broke in Hugh, who had come over to see what was detaining Simon, 'and there was Mother Saxton with her back against a tree surrounded by a mob of young men waving staves at her. I don't wonder she cursed them!'

'Rehearsing the morris, was it?' Page said testily. 'Ten or so of you against one old woman? That's mighty courageous.'

'But Cuddy says she's a notorious witch. His father's told him how she rides through the sky on her broomstick of a night, holds covens in the depths of the woods, turns milk sour and makes cattle fail and has signed away her soul to the Devil.'

'Old Man Banks has all the wit of a flea,' grunted Page on hearing this. He yawned. 'Enough, enough, I'm for my bed and a good night's sleep.' He grinned slyly. 'Which is more than can be said for the bride and groom.'

In the nuptial bedroom under the eaves of the old Manor, the light from the full moon streamed into the bedroom making a silver pathway across the dark, wooden floor. Susan, her long hair tumbling over the pillow, slept soundly, her breathing regular and even. It might be thought that Harry, having taken his pleasure, would have slept likewise. But he lay wakeful, looking up at the ceiling, an expression of deep misgiving on his face.

Chapter 3

The Way Through the Wood

Simon was awoken the next morning by the clatter of a horseman galloping up to the door of the house, followed by a loud banging on the knocker. Next came the murmur of voices then the footsteps of the housekeeper running up the stairs to knock on Hugh's bedroom door. For a little while Simon continued to doze but as the noise from below became more insistent he stretched, yawned, pulled on his clothes and went downstairs to see what it was all about.

He found his friend already booted and spurred standing by the back door, a hunk of bread in his hand, as his groom saddled his horse. 'I'm sorry you've been disturbed, Simon,' he said by way of greeting, 'and also that I have to leave you.'

Simon's gaze took in the horseman standing impatiently outside in the lane. 'I take it you've been called to a patient and that it's a matter of urgency?'

Hugh sighed. 'It's Sir George Rowton at the Hall in East End village. He seems to have had some kind of a seizure, not too surprising in a man of his age and weight but it comes at a bad time. His young second wife's only just come through a difficult childbirth, though she has given him a lusty son, and is, I understand, quite distraught.' The groom brought his horse to the door and Hugh strapped his bag on to it then mounted. 'Make free of my house and go where you will,' he called to Simon.

31

'With luck I should be back before too long,' and with that he galloped off down the lane beside the servant who had brought the summons.

Left to his own devices, Simon ate a leisurely breakfast then considered ways of passing the time. His mind wandered to the man who had died the previous day. No doubt often there were cutpurses and highway robbers lurking in the woods, for hadn't Hugh warned him of them as they had turned off the main road? But he kept recalling the scene with which they had been confronted the previous day, the old woman backed against a tree, the band of taunting youths and their ringleader, Cuddy Banks, who had left them supposedly to follow his mates, but who, according to young Jack, had never actually rejoined them.

A question to the housekeeper elicited the information that the man's body was lying in a disused stable behind the Crown Inn and so he took himself off there to discover what was going to happen; presumably there would be an Inquest either today or tomorrow. A young tapster told him that the 'Crowner's 'Quest' would be held the next day since there had been problems getting word to the Coroner, 'what with the wedding and all'. He was surprised when Simon asked if he might see the body, but after being assured truthfully that Simon was a physician, and untruthfully that Dr Hugh had asked him to do so (he himself having been called away), the lad took Simon through the taproom and out across the yard at the back of the premises.

'He's not been cleaned up nor nothing, since the jury'll have to see him as he is,' he said. 'Once that's done then we'll get him laid out proper. Master James, that's the landlord, sent a letter to his family yesterday afternoon asking what they wanted to do about burial, but they were from home and so it had to be left with neighbours. Dare say they'll have had the sad news by now.'

Shaking his head, the youth left Simon by the rough

wooden coffin in which the man had been laid. The body was now cold and stiff and Simon had some difficulty lifting the head to examine the main wound. It had been a brutal blow. The man was small and slight and his assailant, obviously taller, had brought his weapon down with great force actually causing a depression in the skull.

Simon peered at the wound more closely. Small pieces of leaves and twigs had stuck to the area around it, consistent with the victim having been left to lie on a woodland path; and within the actual wound itself there were minute scraps of bark. Possibly the weapon had been a piece of wood or a branch found near by rather than a proper cudgel. He took a kerchief from his pocket and carefully removed some of the fragments from both in and around the wound, unsure as to what use this might be, but thinking it might prove significant later, especially if the weapon were discovered.

Then, since there seemed nothing more to be gained, he left the outhouse and went into the taproom for a pint of ale. The inn was almost empty, for no doubt most of the honest citizens were either at their work or still recovering from the previous day's celebrations, a point he made to the landlord's wife. She agreed.

'Still, we served a great deal of ale, as well as sack and canary wine, to the wedding guests both before and after church yesterday,' she told him, 'so we can afford to have it quiet now. Would there was such a wedding every week. It must have cost Farmer Carter a pretty penny – and all to marry young Susan off to a penniless squire's son!'

'I'm told it was expected that she'd wed elsewhere,' Simon commented, interested to discover what this might provoke.

'Guy Somerton, you mean?' The landlady poured herself a glass of canary, drew up a stool and settled herself down. 'Well, indeed, so close they'd been for all of a twelvemonth, and he here near by while young Harry was away half the time on Sir Arthur Clarington's estate. It was expected the

33

banns for Susan and Somerton would be called any week, when all of a sudden she ups and says it's to be young Harry. It surprised everyone.'

'Possibly there was a reason?' Simon wondered aloud, stirring the pot.

'The oldest of all, you mean?' returned the hostess. 'Well, it's been much whispered. Indeed,' she continued, leaning towards him in a confidential manner, 'there are those who say if that's the case then it could even be that Somerton was there first . . . if you catch my meaning.'

'But surely if that was so she'd have wed *him*,' Simon pointed out, 'for it would seem he's a far better catch.'

The woman shrugged. 'Your guess is as good as mine, and only the girl herself could tell us. Young Harry's a good-looking lad and nearer her own age, and young women were ever fickle. Not to mention the fact that their fathers were boon companions in their own youth, always drinking and running after the wenches even though Adam Thornton was more or less the squire and Saul Carter a farmer with his way to make. Now things are quite the other way around. Maybe Somerton decided, after all, he didn't want her to be his wife.'

'But he seemed very unhappy about it,' Simon told her, 'and left the wedding party early and obviously in a black mood.' He did not add what he had heard pass between the discarded lover and the bride.

At that point several people came into the taproom for drink and the hostess quickly got up from her seat to greet them. 'Well,' she said to Simon over her shoulder, 'time will tell if we're right or wrong, for there are certain things which cannot be hid.'

Simon left the Crown and, still feeling restless and with time on his hands, decided to return to the wood where the attack had taken place to see if there were any traces of it. A few minutes' walk took him to its outskirts and he easily found the track which led to the Manor and beyond. However, when he reached the Manor gate he stopped short, for from then on the track went off in three different directions, two obviously used by horsemen and one a footpath. It had seemed so straightforward the previous morning when he and Hugh had ridden into Pinner, but now he was totally confused.

At that point a voice called out to him, and turning round he saw Jack Page, accompanied by a younger boy who was shutting the Manor gate behind them. From his appearance, Simon guessed the boy was Jack's younger brother – a supposition that was soon confirmed.

'Father left his tinder-box at the Manor after last night's festivities,' Jack explained, 'and the fire was left to burn itself out. When our mother returned this morning – she's been away for a few days helping our sister with her firstborn – she was furious. Trust men, she said, to carouse the night away while all goes amiss in the kitchen! Paul and I were despatched to fetch it for her as quickly as possible. So what brings you here, Dr Forman?'

'I thought I'd try to find the place where that poor fellow was set upon yesterday, but now I'm here, I've no idea which way to go.'

'That's easily put right.' Jack gave his brother a friendly pat. 'You run off home now, Paul, and give Mother the flint and tinder, and I'll show Dr Forman where the attack took place. Tell her I'll be back by noon.' The lad pulled a face but set off towards home at a brisk trot.

'Please don't stay on my account if you're wanted at home,' Simon told the young man.

He grinned. 'I'm only too happy to have an excuse to stay away. By the time I get back, Mother will have calmed down, the kitchen fire will be alight and she'll have a good dinner cooking over it. Now, it's this way.' They walked on together in companionable silence for about half a mile until they came to a place where the track narrowed. To their left was a clump of bushes or small trees which would obviously give excellent cover for footpads. 'It was about here, I think,' said Jack, going a little ahead. 'Yes,

35

see? Here are the marks of the cart's wheels – and this was where we found him.' He got down on one knee. 'Look, you can still see blood.'

Simon bent down and looked. The tracks of the cart and the feet of the band of lads who had found the wounded man had not only churned up the damp ground but had left a confusing set of footprints, many of which overlaid each other. After trying to make sense of it, he stood up and went over to investigate the thicket. Yes, there was a clear set of footprints coming into it from the far side and then continuing through it onto the track. In one place, however, the footprints were side by side and deeper.

'It looks as if someone stood here for a while,' he said, pointing to the marks, 'so possibly this is where the attacker lurked.'

'But that would make it only the one,' Jack objected. 'Surely there must have been more of them? Two at least – one holding a knife, which the man tried to fight off, and another who came up behind and clubbed him.'

Simon nodded. It certainly seemed the most likely explanation. His mind turned briefly to the disappearing Cuddy Banks. 'And you're certain you saw nothing of your friend Cuddy, after you left us?'

'No. I've told you all I know. We expected him to join us but he didn't. It wasn't all that surprising. He likes to play Jack-the-Lad and doesn't take kindly to being told off in front of others.' He paused. 'Surely you don't think *Cuddy* had a hand in this? All right, so he's loud-mouthed, too ready with his fists, thinks himself cock of the walk and enjoys frightening old ladies, but footpad robbery? Never! Why would he need to? His father and mother indulge him in everything; he always has money enough to spend freely. I only wish I'd half as much.'

Simon was not entirely convinced, but decided not to press the point. He spent a further few minutes fruitlessly searching for the murder weapon, but without success.

Leaves were now falling steadily off the trees and it could be hidden anywhere; most likely it had been thrown away on the other side of the wood. It was time to return home.

'We can go back to the town another way,' Jack informed him. 'We continue on this path until it bears left and leads us to the road.' Once they were safely back on the road Jack soon reverted to his favourite topic of the moment, the coming competition between morris dancers. 'And we've also been asked to perform for Sir Arthur Clarington next month when he comes to his house close by.'

The name Clarington rang a bell. Surely, thought Simon, he had heard it mentioned only very recently. Yes, that was it – the landlady of the Crown had said young Thornton had spent time away on the Clarington estate, but she had spoken as if it were some way away, a point he made to Jack.

'Oh, that's his main residence,' Jack explained, 'over towards Ware in Hertfordshire. But he has a smaller estate with a good house near by which came to him from his mother, though this is the first time for two or three years that he's chosen to visit it. I think that was how he met Harry and offered him the post of some kind of secretary but now, of course, he has no more need to work elsewhere, thanks to Susan Carter's dowry.'

The wood was rapidly thinning out now; Simon noticed smoke rising a little way to their right and soon saw the cause of it. Set back off the road on the very outskirts of the wood was a dilapidated cottage. Smoke rose sluggishly from a hole in a roof which badly needed rethatching. Indeed, the whole place was in a poor state of repair, its only window open to the elements, without even shutters. The front door was also open, hanging askew on its hinges.

'That's old Mother Saxton's cottage,' Jack informed Simon, 'if you can give it such a name. It's more like a barn for cattle, or a pigsty!' It certainly looked uninviting and they were about to turn and follow the road when the old woman herself appeared from somewhere within, accompanied by an unprepossessing-looking black dog.

'Come to ask me for a spell, have you, gentlemen?' she mocked. 'Then come nearer. See, I now have my very own familiar.'

'It's best you don't describe it in such terms,' Simon replied levelly, 'for you'll only provide fuel for those who would seek to make you out a witch.'

She came closer to them, screwing up her good eye. 'You're the doctor from London, aren't you?' she said to Simon. 'You who rode with the other doctor yesterday and recommended me to use hound's tongue salve on my arm.' Her gaze switched to Jack. 'And you're the school-master's son. Oh yes, I recognised you among your friends yesterday. It seems you've learned few lessons in courtesy and good behaviour from that Latin-spouting father of yours.' Then she laid her good hand on Simon's arm. 'Do you cast horoscopes, doctor?'

'I do,' said Simon, somewhat disconcerted. Surely the old crone wasn't going to ask him to cast hers?

She obviously read his mind. 'Never fret. I've no money for fancy pieces of paper and book-learning stuff, but for all that I know many things about many people, some of which they'd rather I did not! I keep my ear to the ground and can see things clearly even if one eye is amiss. And sometimes I can see the future without need of charts, round mirrors or playing cards. Let me tell you something of yours, doctor.'

Simon shivered. 'The last time a woman did that it worked out badly for both of us.' In her case fatally, he added to himself.

Mother Saxton nodded. 'She died, didn't she? Young and at the hands of evil men. I see violent deeds in your past for they still haunt your future.'

It was uncanny. 'That's true,' he replied, with increasing unease.

'As to the future,' the old woman continued, 'your path should be easier at least for a while though you carry within yourself that which will never really let you rest.'

'Do you see a fine wench in his life?' Jack broke in, emboldened by her attitude towards Simon.

'Don't mock, young man,' she returned, 'for what I tell is true.' She looked thoughtfully again at Simon. 'You will never have the woman you want so it's best you accept that now, for it was never meant. Though you may find love by chance one day.'

'Why are you telling me all this?' asked Simon.

'Because you were good to me yesterday when this lackwit and his friends set on me. I owe you a favour and I always repay my debts, all of them and of any kind,' she added significantly.

'Are you *really* a witch?' asked the lad, greatly daring.

'You seemed sure of it yesterday,' returned the old woman, 'and see, within minutes of your leaving me, this black dog arrived. What would you say if I told you he'd come from Satan to claim my soul for him?' Jack stepped back at this awful thought. 'So tell me, boy,' she continued, 'what is said of me in the town?'

'That you can put on curses, cause cattle to fall sick, abort children and fly through the air of a night on your broomstick to attend witches' sabbaths.' He looked askance at the dog. '*Is* he then your familiar?'

The old woman laughed. 'Maybe, maybe not.'

The answer did nothing to reassure the young man. 'We must make haste, Dr Forman,' he said quickly, 'for my mother'll be waiting dinner.'

'Dr Forman, is it?' Mother Saxton considered this. 'I'll remember that. One more thing, doctor. I see death here in the wood – violent death.'

'Then you are too late with your warning,' Jack broke in, 'for a man was set on and killed by robbers yesterday not long after we left you. You probably knew that already, so it needs no witch to tell us that.'

'Oh yes, I knew of *that* man's death, but it's not that of which I speak. There is death still to come. Death and treachery and betrayal. You had a wedding in the town yesterday, did you not? Well then. Love and lust *and* treachery, betrayal and death. Remember. I told you so.' And with that she retired into her cottage.

They walked briskly along the road towards Pinner, for though the sun still shone, the air seemed to have gone chill. 'Do you believe old Mother Saxton's really and truly a witch, sir?' Jack asked as they reached the lane which ran back into town. 'You seemed to find some truth in what she told you.'

'What do we mean when we say someone is a witch?' Simon replied. 'These days, almost any old woman living alone, especially if she's as ugly as that one, soon acquires such a reputation, and if the treatment she receives is the kind I saw yesterday then one can hardly blame her for playing up to it. No doubt gullible young men and women come to her for love potions, others to have her charm their warts away, and when matters go awry in the neighbourhood, cattle sicken or children fail to thrive then it's easier to blame it on a witch than to look for other, more sensible causes. Though having said that, I must tell you that I believe there are things, evil things, with which we should not meddle.'

'And what of her foretelling of violent death in the wood? Is that, too, merely mischief?'

Simon looked thoughtful. 'There are those who have what some call the second sight. Indeed, I have reason to . . .' He shook himself. 'But it doesn't mean witchcraft is involved.'

Some ten minutes later they heard the sound of a trotting horse on the road behind them, and as it came nearer they stepped aside to let it pass. As he saw them, the rider reined in his mount and, after bidding them both good-day, asked if they could direct him to the home of Harry Thornton. He had been led to believe that Harry lived near by.

'He does indeed,' Jack told him, 'and if you continue

along the way we are on now and turn right when you come to the outskirts of the town, you'll find yourself at the gates of the old Manor.'

'Then while I'm so near, have you any objection if I walk my horse and have some company on the road?' Without more ado the young man swung himself easily down from his horse. 'Francis Wynfred, at your service, sirs,' he said, and took off his hat and bowed, revealing a head of neatly cut thick black hair. The eyes he raised to them were grey and widely spaced; altogether he was a good-looking young fellow.

'I am Dr Simon Forman and this is my young friend, Jack Page,' returned Simon courteously.

'Then we are well met, sirs,' returned Wynfred. His voice was exceptionally sweet and pleasant, so much so that Simon wondered if he might be an actor, though the sober cut of his doublet and its dark colour did not suggest a member of the profession; however he voiced the suggestion to his new companion.

Wynfred laughed. 'When I was a young lad, every time one of the acting companies came to town I thought it might be fine to be a player and strut the stage, but I soon grew out of it – and anyway, my family had other ideas for me.' Looking at the fine-featured face so close to his, Simon was struck by its pallor and it occurred to him that Wynfred might be recovering from a recent illness. Suddenly aware of Simon's gaze upon him, the youth flushed slightly.

'I must beg your pardon for staring at you so,' said Simon. 'I'm a doctor, and I suppose I see everything through the eyes of a physician. I thought, possibly wrongly, that you looked as if you might have experienced sickness of late. Forgive me, it is in a doctor's nature always to diagnose!'

Wynfred looked momentarily grave. 'You have a shrewd eye, Dr Forman, for I have indeed been sick, of the bowel flux, though I am now more or less restored to health.'

'A very debilitating disease,' Simon nodded, 'and will lay waste any of us. What did your doctor prescribe for you?'

Wynfred hesitated, obviously casting his mind back. 'Celandine, mixed with white of egg – I think,' he added cautiously, 'but an old wife dosed me and I could be mistaken. Oh, and I'd a plaster to my stomach made from feverfew and some other herb.'

Simon was surprised. 'You were not given the fluxweed with comfrey to take, then? Or, my own preference, hartshorn burnt, then distilled in white wine?'

The young man shook his head. 'I might well have been but I felt so sick, I cared only that it might make me feel better.'

A few minutes later they came to the place where a path led off to their right. Jack stopped and pointed the way to the Manor. 'It will take you barely five minutes on horseback,' he said, then a thought struck him. 'Heavens! Did you come for the wedding? If so, you are out of luck for it was yesterday.'

Wynfred looked puzzled. 'Wedding? What wedding?'

'Why, Harry Thornton's, of course.'

The news had an immediate effect for Wynfred looked startled and turned, if anything, even paler. 'No,' he replied, obviously shaken, 'I knew nothing of any wedding. Harry never sent word to me.'

'Well, it was rather sudden, so much so that they say—'

Simon nudged Jack, giving him a meaningful look. 'I'm a stranger in Pinner, here at the invitation of a colleague,' he said smoothly, 'but I understand arrangements for the marriage were made in some haste, and no doubt that's why some of those who should have been told were not – and you among them. You are then a friend of Thornton?'

Wynfred nodded. 'A close one, or so I thought. We were both in the service of Sir Arthur Clarington near Ware,' he explained, thus raising the name for the third time that day. 'Harry was his secretary and I was also in his service. Harry left some five months back, I think, but I had already gone some time before, which is possibly why the invitation went astray – for I'm sure he would have told me of so important an event in his life and invited me to dance at his wedding.' He paused. 'Perhaps it's best I not call on him so soon after his wedding day.'

'Nonsense!' exclaimed Jack. 'If you are good friends and also worked together then I'm sure Harry will be delighted to welcome you to the Manor, and no doubt will be mortified you were not invited to the festivities. The young couple are to live at the Manor,' he continued cheerfully, 'and they say the bride's dowry came not a moment too soon to put new glass into the windows!' Wynfred smiled and the three shook hands before he remounted his horse and, with a friendly wave, set off towards the Manor.

'He seems a handsome, well set-up young fellow,' commented Jack as they watched him go.

'Yes,' Simon agreed thoughtfully. 'Very pleasant and well spoken. Somewhat surprised, though, that his friend hadn't told him of his marriage.'

'Well, you heard what he said – both he and Harry left Clarington's employ months ago, so it would be easy enough for a letter to go astray. Harry may not even have known his new direction.' Simon nodded. Surely that was the explanation for it, but he wondered why he was left with a feeling of doubt.

Harry and his new bride were at dinner with his father when a servant came in and informed the company that there was a young gentlemen outside claiming he was a friend of Master Harry's and asking if he could see him. Harry told her to go and fetch him. 'I imagine it must be some old friend come to wish us well,' he told Susan, 'and if that's the case then he must dine with us.'

A minute or so later the servant returned bringing

Francis Wynfred with her. Harry looked up. He had just taken a mouthful of soup and appeared to swallow the wrong way for he choked and coughed until his eyes streamed and his wife thumped him on the back.

Susan smiled at Wynfred. 'You'd best come in and sit down while Harry gets his breath back. Have you dined yet?' Wynfred shook his head. 'Then you're most welcome to sit with us and share our dinner.' Harry, who had finally stopped coughing, looked across at Wynfred with blurred vision. 'Aren't you going to greet our guest,' demanded Susan, 'and introduce him to me?'

'Francis Wynfred, mistress,' said Wynfred, taking off his hat and bowing, 'and I will gladly accept your invitation to dinner.' He sat himself down at table opposite Harry, after having shaken hands first with his father, then leant across the table. 'So,' he said, 'you are full of surprises, Harry. I hear I'm to wish you joy.'

Harry still stared as if he could not believe his eyes. 'Yes,' he managed finally, 'we were married but yesterday. This is my bride, Susan.'

'Then let me wish you both all that you would wish yourselves,' declared Wynfred. 'But I must take issue with you on one thing, Harry. Why didn't you send your good friend word of your wedding? But perhaps you did and it went astray? Was that the case?'

Harry stammered that it must have been, 'For I'm sure I did send to inform you of it.' He continued to stare at Wynfred. 'Yes,' he said in a low voice, 'that must have been what happened. My letter went astray.'

Chapter 4

Plague

Simon returned to Hugh's house to find his colleague had arrived only minutes before him. He looked tired and strained.

'How is the patient?' asked Simon.

'As well as can be expected following so severe an apoplexy. At least he's still alive, though I fear he may have lost some of the use of the limbs on his left side. I've bled him and got him to drink an infusion of fox-glove leaves with honey to quieten the heart and cleanse the body of ill humours, and have left with his wife a distillation of the flowers of lily-of-the-valley in white wine to strengthen the brain. After that it is in the hands of God. I've told the household that I must be sent for at once should there be any change.'

As they sat over their dinner Hugh gave Simon more details of his patient's condition. 'Are you going to cast a horoscope to discover its outcome?' Simon enquired at the end of it.

Hugh shook his head. 'Since his wife has not asked for it, then I think it better not.'

The housekeeper came and removed their dinner plates, setting down a bowl of fruit and a wooden platter on which was a good piece of cheese. 'What would you prescribe for the flux?' asked Simon as he cut himself a slice.

Hugh looked surprised. 'Why, burnt hartshorn for preference, surely?'

45

'So I would say, with or without some use of the fluxweed,' Simon agreed. 'So what would you say to celandine in white of egg and a compress for the belly of feverfew and comfrey?'

'That it was most odd. Have you had it recommended to you then?'

'Not recommended but apparently proposed as a cure,' Simon replied, and told Hugh of his meeting with Francis Wynfred and how the young man had come to Pinner in search of his friend, Harry Thornton. 'As we spoke I thought he looked overly pale,' he explained, 'and somewhat impertinently queried if he'd been ill; he said he'd but recently suffered from the flux. When I asked what he had taken for it, his reply was celandine in egg-white and the application of a compress.'

'Perhaps it was prescribed for him by some mere hedge physician,' shrugged Hugh. 'Did he say where he came from?'

'Not as of now, though he said that previously he'd been in service with Harry on Sir Arthur Clarington's Ware estate. He seemed no little surprised and put out when young Jack Page told him he'd missed Harry's wedding by a day, especially as he professed the closest of friendships.'

'Well, you know what young lads are like. Fast friends from childhood while they steal apples and go birds' nesting, then, as youths they ride together, drink together, visit the taverns and playhouses, eye the girls and swear eternal friendship until one or other of them sees a young maid trip across a room or gazes into the depths of a pair of blue eyes and is lost to all but the object of his desire. Then friendship, I fear, is likely to fly out of the window!'

Simon agreed. 'I don't imagine these two knew each other as lads but they must have been much thrown into each other's company, both away from home and serving together on a large estate miles from anywhere. Perhaps Harry thought that if he spoke too much of Mistress Susan's beauty he might fire Francis Wynfred to go and see the lady for himself and even supplant him in her favour. It has been known.'

'What was he like then?'

'Very personable – quite handsome, in fact. Well spoken too, so much so that I thought he might be an actor.'

'And is he?'

'Apparently not. He said that, like many another, each time a company of players came to town he thought it would be a grand notion to join them, but that common sense and family wishes had prevailed. An interesting young fellow though.'

'Well, no doubt we'll hear more of him, local gossip being what it is,' said Hugh and the subject was dropped.

The next two or three days passed pleasantly enough and the two men parted at the end of it, happy to have renewed their friendship and with promises of meeting again in the near future. As Simon set off back to London he had mixed feelings. He was grateful his patients had not deserted him during his sojourn in Scotland and he was kept busy, yet his life seemed lacking in substance. He wondered, with increasing frustration, if Avisa would ever be sufficiently free from the bonds of domesticity to spend much time with him. He had been so carried away by her response when he had returned from the Border country that it had taken a while for him to realise fully that in all but one way the situation was unchanged. Yes, she had finally come to his bed, but failing the death of her husband and her thus becoming a widow, there seemed little more he could hope for. Old Mother Saxton had been uncannily accurate.

When he reached the northern outskirts of the city he became aware first of one bell tolling, then another, and as he rode over London Bridge yet a third began to ring out from nearby St Mary Overy. Automatically he started counting them, for they announced a death; nine taylors for a man, thirty for his age: he wondered if he knew him.

Then, looking over towards the Rose Theatre he saw the flag was no longer flying, which meant there were no performances. He was soon to know the reason why, for seeing several notices pasted on walls, he dismounted on reaching the south side of the Bridge in order to read one. He discovered that it was an official decree, informing everyone that from now until further notice all playhouses, bear pits and other places of public amusement were to close owing to the growing prevalence of the Plague.

So now he was likely to be busy, he thought grimly, not least because it was widely known that some years earlier he had caught the Plague and yet survived it. Indeed, he owed his unwanted reputation as a necromancer to that fact for, argued the credulous, how was it he had survived death when so many of the good and virtuous had not? People who regularly attended church and turned from drink and fornication, little innocent children with their lives before them; God had taken so many such to Himself. Had he struck some deadly bargain with Satan – his soul in exchange for a cure? Simon sighed. No wonder Kit Marlowe's *Doctor Faustus* had proved so popular and that country simpletons believed every old limping woman to be a witch!

Later that evening, over supper with the Bradedges, he caught up with what had been happening while he was away. Apparently there had been a sudden upsurge in cases of Plague almost within hours of his leaving home, and panic was soon sweeping along both sides of the river, Bankside and City. A host of people had come to the house asking for him, and no doubt they would be back once word got around that he was home. Hardly had he voiced this to John and Anna, when there was a loud knock at the door. Simon motioned Anna to remain where she was and went and opened it himself, his heart sinking at what the summons might mean. But it was only his actor friend, Tom Pope.

'God send you don't come with news of sickness,' Simon said as he ushered him in.

'Heaven forfend! We are all of us fit and well, but no doubt you've heard that the playhouses have been closed; hardly surprising in the circumstances. No, I came to see you before leaving for Oxford. I'm taking Jenny and the children to her father for a few weeks until we see how matters progress. I know Plague doesn't halt at the city boundaries but so far there are few cases further north, so I'm told. As for us, Philip Henslowe won't allow the Lord Admiral's Men to be idle, of course, so once again we're off on tour – without the problems that so beset us last time, I sincerely hope, and for which we had to call on your services!'

Simon took him through to the kitchen and Tom joined them at table for a tankard of ale. He had come, he said, to give Simon this information and to ask him if he would kindly keep an eye on their small house near by. Neighbours would do the same, but he felt it wise to tell as many people as possible since on previous occasions when folk had fled the city during outbreaks of pestilence, there had been instances of villains, realising that a house had been temporarily abandoned, moving in and making themselves at home.

'I suppose you're inundated with people wanting you to prescribe against the sickness?' he asked, having had his say.

Simon explained that he had been out of town for a few days, but now that he was home, that would inevitably be the case. 'It is always the way. They hope against hope I can offer them a miraculous preventative or magical medicine which, of course, I can't and nor can anyone else unless they're coney-catchers or whoreson rogues looking to profit from the misfortune of others.'

'There are already plenty of those abroad,' said John Bradedge. 'Every cheapjack on the street corner is offering nostrums of some kind.'

'Not to mention more blatant cheats,' added Tom, with a laugh, 'for I came on one, Simon Kellaway, selling small scrolls tied with red ribbon which he advertised as *A Defensative Against the Plague* and was selling for a shilling a time. One of the simpler members of our company who was with me insisted on buying one. He opened it up, only to find there was nothing inside except two words written in Latin which he couldn't understand so he asked me to read them for him.'

'And what were they?'

'Fugi loci!'

Simon smiled. 'Flee the place! Well, I suppose that's as good a piece of advice as any for those who are able to do so, but it seems somewhat rich to charge people a shilling for it.'

'Do you think it unsafe then for children to remain here?' asked Anna, anxiously looking at the ceiling above which her son, small Simon, was fast asleep.

Simon shook his head. 'I truly don't know, Anna. Let's see how it develops. Last year at this time, the Plague raged for only a short while. Yet we must take all possible precautions. Make sure any coins you are given by shop-keepers or stallholders have been put into vinegar first, keep from crowded places, even church – I'll pay your fine for you if necessary. And sit outside in the garden with the child when the weather's warm enough.'

'So tell me, Simon,' enquired Tom, 'how *did* you survive the Plague? I've yet to be persuaded the Black Arts were involved!'

'Certainly not, though possibly good luck and the Good Lord were involved. No, quite simply I treated myself as I had others who survived it. As you must know, Plague comes in two guises, the black and the red. The black is under the sign of Saturn, the red under that of Mars, especially when he is in Leo or Sagittarius. Both produce the boils under the armpits or on the groin, though those of Saturn are long in rising and seldom break. I've often lanced them or cut them whereupon they release only a little matter but much water. Those of Mars fast come to a head and often break of their own accord, and you must always be careful about dressing these as they are most dangerous and infective.

'Most of those who suffer from the black Plague die for there's no real remedy. But for those who are taken with the red Plague, there's hope if you lance the boils quickly enough and with a clean instrument. Also, though, as I've often told you, I rarely advise bleeding, I do so moderately in this case for it helps purge the body of poisons.

'So that is what I did when I realised first that I'd caught the pestilence and then that it was of the red variety. Fortunately, all the boils were in the groin so I was able to lance them, after which I bled myself. I'll tell you now I felt so ill I was convinced my time had come and prayed long and hard to my Maker!

'The day after that I crawled out of my bed and called from the window to a passing lad, threw some coins down and asked if he would go to the apothecary for me, doing my best the while to look as if nothing was amiss. I asked him to fetch dried hops and various herbs and flowers peculiar to the sign of Venus (who, you know, held Mars in thrall), and also to pick me fresh nettles. When he returned I bade him leave them at my back door for me since I'd sprained my ankle and had difficulty getting up and downstairs. Then I dosed myself with a nettle posset, syrup of hops in honey and white wine, and many other things and, as you see, here I am. Though it took me weeks, if not months, to recover fully.'

Tom shuddered. 'God save us, man, you make me feel ill thinking of it.' He stood up and thanked them for the ale. 'And now I'll get home to Jenny and help her pack. Her father's sending a carrier and he should be with us by first light tomorrow morning. I'll go and see them safely settled before rejoining the company.'

Simon slept only fitfully that night, thinking uneasily of

51

Avisa. Although a merchant's wife she had no small skill in the distillation of herbs and it was commonplace for friends and neighbours to ask her for help. No doubt they were now pressing her for help to ward off the Plague and if that were the case, then might she not be at greater risk than most of catching it from one or other of them? It made him feel cold to think of it. At first light he wrote her a letter (which could be read by any who might see it), asking after her husband, if he were now recovered, and expressing his hopes that both he and she were doing all in their power to avoid the pestilence; immediately after breakfast he sent John Bradedge over the river to deliver it.

Hardly had he risen from table when the first of the morning's patients arrived. Master Matthew Pym owned several properties on the Bankside as well as a substantial tavern on the other side of the Thames almost opposite Simon's house. He sat down heavily on the chair provided for him, reached into one of his capacious pockets, and brought out a heavy purse which he dropped down in front of Simon. Simon raised an enquiring eyebrow.

'For you,' Master Pym informed him.

'I don't understand,' Simon replied.

'I want two things. First a guard against the pestilence, no matter what it costs; secondly, in case it does not prove effective, a cure.'

Simon pushed the bag back across his desk. 'Then you have come to the wrong man,' he said, 'for neither I nor any other physician can offer you a sure guard against Plague. Nor, as you must know, can I give you physic to ensure you survive it no matter how much you might pay me. I cannot play God.'

Master Pym looked taken aback. 'There are thirty crowns in there.'

'If there were three hundred, I still couldn't promise what you ask. You are welcome to find out what other doctors have to tell you, though I fear if they take your money it will be under false pretences.'

'Then what shall I do?' quavered Pym.

'Keep from crowded places; carry a pomander or ask the apothecary to make you up a packet of herbs that your wife – I take it you have a wife? – can sew into kerchiefs for you all to put to your noses when you go abroad; buy from those who put their coins in vinegar; and pray to God to keep you safe. And for that,' he added, standing up to show the consultation was at an end, 'you may pay me two shillings!'

Pym drew himself to his feet, grabbed the money bag and threw down two coins. 'Call yourself a doctor?' he bellowed. 'I'll waste no more of my time with *you*! I shall go and find one who knows what he's about!'

Pym was followed by at least a dozen others, some demanding as he had done, that he tell them how to avoid the pestilence while others, suffering merely from pimples or warts, had convinced themselves that these were the dreaded buboes heralding death. To the former he gave the same advice as he had to Pym, thinking to himself ruefully that at least the apothecary would benefit from it in increased sales.

As to the latter, after assuring them that they were free of all deadly symptoms, he sold them small phials of a soothing mixture for the nerves made from marjoram, mint, sage, rosemary and honeycomb, steadfastly refusing to cast horoscopes to see if they would fall victim or not. They would know soon enough and the mere fact of being told that they were likely to succumb might well bring it on to them.

Then, towards the end of the afternoon, Anna showed Avisa in. After embracing her, Simon looked at her long and hard to assure himself she was in good health, before kissing her again. She responded with such passion that he was almost taken aback. 'How long can you stay?' he asked, with a sharp intake of breath.

'An hour, no more, but maybe . . .?'

He went at once and told Anna that he must not be disturbed for some time since he would be in his small sitting room discussing important medical matters with Mistress Allen; any patient who came asking for his services should be told to return later. John Bradedge rolled his eyes at his wife at this but said nothing until his master had disappeared.

'He must think we came down with the last shower of rain!' he said as the door closed behind Simon. 'Important business, is it? Behind-the-door business, heavy stairwork, smock lifting . . .'

'Hush,' Anna remonstrated. 'It's nothing to do with us. He's a good master and we should be glad of it.'

Later Simon and Avisa lay side by side on the day bed in the sitting room. Then she began to laugh. 'Don't you remember, my dear, how I came upon you in just such a position with that black-haired witch, Emilia? And she without shame or even her shift. Your face! And all after I'd plucked up courage to come and tell you that I loved you.'

'I remember it only too well. I thought I'd lost you for ever.'

Avisa sat up on her elbow and stroked his cheek. 'I fear you are to lose me for a while. That was one reason for my coming here.'

His heart sank. 'What do you mean? Where are you going?'

'William thinks it best that I go into Kent to stay with my mother until the worst of the pestilence is past. She sends word that so far there are no cases of it in her village, and already here it has struck two families in our own street.'

Simon saw the sense of this. 'Then you must go, my love. Maybe I can visit you?'

She smiled. 'I see no reason why not, though we will need to be discreet. My mother is no fool.'

'When do you go?'

'The day after tomorrow. I doubt if I can come again beforehand.'

A thought struck Simon. 'My servant Anna is worried for the safety of her two-year-old child, my Godson, Simon. Would it be possible, if she were agreeable, for you to take her and the little one with you for a while? That is, if your mother has room. I will pay her keep and she will do anything you ask most willingly.'

Avisa said at once that this would not be necessary since she would ensure that her mother was not out of pocket; the old lady might well find Anna's help useful since she was getting on in years. They dressed in sombre silence and he tidied the day bed while Avisa pinned up her hair. Then he went and fetched the Bradedges and told them of his plan.

'But I couldn't leave you or John,' protested Anna.

'Don't be foolish, woman,' her husband told her firmly. 'The doctor and I can manage perfectly well and it would put my mind at rest to think you and the boy were safe out of harm's way.' So, with some reluctance on Anna's part, it was agreed. Avisa would tell her husband that she was taking Anna with her to help her mother in the house. She was to have the carriage to take her into Kent and so would call for Anna and little Simon on her way.

As matters turned out, both men were glad the decision had been taken, for over the next few weeks the tally of deaths from pestilence rose relentlessly. It took rich and poor, young and old. It showed no mercy. Simon, coming grim-faced from yet another deathbed, heard from a shopkeeper that the unbelieving Master Pym had succumbed. So much for finding a doctor who knew what he was about, thought Simon.

He felt exhausted, yet still his mind raced. At the Bankside end of London Bridge he stopped and leaned on the wall close to the watersteps, taking in great gulps of clean air for the tide was running in bringing with it the smell of the sea. Over on the opposite bank, early risers were lighting their candles and lamps. Then a hand fell on his shoulder and he turned to find it was the poet from the Rose Theatre, Christopher Marlowe.

'How are you bearing up?' Simon asked him.

'How do you expect?' responded Marlowe, his face gaunt. 'I've been with Walsingham in the country for a few days only to return to find my old friend, Thomas Watson, dead of the Plague and no doubt thrown into some pit somewhere for I can find no trace of his burial. What an end for a fine poet!'

Simon thought for a moment. 'Has he not recently had some success at Court?'

Marlowe nodded. 'God's Death, to be taken now when at last he had recognition! Did you know we once went to gaol together for killing a man?'

Simon had heard rumours. 'How was that?'

'This piece of devil's trash, a drunken jolthead son of an innkeeper, came seeking Thomas in Hog Lane swearing to have his blood for some imagined slight or other and found my goodself instead. "Sodomite!" he greeted me merrily, so without more ado I drew on him and could have easily killed him myself had not poor Thomas arrived at the wrong moment, whereupon this pig's tripe turned on him and spiked him through the thigh. He drove Thomas until his back was against a wall and I had actually raised my dagger to stab the lout, when Thomas, in desperation, lunged forward and more by good luck than skill ran him through the heart.

'So the constable was sent for and we were duly put in gaol though we pleaded self-defence. I was lucky, for the Walsinghams extracted me within days, but it took longer to release Thomas, by which time his leg wound had festered. It took months to recover; in fact, he had only recently been fully restored to health. And for what? Simply to die in so disgusting a fashion.

'First Robin Greene,' he continued bleakly, 'now Watson. Who next, one asks oneself? I've been trying all night to drown my sorrows, but a pox on it, the drink no longer seems to work.'

Simon looked at him with compassion, for he and Kit Marlowe had shared much together in Scotland, and difficult and rude as he could be to both friends and enemies, as a poet Marlowe ranked with the greatest; also, when the mood took him, he could be as sparkling and witty a companion as one could wish.

'You need rest,' Simon told him gently. 'If you wish me to give you something to help you sleep then come back with me now.'

Kit shook his head. 'No, leave me to my devils. They ride me hard but I might well take you up on that later.' Dawn was now beginning to break; the smell of the sea grew even stronger but the streets remained uncannily quiet. Then they heard the sound of wooden wheels and round the corner came a cart. It was obvious what it was carrying for, from beneath the canvas that covered its burden, they could see the white arm and head of girl, her face concealed, her long red hair hanging halfway to the ground.

'Then take care of yourself,' said Simon, holding his kerchief to his nose, 'for I hope to see another Kit Marlowe play at the Rose before long.'

'I fear you will be disappointed then,' returned Marlowe, 'for try as I might, I find I cannot write.'

Day followed day with dreary similarity, Simon even going so far as to allow John to dispense simple medicines and salves he was so overwhelmed with work, then suddenly, towards the end of October, the number of dead began to fall off and while the pestilence did not go away altogether, at least it relaxed its grip.

A week later, with the daily tally now down to single figures, Anna and the child returned unexpectedly one morning to be greeted with relief by both master and man. Avisa, she told them, would follow in a week or so but as a friendly carrier had offered to give Anna a lift to

London she had happily accepted, for word had reached them that matters were much improved.

'She gave me this letter for you, doctor,' she finished, then looked round at the state of her usually immaculate house. 'I shall want water,' she told her husband, 'a great deal of it. And a big new scrubbing brush.' Peering into her kitchen she looked in awe at the mountain of dirty platters, cups and tankards. 'Have you washed *anything* in the last few weeks?' she demanded. But she said it with a smile and, sending the little boy out to play in the garden, she at once kilted up her skirts and set to work.

Simon went into his study and opened Avisa's letter:

Dear heart, he read, *I hoped and prayed you might have been able to visit me in Kent but, hearing the news from London, I realised what you must be about. Though we don't share a faith, believe me, my dearest, I prayed to the Holy Mother every day and burned a candle with my prayers. God keep you safe and well. I hope to be home within a week.*

Simon stretched and yawned. He was tired to the bone. Then he came to a decision. He went into the yard and, taking off his shirt, sluiced himself under the pump. Then he ran upstairs and changed out of his dirty clothes, came down again, pulled on his riding boots and went through to the kitchen.

'I've worked day and night without ceasing,' he told the Bradedges, 'and now I'm away to Kent for a few days. I feel I've earned it.'

So it was that he spent three days with his love, unworried by who might see him and by the lurking presence of her husband. If her mother realised the situation she gave no sign of it, though the stealthy creak of feet along the landing in the middle of the night might well have given them away. It was an unexpected and wonderful interlude after the nightmare of the last weeks.

He rode back to London beside her carriage until they reached the Bankside where, for the sake of discretion, he left her. Anna opened the door to him and he marvelled at what she had achieved in his absence. Once again the house was swept clean and tidy, the furniture polished, a bowl of late flowers standing on the small table in the hall. Through the kitchen door he saw the light of the fire reflected in the clean plates along the dresser. All was well with his little world.

John Bradedge broke into his reverie. 'This came for you, doctor,' he said, handing him a letter. 'The day after you went into Kent.'

Simon sighed and opened it. It was from Hugh in Pinner. *I can imagine how hard pressed you must have been,* he wrote, *and hardly dare bother you but, if it is at all possible, could you come again to Pinner for I need your help. I fear they mean to kill a witch!*

Chapter 5

The Love Charm

In the event it was nearly two weeks before Simon felt able to leave London again. In the aftermath of the Plague, almost every day brought a sad procession of those who were fortunate enough to have survived but remained very weak, others worn down with nursing family members, yet more suffering from the coughs and colds of autumn and even a handful feeling optimistic enough to wish to have their horoscopes cast.

But finally, as the new cases of Plague remained steady and the numbers of the afflicted knocking on his door diminished, he sent word to Hugh that he would be with him the following day. Having done so, he decided he would like to take John Bradedge with him, not least because he too had worked so hard during the peak of the Plague weeks but, unlike himself, had taken no rest afterwards. On the other hand, though, he had been parted from Anna and his child for the best part of two months and, understandably, might not want to leave them again so soon.

However, both John and Anna were quite happy for John to go into Middlesex with his master. Anna, because she thought the country air would do her husband good, John because he was convinced his master was ever attracted to trouble like a moth to a candleflame and that therefore he should be at his side to rescue him from his own folly if need be. This was no idle whim since on at

61

least two occasions he had had to do just that.

The day was cold but fine as they rode out of London, and Simon had been pleased to see, as they crossed London Bridge, that the flag was once again flying from the flagpole of the Rose. So the actors must not only be back but giving a performance that very day. As they took the road towards Pinner, Simon wondered if he would remember Hugh's short cut through the woods which had brought about his first meeting with Old Mother Saxton, but it was easy to see the path they had taken before as so many trees had shed their leaves. Before turning off the road he warned John that the wood had a reputation for concealing footpads.

'Indeed,' he said, 'while I was in Pinner last time a poor unfortunate fellow was brought in dying from being bludgeoned about the head, having been robbed of all he had on him.'

John looked unimpressed. 'Forewarned is forearmed,' he returned, flourishing a serviceable dagger, 'and there are two of us. And it will be harder for a cutthroat to conceal himself now than it was when you came through here two months back.'

But all was peaceful and they met with no one during their passage through the wood. The glade where Simon and Hugh had come on the old woman besieged by the youths lay quiet and empty, the only noises those of birds and the odd rustle of some small animal in the dried leaves. When they reached the edge of the wood Simon paused for a moment trying to decide which was the quickest route to the town. Having made his decision, he soon discovered that he had been right, for through the now thinning hedges he could see the Thornton Manor house over on their left. Within minutes they were almost up to the gate.

A man and a woman were standing immediately outside in such deep conversation that they did not even look round at the sound of horses' hoofs. As they drew nearer

Simon recognised Susan Thornton as the woman and Guy Somerton as the man. She seemed almost to be pleading with him while he was responding with some vehemence, tapping his hand impatiently against his thigh, the while. Simon was about to call out a greeting then thought better of it. Whatever there had been between those two was obviously not yet at an end.

'When you see a tearful wench and an angry gallant, it usually means there's trouble afoot,' commented John sagely. 'Perhaps the oldest of all and she's pleading with him to make an honest woman of her. They took no more notice of us than if we had been a pair of wooden posts!'

'Certainly they seemed engrossed in their own affairs,' Simon agreed, 'but you're wrong about the rest. You remember I told you I'd been to a wedding when I was here last? Well, she was the bride but not he the bridegroom.'

'Perhaps the husband didn't live up to her expectations in the realm of bedwork then,' replied John with a broad grin.

'Gossip has it he lived up to it only too well beforehand and that she was with child when the marriage took place. The man you saw with her is an old admirer or lover depending on whom you believe. He took her preference for another very badly indeed and even at the wedding feast was full of dark threats towards the bridegroom. Perhaps she's now regretting her choice.'

Within ten minutes they were riding up the High Street towards Hugh's house, to be warmly welcomed at the door by the doctor himself. Hugh looked enquiringly at Simon at the sight of John Bradedge. Simon felt he had always looked somewhat askance at his servant with his scarred face and obvious familiarity with his master.

'You know my man, John,' he said at once, 'and how valuable he has been to me on many such occasions as this. He's also my eyes and ears very often when I'm from home, and during these last dreadful weeks he has been my right hand, helping dispense salves and simple medicines to those coming to us for aid. I thought he might be useful to us and hoped you could find him a bed.'

Hugh agreed that he could. 'One day I shall ask you about your adventures, Master Bradedge, but for now, take the horses round the back to my stable and ask my housekeeper to make ready one of the attic rooms and also give you some dinner.

'You still look tired to death,' Hugh commented, leading Simon into the house as John took the horses away. 'I suppose it's only to be expected.'

'It was very grim,' Simon agreed, 'the worst thing being, of course, that one was able to save so very few. Did you keep free of it here?'

'We were comparatively fortunate. We had only five deaths, all in a single family, and we know how it reached them. The son of the house, always a wastrel, had run off to London some years ago and was living off his wits as a pedlar of goods of doubtful provenance and, so it's rumoured, as a petty thief. He arrived at his mother's house on the run from the law and begged her to take him in which she did, only to discover he'd brought the pestilence with him. Fortunately for the rest of us they lived on the far outskirts of the town and it did not spread. But, yet again would you believe, the mere fact that there was any Plague at all was blamed on our witch.'

According to Hugh, since Simon's visit the feeling against Old Mother Saxton had continued to grow, egged on not only by young Cuddy Banks, but by his father too: 'A man with not so much brain as ear wax! From that day when we found her set upon, no cow has run dry, fowl not laid, child not thrived or bad luck befallen a neighbour but it is blamed on Lizzie Saxton.' Hugh shook his head. 'I suppose one can hardly condemn her that she now plays up to it. Half the town think that black dog of hers is her familiar and she makes no effort to disabuse them, rather the reverse. Several women claim to have seen her whistling over the rooftops on her broomstick while every miscreant from the lad who thieves apples, to the drunken fellow who beats his wife or sets about his fellows in the street, piously ascribes his behaviour to his having been bewitched! The town is running mad and I fear that if this hysteria is not curbed, within days we'll have a witchhunt.'

Simon listened sympathetically but felt somewhat at a loss. 'I see the danger of the situation, Hugh, but quite frankly don't know how I can help.'

'Two heads are surely better than one,' Hugh responded. 'I hoped you might help me to knock some sense into the population before it all gets totally out of hand.'

Simon remained unconvinced but consoled himself with the thought that Pinner was a pleasant-enough place in which to spend a few days and, as Hugh had observed, he was still exhausted from the rigours of the Plague.

That evening Hugh held a supper party to which he had invited the widow, Mistress Jessica Morrell, to whom he was now paying open court, and Andrew Page, the schoolmaster, his wife and son Jack, who was as exuberant as ever. John Bradedge, who had also been invited, declined – preferring, he told Simon, to spend a quiet and pleasant night in the Crown.

'Very well,' said Simon, 'but as usual keep your ears open. They talk of witchcraft here. Find out what it's all about.'

John, always superstitious, took a pace back. 'Witchcraft! Are you serious, doctor?'

Simon laughed. 'I'm serious that they talk of witchcraft and witchhunts. I'm not serious that the poor old crone in question is a witch.'

John looked thoughtful. 'Perhaps I should find some garlic to hang round my neck?' he suggested. 'Just to be on the safe side.'

'You'll hardly be welcomed in the taproom if you do,' his master chuckled. 'People will flee from you as soon as you set foot in it.'

The evening proved to be a pleasant one. It was obvious from the glances that passed between Hugh and Jessica that matters had moved on considerably since Simon last saw them together, and again he was aware of a feeling of envy. He was also pleased to renew his acquaintance with the Pages, for the schoolmaster had a dry wit, his wife was pleasant and young Jack, as usual, was full of beans.

'So how's the morris dancing?' asked Simon when most of the plates had been cleared and the housekeeper had brought in a dish of pieces of marchpane.

'It goes very well. We were much commended when we danced at the festival I spoke of when you were here before. We're still waiting to perform before Sir Arthur Clarington. He should have paid a visit to his estate last month but he never came.'

'That's the landowner with his major seat near Ware, is it not?' Simon asked idly. 'I also seem to remember it was where Harry Thornton was employed before his marriage, along with that other young man – now what was his name – Winfrith? Wynford? – that Jack and I met up with.' He turned to Jack. 'Do you recall him? He came seeking Thornton. A pleasant young fellow, I thought.'

Jack nodded. 'You mean Francis Wynfred? He's pleasant enough, I suppose, but keeps himself very much to himself – or at least to a select few,' he added darkly.

Simon was astonished. 'Keeps himself? Do I take it then that he's still here? He spoke only of a brief visit.'

Mistress Page leaned forward, eager to impart gossip. 'It's become something of a talking point, if not a scandal. This young man Wynfred seems to have moved in permanently with the Thorntons, for he shows no sign of leaving and has become close, very close, with —'

'Surely not with the bride!' exclaimed Simon, recalling the scene he'd observed only that morning and beginning to wonder if Susan Thornton was set to rival legend's false Cressida as a light wench.

'No, Dr Forman,' Jack broke in, hugely amused. 'With

the *bridegroom*. Thornton and Wynfred are inseparable: they go everywhere together. Susan's nose is quite put out. No wonder she looks drawn and pale.'

'Possibly there's another reason for that,' Simon suggested.

Jack shrugged. 'Nothing's been said.'

'Well, it does sound somewhat odd, but where lies the scandal?' prompted Simon.

'Because,' Mistress Page's face took on a look of great disapproval and she lowered her voice, 'because it's now being said that what's between them is unnatural.'

'God's Breath, wife,' Andrew Page exploded, 'do you think we came here to peddle housewives' gossip? Keep it for your fellow spinners when you meet together to pass the time while at your wheels.'

Simon turned to Hugh. 'What do you say?'

Hugh shrugged. 'I don't know what to think. It's scarcely usual for a young married man with a pretty wife to spend all his time with another man, even if they are old friends.'

'Perhaps,' said Jessica Morrell hesitantly, 'Harry Thornton is one of those who prefers the . . . the *company* . . . of his own sex but was persuaded to marry for the sake of the family and to keep up appearances.'

'Are there such, then?' queried Mistress Page.

'It's not unknown,' Simon told her, 'indeed it was rumoured, when I was in Scotland lately, that King James himself is such a one. But to my mind if one is that way inclined then it's better by far not to wed at all and remain a bachelor, not least for the unfortunate woman cheated into a false marriage. The great poet of the Rose Theatre, Kit Marlowe, he who wrote *Tamburlaine*, is quite open about his preference. Indeed, he publicly proclaims that all who love not boys and tobacco are fools! Unwise, maybe, but he was ever honest and would never marry for convenience either to quell gossip or for anything else.'

'I suppose it's a possibility,' Hugh agreed cautiously, 'but if that's the case then he showed no sign of it earlier.

Indeed, I'm led to understand his reputation was quite otherwise.'

'And so it was,' continued Mistress Page. 'He was one of those of whom it was said you should lock up your daughters if you wanted to keep them safe. No,' she concluded triumphantly, 'if you ask me, if he's been tempted into unnatural vice then it's because he's been bewitched.'

Andrew Page turned his eyes heavenward. 'Good Lord preserve us! Have I, after all, married a fool? This is plain superstition, Alice, egged on by troublemakers, and I can quite imagine where it started: with that fool Banks's wife and her two cronies. They look like a trio of witches themselves!'

'So what of the other players in this drama?' asked Simon. 'Her old admirer, for one?'

'It's beginning to look as if Somerton will be marrying into the Carters after all,' said Hugh, 'for he and Susan's sister Phillipa are now always in each other's company.'

'Aye, and she's worth two of the other one,' Page added. 'A very bright lass indeed. I wish I could have had her as a pupil at my school. She'd have beaten all the lads for she's a wench of much wit.'

Jack, who had been unusually silent throughout all this, suddenly began to laugh. 'Did you know Cuddy Banks is in love with Phillipa?' he announced.

This caused general mirth all round. 'Then he's doomed to disappointment,' commented Jessica, 'for even if she didn't feel fond towards Guy Somerton, which she did even when he was courting her sister, she'd never consider such a loon in a month of Sundays!'

'He says that for all her airs she's but a farmer's daughter and he's a farmer's son, so why not?' Jack continued. 'Do you know, he's even talking of buying a love potion to make him desirable in her eyes? Though where he'd get such a thing, I can't imagine. Perhaps he'll try Old Mother Saxton,' he concluded, laughing even louder at the thought.

The talk then turned to more general topics until, just before midnight, the party broke up. Andrew Page yawned. 'Come, Alice and Jack, I'm for my bed. It's school in the morning and I must be there betimes.' They left after much handshaking, suggesting a day when Simon might dine with them. Hugh, meanwhile, was putting her cloak round Jessica's shoulders.

'I'm just going to see her safely across the road,' he told Simon with a satisfied smile. 'I'll see you in the morning.'

Simon went through to the kitchen to see if he could find John Bradedge, but there was no one about. Possibly he had come in earlier and was now asleep in the attic room assigned to him. Simon slept heavily that night and dreamed, somewhat unpleasantly, that he was in the middle of a wood sitting with some who were condemned to die, whereupon he found he had suddenly acquired the ability to fly by virtue of eating large red plums off one of the trees. When the persecutors came to round up the condemned, Simon fed them all with the plums then made them all hold hands, and in a great chain they rose off the ground and flew through the sky though quite low, merely skimming the rooftops. They flew over fields, hedges and water until they were suddenly set down in an open place on a hillside. At which point he woke up.

Jack Page had not been joking when he told Hugh's guests that Cuddy Banks was determined to obtain a love charm or potion to compel Phillipa Carter to yield to his passion. Every effort he made to endear himself to the lady was met either with ridicule or annoyance, and this was not only stoking the flames of his desire but making him feel foolish as well – and this he could not bear. He'd show her! Just imagine the triumph of seeing her pleading for his love, desperate for him to bed her. Then the marriage for, after an appropriate period of time for her to consider the position she found herself in, he would grandly agree to make an honest woman of her. Pictures formed in his mind of the grand wedding in Pinner Church, conducted not only in front of all his disbelieving companions, but also of arrogant Guy Somerton, now rejected for the second time.

Thus it was that while Hugh was entertaining his guests, Cuddy set off along the lane which led to Mother Saxton's hovel. He had chosen to make his call in the early dusk when few people were abroad and he was unlikely to be recognised, but as he came nearer to the place he began to feel increasingly uneasy. There was no doubt she would recognise him as the ringleader of the youths who had attacked her and, while not prone to soul-searching, he knew that he was largely responsible for bringing about the town's current obsession with witches and witchcraft, for he had given his parents a lurid account of what had happened in the wood that day, suitably embellished to extract the last ounce of drama. Unsure therefore of Mother Saxton's attitude towards him, he had brought along some silver coins, half a cheese from the dairy and a bundle of sticks for her fire.

As he arrived outside her door he realised she must be in, for a dim light showed through a crack in the boarded window. Screwing up his courage he raised his hand and leaned forward to give a hearty knock, at which point the door suddenly opened and he almost fell over. The old woman stood there, the black dog at her side. She gave him a disparaging look out of her straight eye.

'Well,' she snapped, 'what's your business, young Banks? To hit me again? Have me whipped through the town?'

'No, no,' returned Cuddy obsequiously. 'See here. I've brought you cheese and firewood and three silver coins.'

'In recompense for what you did the last time we met?'

'No, Mother Saxton, though I *am* sorry for it,' he answered, quailing before that one-eyed stare. 'I've come on business.' The old woman said nothing. 'I've come because I must have something to make a maid love me.'

The old woman swivelled her wall eye towards

him, which was even more disconcerting, then burst out laughing. 'Love, is it? Aren't you frightened that I'll bewitch you or put a curse on you?'

'I'm already bewitched,' wailed Cuddy, 'by Phillipa Carter.'

At this Mother Saxton smiled a deeply unpleasant smile. 'I see. So you want me to help you gain your love? Tell me, why should I do that?'

This was not going at all well. 'Because,' said Cuddy desperately, 'nothing else has worked. And I have brought you payment as evidence of my good faith.'

Mother Saxton appeared to think this over then finally she nodded. 'Very well. I'll see what I can do. Do you want a charm or a potion?'

Cuddy thought hard, a slow process for him, but finally concluded that persuading Phillipa Carter actually to drink a strange potion or to find a means of putting it into her wine or water without her knowing, was likely to be beyond him. 'A charm, I think,' he managed at last.

'You'd best come in then,' the old woman replied, and led him into her dark dwelling, the dog always close at her heels. 'Sit there and don't move,' she commanded once they were inside, pointing to a stool which had lost a leg. She went over to her fire, calling the dog over as well. Then she knelt down and rocked back and forth, muttering strange words for at least ten minutes. It made the hair stand up on the back of Cuddy's neck. Finally she rose, took something from a shelf beside the fireplace which she placed carefully before the fire on a small metal plate. Next, she took some powder from a jar and threw it onto the burning embers. Immediately the fire turned bright green and gave a great roar.

'Holy Mother of God!' screeched Cuddy, reverting to the old form of appeal, falling off his unsteady stool with fright. The bright light affected his eyes so for several minutes he saw only green spots in front of them, but finally the spots cleared and through his streaming eyes he saw that all was as it had been before.

'Here, take this,' said Mother Saxton, thrusting something into his hand.

He looked down and saw what looked like a piece of blackened, twisted twig. 'Is that all?' he demanded. 'Is this it?'

' "It" is a piece of mandrake root. Take good care of it, for it is very powerful.' Then suddenly a kind of trance seemed to come on the old woman and she began to speak in a high, sing-song voice. 'The stile . . . the stile at the end of your father's peasefield on the edge of this wood. Be there at sunset on the night of the next full moon and you'll find your love there waiting for you. Approach her bravely. She may seem wantonly coy and flee thee, but follow her close and boldly. Do not fear to take her in your arms, even should she struggle, for then she will be thine!'

Then, just as quickly, she appeared to come out of it. 'Did I speak just now?' she enquired.

'Yes,' replied Cuddy, staring at her wide-eyed. 'Weren't you aware of it? You told me to be at the stile at the end of the peasefield three days from now at the next full moon when the girl would be mine!'

Mother Saxton appeared to consider this. 'That must have been my incubus speaking through me. He's never wrong.'

Cuddy strode off back home with a spring in his step, lighter by a few coins but with the piece of mandrake root secured within his shirt. Full moon was in three days. In three days' time, Phillipa would be his. Mother Saxton watched him go, scarcely able to contain her mirth. It would be quite easy, in three day's time, to terrify some passing child into going first to Phillipa Carter telling her Guy Somerton needed to see her by the peasefield stile *before* sunset as a matter of urgency, then on to Somerton to warn him that Phillipa's life was in danger if he did not reach the peasefield stile by just *after* sunset. She would just have to hope that they were not together at the time. Then, if her scheme worked, she would lurk in the shadows to watch the subsequent entertainment.

Had she really had the powers she claimed, however, she would have thought better of such a potentially disastrous plan.

Over breakfast the next morning, John Bradedge was full of tales of witchcraft which he had learned in the Crown the previous evening. 'People can talk of nothing else, doctor,' he assured Simon, 'and even you might think there's something in it, for it seems that there has been nothing but bad luck here in recent weeks. Women have miscarried, horses been stricken with the staggers, the apples in the apple-lofts rotted, the . . .'

'So I've heard – so spare me any more, please,' said Simon firmly. 'Have these good burghers also considered what *good* luck they have had of late? Only five cases of Plague, for instance? Surely if this witch is as powerful as they claim, then she must also be responsible for their good luck too.'

John gave his master an obstinate look. 'You never will be told, will you, doctor? If you don't believe me, go into the Crown yourself and listen to what people say.'

'Yes, do that, Simon,' Hugh agreed. 'I have some calls to make and when I return we'll sit and discuss how best to try to stem this tide before there is serious unrest. You might have a word with James, the landlord. He's got a sound head on his shoulders.'

'Have you had any more thoughts as to what to do?' Simon asked him.

'I'm going to arrange a meeting here of those holding some authority – the parson, the constable, Andrew Page and any other that comes to mind.'

'You mention the parson. What are his views on it?'

Hugh sighed. 'Wytherley is a vain man with a great deal of the Puritan about him. He sees himself as single-handedly stemming a tide of evil, though so far I've managed to persuade him not to preach "Thou shalt not suffer a witch to live!" from the pulpit.'

Later that morning, Simon went into the Crown as promised and, having ordered his ale and there being few folk in the taproom, asked the landlord what he made of the talk of witchcraft. James looked thoughtful. 'I don't reckon much to most of it. By the time a tale has passed through the mouths of a gaggle of silly women and a handful of want-wits, it has grown out of all proportion. But it concerns me that the old woman, Mother Saxton, is now proclaiming herself to be a witch, and warns any seeking her harm that they do so at their peril. That acts like a red rag to a bull. Now here's another pretty piece of work,' he continued, looking towards the door and dropping his voice as Harry Thornton and Francis Wynfred entered.

Simon greeted them in a friendly manner and both looked at him somewhat startled. 'My name is Forman, Dr Simon Forman. I came to your wedding, Master Thornton,' he said, 'though we hardly met. I was brought along by your doctor, Hugh Brett. And you, sir,' he continued, turning to Wynfred, 'I met at the edge of the wood the day afterwards, seeking out your friend here.' Was it his imagination or was this explanation greeted with some relief?

'Dr Forman!' Thornton responded. 'Of course – I should have recognised you.'

Simon smiled. 'There's no real reason why you should, for we'd never previously met and you must have had the best part of three score people at your wedding celebration. As for your friend, he and I met but briefly as passing travellers.'

The two young men were friendly enough, but Simon sensed that they preferred their own company and therefore took himself off to a bench in the corner, along with a treatise on the effect of the planets on certain illnesses.

74

James was called over to see to the wants of two old men sitting at the far end of the room, thus leaving Thornton and Wynfred alone. As Simon glanced over the top of his page he saw Thornton, who was standing behind Wynfred, momentarily rest his chin on his friend's dark hair – a gesture more like that of a lover than a friend. So, he thought, immediately looking away again, perhaps there is some truth in the rumour after all. Poor Susan.

A minute or so later the landlord returned. 'Fine day,' he commented. 'What can I get you gentlemen?'

'Two pints of ale please, landlord,' said Wynfred, proffering some coins.

'Take a seat then, if you like,' James said, 'and I'll bring it to you.' When he came over to where they were sitting at a small table and put two foaming tankards down in front of them, he announced: 'I've heard news that might interest you, Harry. Did you know Sir Arthur Clarington's due here in two or three days' time?'

Once again Simon peered over his book and noted that Thornton looked shaken while Wynfred had lost all his colour.

'No. No, I did not. Why should I?' Thornton managed at last.

James seemed surprised. 'But wasn't he your master for some time? Weren't you his secretary until a few months before your marriage?'

Thornton appeared to recollect himself. 'Certainly,' he replied, 'and very hard he made me work, too. But it was always understood to be a temporary arrangement, and that eventually I would come back here, so there's no particular reason why his visit should be of interest to me now. I'd heard a few weeks back that he was due to visit Pinner, but as he never came, I gave it no more thought. Do you know what brings him here? In my day he spent little or no time on this estate.'

'They say it's because of the witch,' James informed him. 'It seems some of his tenants have been sending to him to know what can be done about her. That cottage of hers is right on the boundary of his land, you know. So he's come to see the position for himself and I'm told he's bringing a magistrate down with him to question her.'

Before he could say any more, a group of travellers arrived wanting beds for the night and once more Thornton and Wynfred were left to their own devices. That end of the taproom was relatively quiet and therefore Simon, still apparently absorbed in his book, heard quite clearly what passed next.

'Two or three days!' whispered Wynfred. 'God's Breath, Harry, *what are we to do?*'

Chapter 6

Full Moon

'But sister, is it quite impossible for you to talk to Harry about it?'

Susan Thornton, her eyes full of tears, shook her head. It was the day after Cuddy Banks's visit to Old Mother Saxton, and she and Phillipa were sitting side by side in the Manor parlour.

'He either dismisses it or flies into a temper,' she replied dismally.

'But he's your husband, your new husband,' insisted Phillipa. 'He married you, even knowing that you'd once virtually been promised to Guy. Then, of a sudden, this youth appears out of nowhere and Harry dances attendance on him, morning, noon and night. Surely you realise how much talk there is in the neighbourhood?'

'So I must suppose, though little of it reaches me. What do they say then? You'd best tell me, now you've begun.'

Phillipa took a deep breath. 'That what is between your Harry and Francis Wynfred is . . . is *unnatural*. That he married you for your dowry to save this old house and the estate, but that his affections really stray towards young men. At least, that is what polite people say. Young men like Cuddy Banks and his kind put it in a cruder fashion.'

Susan's tears broke out afresh. 'Guy hinted as much when I met him by the gate the other day. He was most incensed, even going so far as to offer to demand an explanation from Harry and I'd much ado to persuade him otherwise. But I can't believe it can be so, not of Harry.' She felt for her handkerchief to mop her eyes. 'I'm sure he is as other men.'

'Then might there be some other reason for this curious friendship?' persisted Phillipa. 'Could this young man have some hold over Harry, such as a formidable debt? Or could he know something that Harry wishes to keep hidden and so forces his hospitality by threatening to tell you or his family?'

'How can that be either?' wailed Susan. 'Father paid off all Harry's debts before we wed – that was part of the marriage settlement – and surely had there been some major sum outstanding, he would have said so. As for the other, could Wynfred possibly know anything that would threaten Harry? Harry is known to everyone in Pinner. His family have lived hereabouts since before the wars of York and Lancaster. Harry was born in this house, grew up here, went to school to Master Page.'

'He was away in Hertfordshire for some good time though,' her sister reminded her, 'and it was there he met Wynfred. Perhaps something happened while he was with Sir Arthur Clarington which he is too ashamed to admit even to you or his family.'

Susan rose to her feet. 'No,' she said passionately. 'No. Even if it were true that he owed Wynfred money or feared he would reveal some hidden secret, it could not explain the affection Harry obviously feels for him. Affection which I'm sure, though most hurtful to me, is *not* unnatural, even if he does spend more time with him than with his own wife.' Her voice quavered again.

Phillipa looked at her sister, her pity mixed with exasperation. She found Harry's behaviour unforgivable and was minded to ignore Susan's feelings and tell him so in no uncertain terms. 'Well,' she said at length, 'if it persists much longer then perhaps you should let Guy speak to him.'

Susan shrugged. 'Harry would just think it the jealousy

of an old lover.' She paused. 'And how are things between you and Guy?'

Phillipa coloured slightly. 'Very well. Though I'm not sure it's what you want to hear.'

Susan sighed. 'Whatever there was between myself and Guy was lost when I fell in love with Harry. If he now prefers you, then I wish you both joy.'

Phillipa put her arm around her sister. 'I'm sorry I drove you to tears, Susie,' she said, reverting to the old name of childhood, 'but believe me, it's only out of care for you.' She stood up then added reluctantly, 'The other thing I can't understand is why he insists you tell no one of the child. Father in particular would be so delighted, as would all your friends.'

Susan looked round. 'Shush, keep your voice down! I'm not even supposed to have told *you*. Harry says it's because of the witchcraft in this place, that while a curse hangs over the town it's best to keep the matter secret as long as possible to avoid any harm to myself or the baby.'

Phillipa shook her head. 'Susan, Susan, you are so credulous! There is no curse over the town other than that conjured up by fearful and superstitious simple folk. Mother Saxton is an ugly and malicious old crone, but that is all. She's no more capable of causing you to miscarry than she has of flying the skies on a broomstick!'

She was about to elaborate on this when the door opened and Harry came in. He seemed in a good mood and smiled at the two women. If he noticed his wife's red eyes, he gave no sign of it.

'Now, Susan,' he began at once, 'what do you say to a visit to London, now that the Plague seems to have diminished? We've had no wedding journey and I thought the change might do us both good.'

Susan's face lit up. 'Oh Harry!' She jumped to her feet and went over to him. 'Do you really mean it?'

'Most certainly. We'll go to the playhouse too, since I know that's something you've long wanted to do.'

Susan looked at Phillipa, her face suddenly radiant. 'Isn't this a fine piece of news?'

'Very,' returned Phillipa dryly.

'You must take me to the silk merchant to buy cloth for at least two new gowns,' Susan told Harry. 'Perhaps we can go this very day and then I can ask Mistress Ramsay to make them up for me. She's most quick and neat and can surely do that within a fortnight or so.'

'Fortnight!' exclaimed Harry. 'My dear girl, I'm proposing we should go tomorrow.'

Susan looked astonished. 'But why so much haste? You've said nothing of such a plan before.'

There was a slight pause then Harry replied, somewhat irritably, that surely she could not have imagined they could go until they were reasonably sure the Plague had abated.

Phillipa looked at him thoughtfully. 'And Francis Wynfred?' she queried pointedly. 'Does he go too?'

'No, he does not,' snapped Harry. 'Why on earth should he?'

'Because he seems to go everywhere else with you,' Phillipa replied, unable to contain herself any longer.

'Francis is my dear, good and long-standing friend,' he told her coldly, 'and as such is welcome to my hospitality whenever he should choose to visit the Manor. He will travel with us for a short part of the way then leave us to visit another friend before returning home to Hertfordshire where his mother lives.'

Susan was so delighted at the turn of events that all thought of what had passed between her sister and herself was forgotten in anticipation of the forthcoming treat. She went over to her husband and put her arms round his neck. 'Oh Harry, I'm so excited. Come upstairs with me, Phil, and help me choose which gowns I should take to London. Oh, and Harry, I'm told Dr Forman is back in Pinner, staying with Dr Brett. Perhaps we could ask him what best to see at the playhouse?'

★　★　★

Later, much later, Simon was to see a pattern in what, at the time, appeared to be a disconnected set of events. The same morning saw him out with Hugh visiting the growing number of his patients who were convinced they had been bewitched. Yet never had there been a more disparate variety of illnesses or symptoms: headaches, pains in the gut, dropsy of the legs, quinsy, gout, the tertian fever, even constipation – all were blamed on the evil influence of Mother Saxton. The young wife, delivered of a stillborn first child, sobbed into her pillow that it was 'all along of that witch', while her husband threatened to take his cudgel to the woman.

Nor did the afflictions stop there. She had sent folk demented, the doctors were solemnly told, causing them to fall on the ground and froth at the mouth while others, hearing through rumour that a curse had been laid on them, simply took to their beds and waited to die. Hugh's assurances, fully supported by Simon's second opinion, that all the maladies could be put down to natural causes, were greeted with various degrees of disbelief.

'God's Death, Simon!' exploded Hugh as they rode home. 'Have you ever heard such a farrago? The place has run mad. For every one of those people we have seen today, there is a perfectly sensible explanation for what is wrong with them. Old Man Davy, he with the gout, has suffered from it these last ten years and will continue to do so until his dying day, unless he drinks less sack! And as for fevers, they are all too prevalent here at this time of year. It's sad poor little Betsie Miller lost her baby, but she was a long time in labour and, as you well know, it is not uncommon with a first child. She'll have others. Well, we'll see what the parson and Page have to say when we meet later today.'

They returned home, much dispirited, and were just finishing their dinner when John Bradedge knocked on the door and asked if he might have a word.

'I thought you might both like to know – if you've not heard it already – that Sir Arthur something or other is apparently due at his estate tomorrow late and is to be joined by a magistrate who is to see what Mother Saxton is up to and, if necessary, order her arrest.'

'Where did you learn this?' Hugh said, aghast.

'In the Crown. But the whole town is talking of it.'

'I must say I heard the same thing myself yesterday,' Simon admitted, 'but it somewhat slipped my mind.' As he spoke, he recalled the strange scene he had witnessed between Thornton and Wynfred, and was on the point of telling them of it when there came a frantic knocking on the front door and almost at once the housekeeper showed in a young man who, from his muddied appearance, had ridden hard.

'I apologise for coming in on you like this, Dr Brett,' he began, still breathless.

'Catch your breath, son,' advised Hugh. 'You're Farmer Wilkins's son from Home Farm, aren't you? And no apologies are needed. From your appearance I imagine it's a matter of some urgency?'

The young man nodded, still breathing hard. 'We have two badly injured men back home. Father found them on the roadside this morning, not far from Mother Saxton's cottage, and got his men to carry them back to the farm. One's been hit over the head and will not wake while the other has lost much blood from a stabbing. We felt neither would survive being jolted in a cart so I've ridden over to beg you to come out to them.'

'Hit over the head, you say?' enquired Simon. 'It sounds as if they have met up with the same villains who killed that poor fellow when I was here before.'

'I'll come with you at once,' said Hugh, from the table. 'You needn't disturb yourself, Simon, unless you wish.'

'I'd much prefer to come along too, if you're agreeable,' Simon assured him. 'Nor would it be a bad idea if we took

John with us too, in case these cut-throats are still in the vicinity.'

Home Farm was only a mile or so along the road beyond Mother Saxton's cottage, but if she was inside as they passed, she gave no sign of it; all was quiet. Hugh reined in for a moment and looked back. 'Do you think she might be in league with the robbers?'

Simon shook his head. 'I doubt it very much, but it's possible she saw something. I imagine she doesn't miss much of what goes on hereabouts. It might be worth trying to find out later.'

Mistress Wilkins had put both the injured men in one of her spare bedrooms, each on a pallet bed. The man with the head injury lay on his side, breathing noisily, dead to the world, while the other, deathly white, moaned and tossed from side to side. Hugh at once knelt beside him, motioning Simon to attend the other man, after explaining to the farmer's wife that his companion was also a physician.

She had done her best in the circumstances, bathing the head wound and placing a pad of linen against it. 'I didn't know what else to do, doctor,' she explained as Simon removed the linen and peered closely at the wound. Certainly it was very similar to that suffered by the dying man in the cart whom he had examined two months before. Yes, in spite of Mistress Wilkins's ministrations, once again there were minute specks of bark and wood present around the contusion, a fact he imparted to Hugh.

'I would say it's highly likely he was attacked by the same fellow, a man who makes himself a weapon from what he finds to hand in the woodland – a weapon that he can throw away afterwards without anyone realising what it is. Happily, I think that this time, the blow will not prove mortal, for our friend here is taller and more robust than he who died outside the church that day. Though whether he'll remember anything of what happened to him if he does live remains to be seen.'

'So you think he'll wake, then?' Mistress Wilkins asked anxiously.

'I am hopeful, but it's in God's hands,' replied Simon, 'for we can't know the extent of the damage – how much bleeding there is inside the skull that we cannot see. In the meantime, he must be kept quiet and I know Dr Brett has a salve in his bag which is of great assistance for the treating of head wounds. It is made from shepherd's purse and is under the dominion of Saturn, and therefore of a cold and binding nature, like to him, so first we will apply it to the wound.'

Hugh turned aside from his own patient and took a jar out of his bag. 'Put this thickly on the pad of linen and do as Dr Forman asks, my dear. I will also bleed him a little before I go to relieve the pressure, though it is ironic for this poor fellow here has too little blood.'

Mistress Wilkins sighed. 'He was fair drenched in his own blood when my husband found him. So we cut off his doublet and shirt, then I made another pad out of linen and bound it to him as tightly as possible to try to staunch the bleeding.'

Hugh carefully removed the bandage. The wound was bleeding only sluggishly now. 'You did well,' he praised the woman. 'Come and see here, Simon. He must have been grappling his assailant when he was stabbed in the chest. The dagger went deep, but the ribs seem to have deflected it from actually penetrating the heart, though I fear it might have pierced other vital organs. He is in a very bad way. Even more is this one in God's hands. But I think his wound too will benefit from the salve, and I'll also leave you something with which to make a posset should he recover sufficiently to drink it. You have honey and vinegar in the house?'

The farmer's wife nodded.

'Then take this powder – it comes from the plant "one-blade". It's a herb of the sun, and half a dram of the root taken in vinegar with honey helps both to heal the wound and sweat out any poison.'

'My hostess on the Borders would, no doubt, have taken needle and thread to the wound,' Simon remarked.

'Lord preserve us!' exclaimed Mistress Wilkins. 'What an idea! Do you want to kill the man?'

In answer Simon undid his doublet, untied the strings of his shirt and pulled it aside sufficient for her to see some of the scar crossing his shoulder. 'That wound was longer than this here, if not as deep. I was already failing rapidly for loss of blood, and by sewing up my wound she prevented my losing any more.'

The woman looked doubtful. 'It sounds a pagan practice to me,' she asserted.

'There is much that is pagan on the Borders,' said Simon, with a smile. 'But I see no point in putting it into practice here, even if Hugh would allow it. As I said, the wound is deep rather than long and bleeding has almost stopped.'

As Hugh finished rebandaging the man, he stirred, moaned and opened his eyes. 'Where am I?' he croaked, running his tongue over dry lips.

'Safe among friends,' Hugh assured him, and motioned the woman to bring some water. 'Raise his head,' he told her when she had done so, 'and I'll see if he'll take a little.'

The wounded man swallowed, then gulped down some water. 'Can you tell us what happened?' Simon asked.

The man frowned. 'What happened,' he repeated in a faint voice. 'What happened . . . Joseph and I were walking down a lane alongside some woodland. We'd been warned against going through it . . .' His voice trailed off and he seemed once more in a swoon.

'Then what?' Simon urged him. 'Please try to help us so that we can catch the villains who attacked you.'

At this he opened his eyes again, struggling against faintness. 'Suddenly, we were set on. Joseph was hit over the head by one man, I wrestled with another . . . I don't remember any more.'

85

'Can you recall what they looked like?'

The man shook his head weakly. 'Not clearly. He who struck Joseph was thickset, but not tall. As to my man, he wore a leather mask over his face . . .' His eyes closed again and this time he could not be roused.

'Best leave him,' said Hugh. 'If he is to live then he must rest as much as possible. Can you manage to nurse them both?' he added, turning to Mistress Wilkins.

'I'll do my best,' she replied. 'The girls will have to help. We've a busy farm to run.'

Hugh thanked her. 'I'll call in again tomorrow. In the meantime, if there's any change, send your boy for me.'

Simon went down to find John Bradedge. 'See if you can find out for me exactly where the two men were found,' he instructed him, 'and anything else you might think useful. Then follow us back to the town.'

Hugh and Simon rode home to find the schoolmaster, the parson, the constable and several other worthies already ensconced in Hugh's parlour impatiently awaiting their return. Hugh apologised for keeping them, explaining, to a murmur of concern, the reason for the delay; he ordered refreshments for them while he and Simon recovered from their ride. He trusted, he told his guests, that the meeting would not need to be a long one – a hope with which Simon heartily agreed, feeling privately that their time would have been better spent discussing the growing threat of highway robbery rather than the possibility of witchcraft abroad in the town.

It soon became clear that there was no firm notion as to what should be done, though few present felt it right that the local people should take the law into their own hands.

'But if we cannot calm the people down, then it is extremely likely that is what will happen,' said Hugh. 'And once an angry mob has stormed out to Mother Saxton's cottage and created mayhem there, how will we prevent them from going on to commit further excesses?'

The response to this was mixed. Schoolmaster Page

86

still considered the whole thing to be a lot of nonsense whipped up by those who should know better, while the parson, quite genuinely fearful, opined that there might well be something in it since the Scriptures themselves warned against such creatures. As to the town worthies, their opinions ranged from he who wanted to march on the witch's cottage immediately and get rid of the problem once and for all, and the rest who still insisted there should be recourse to the law. It was at this point that the constable reminded all present: first, that it was his bounden duty to see there was no public disorder and second, that since it was known that Sir Arthur Clarington was due that same day, bringing with him a magistrate to look into the very situation they were discussing, then surely it should be left to him. At this common-sense suggestion, the meeting broke up.

'You'd be better seeing what can be done about those villains who lurk outside the town preying on travellers,' remarked Page, voicing Simon's unspoken thoughts. 'Are the two poor fellows likely to recover, Dr Brett?'

Hugh sighed. 'Both are in a bad way, one bludgeoned over the head, the other stabbed and neither the better for having lain at the roadside since yesterday.'

'There you are then,' continued Page, turning to the rest. 'If you talk of wanting to form a pack to scour out evil, then surely bringing these people to justice should take precedence over chasing after one old woman.'

'But in the case we've been discussing, we are dealing with the supernatural, with one flying in the face of God's holy ordinance,' the parson pontificated.

'I'd have thought murdering honest folk was also flying in the face of God's holy ordinance,' Page retorted, 'though it requires more courage to tackle *that* than the other.'

The morning of the night of the full moon, Hugh set off once more to visit the two injured men, planning to call in on another patient on the way home. This time Simon did not ask to accompany him. He was becoming restive. He had work to do at home and could see little point in remaining in Pinner much longer, since his repeated confirmation of Hugh's assurances to the sick that Mother Saxton had nothing to do with their illnesses, continued to be disbelieved. He decided, therefore, that he would see what the outcome of the magistrate's visit would be, then make his excuses and return to London.

As soon as Hugh rode off, he sought out John Bradedge. His servant had told him that there was nothing on the roadside where the two men had been found, apart from a smear of dried blood, but that there was a track near by going into the wood which might be worth investigating. He had thought of doing so himself, then decided against it. 'If there are two of these villains, doctor, then one man on his own might well be in hazard.'

They rode companionably together, both remembering other such times in the past, not least their wild trek across the Borders. When they reached Mother Saxton's cottage, Simon dismounted, telling John to stay with the horses. His servant was only too pleased: cut-throats and villains were one thing, witches something else.

Mother Saxton came to the door as Simon approached it. 'And what do you want this time, doctor? Not come for the same thing as young Banks, I trust?'

'Young Banks – he came here? What on earth did he want with you?'

'A love charm!' she cackled. 'Much good may it do him.'

'And when was this?'

'The day before yesterday. Begged me, he did, brought me firewood, silver coins and a cheese. He must have the girl or die!'

'Which girl is that?'

'The older Carter wench. Phillipa they call her.'

So young Jack Page was right but, more to the point, once again Banks had been near to the scene of an attack.

'Did you see where he went when he left you?' Simon asked the old woman.

'Towards the town, I think,' she replied, 'but I could be mistaken.'

'Have you heard that two men were set on near here on the same day?'

She looked at him keenly. 'That's the way your mind works, is it, doctor? Yes. I know of it.'

'Did you hear or see anything?'

She shook her head and began to close the door. He thanked her and was about to return to his horse when a thought struck him. 'Do you also know that Sir Arthur Clarington is planning to visit you tomorrow, bringing a magistrate with him?'

This obviously did come as a surprise. 'No. I did not.' She paused. 'Sir Arthur Clarington, is it? Well, now, that is interesting.'

'You know him then?'

'Oh yes,' she replied. 'I know him.'

John led Simon to the place where the two men had been waylaid. They dismounted, hitched up their horses and set off to investigate the track John had found. It was quite broad, a yard at least, and the ground was much disturbed both with hoofmarks and those made by boots, but it was impossible to read anything into them though it seemed likely that the robbers had lurked near by while waiting for unsuspecting travellers. Finally Simon called off the search. It was not, after all, his business and within a day or so he would be gone. As they came up to the Manor gate on their way back to town, they found in front of them a scene of much activity.

Susan and Harry Thornton, dressed for a journey, were bidding farewell to their respective families, while Francis Wynfred, his saddlebags secured, was mounted and ready to go. Hearing the sound of horses, Susan turned and saw Simon and John and beckoned them to stop.

'I'd hoped to see you before we left, Dr Forman,' she

said, 'but our decision to visit London was a sudden one. Can you tell me what we should see at the playhouses? That's if they are open again now.'

Simon smiled at her beaming face. 'You are in luck, my dear. The Lord Admiral's Men are now playing again at the Rose and, I imagine, the Lord Chamberlain's Men at the Theatre. Both companies are excellent, but if you can, you should certainly try to see *Doctor Faustus* at the Rose and *The Tragedy of King Richard III* at the Theatre.'

'Come, Susan,' Harry called out impatiently. 'The morning's far gone and it's more than time we were off.'

'Which way do you intend to take?' asked Simon.

'Almost straight through the wood,' Harry replied. 'It cuts the best part of six miles off our journey.'

'Do you think that's wise, sir?' John Bradedge broke in. 'It's only two days since a pair of travellers were attacked on this very road, let alone within the wood. If there's a safer way, wouldn't it be better to take that? Rather an extra six miles than risk meeting up with thieves.'

Harry obviously did not take kindly to the advice of one he considered a mere servant. 'I've ridden through these woods since my boyhood,' he said sharply, 'and see no reason to stop now.'

'And I shall be at hand, should we be attacked,' added Wynfred, who had been listening.

'You visit London too?' Simon asked politely.

'No. I travel with them for part of the way then have business of my own.'

Simon and John rode on to Pinner while Susan and Phillipa embraced once more. Then Harry mounted his horse, his father helped Susan up onto the pillion behind him and with a flurry of farewells they were gone.

Phillipa looked after them, wondering why she should feel so much misgiving. She had obvious fears for their safety on the road, but it went deeper than that. What was behind Harry's sudden decision to go to London? There seemed no good reason for it. At least, though, it looked as if they were finally to be rid of Francis Wynfred. It was then a small boy arrived with a message. Would she meet Master Somerton at the stile at the end of Banks's peasefield outside the wood after moonrise, on a matter of great urgency. She must tell no one of their tryst.

Phillipa was somewhat disconcerted. It was unlike Guy to ask such a thing of her nor was it necessary, since as a suitor for her hand, he could see her whenever he liked. 'Are you sure of this?' she said thoughtfully.

The small boy solemnly assured her that he was. 'Very well,' she said, 'tell Master Somerton I'll be there.'

The sky had cleared by evening, which was as well, since otherwise she would not have been able to see whether the moon had risen or not. However, although it was full, clouds continually scudded across it, obscuring its light. Wrapping herself in a dark cloak, Phillipa let herself out of the door and set off for the peasefield stile about fifteen minutes' walk away. She had hoped Guy would already be there waiting for her, but when she reached the edge of the wood, there was no one there.

It was eerie in this place. When the moon did break through, the boughs of the trees threw strange shadows across the path in front of her, and it was only too easy to imagine something crouching there. There were odd noises too – animals rustling in the undergrowth, an owl hooting, and once she thought she heard a faint voice crying out from far away, but it did not recur and she put it down to her imagination. More time passed. She could not understand what had happened to Guy, and suddenly losing patience, decided to go back home to light and safety. Then she saw a movement on the other side of the stile.

'There you are, Guy,' she said with relief, climbing over the stile into the wood. 'I thought you'd never come. Why in God's good name have you brought me out here?'

A man loomed up in front of her and grabbed her round the waist. Phillipa's first thought was that she was about to become another victim of the highway robbers –

then immediately she discounted it as they could not possibly have sent for her in such a manner. She struggled to get free, but succeeded only in being able to turn and face her attacker.

'Don't try to run away,' Cuddy told her triumphantly, 'for willing or no I'll have you tonight.'

'Cuddy Banks!' she exclaimed in amazement. 'Have you run mad?'

'Mad, no,' he replied ardently, 'or if so, only with love.'

Tugging a hand free, she smacked him across the face, whereupon he seized it and twisted it behind her back until she cried out. 'Best you get down now on the ground and enjoy it,' he leered, 'for there's no escape. Didn't I get a charm from the old witch to make you want me.'

'But I don't want you. I'd never want you if you were the last man left!'

Cuddy laughed. 'The witch told me you'd say that, and to take no notice.'

But in spite of all his efforts, he failed to wrestle Phillipa to the ground; nothing daunted, he pushed her relentlessly towards a stout tree until she was backed up against it.

'Well now, my pretty,' he panted, 'if you won't have me in comfort lying down, this way will have to do.' He sniggered. 'Do you scorn me still, Phillipa? Am I still a figure of fun to you?'

She spat in his face and, disgusted, he wiped it away. For the first time it began to occur to Cuddy that Mother Saxton had mistaken the effects of the mandrake root . . . but by now his blood was up.

'What kind of a woman do you imagine I am?' hissed Phillipa, still trying to fend him off. 'One of those stales you buy for your lewd and wanton behaviour?'

'You wait, you'll find you're just like all the rest – hungry for it.' Securing her as best he could, he loosened his breeches, put his knee into her stomach with all his weight behind it, then reached down and pulled up her gown and shift.

Really terrified now, Phillipa screamed for help as loudly as she could, though with little hope of salvation. To her amazement, there was an immediate reply as Guy Somerton himself vaulted over the stile. As he did so the moon came out again from behind a cloud, illuminating a scene which required no explanation. It took only seconds for Guy to dash over and wrest Cuddy Banks away. He then flung the youth face down on the ground and pulled off his breeches.

'You walking fundament, you vile clotpoll, you whore's bastard!' he shouted, applying his riding whip to the youth's backside. 'You bedlam, brainsick worm!' He hauled Cuddy to his feet, shook him until his teeth rattled, then shoved him towards the tree where Phillipa had stood, and banged his head against it a few times.

'Mercy, mercy, Master Somerton!' begged Cuddy. 'It wasn't my fault.'

'Not your fault?' roared Guy, grabbing him round the neck. '*Not your fault?* If you intend to put the blame on Phillipa, I'll knock your lying teeth down your throat!'

Cuddy tried feebly to shake his head. 'It was the witch's fault. I went to her for a love charm. She said it would make Mistress Carter mad for me even if she protested otherwise.'

Guy banged Cuddy's head back again. 'That excuse will prove of very little value when I go and tell your father you tried to rape Mistress Carter.'

'Take me home, Guy,' said Phillipa, still shivering from the shock of the attack.

He came over and put his arms round her. 'Did that disgusting creature harm you?'

'He twisted my arm till it hurt and I've scratches and bruises with fighting him. But the end to which it was all leading – no, thank God. He was stopped just in time.' She faltered, tears rising. Then: 'Guy, I came because I'd a message asking me to meet you here.'

'Likewise, so did I.' Her lover frowned. 'Someone has

been determined to make mischief.'

They clung together for a moment. Cuddy, painfully levering himself away from the tree, saw his chance and limped off into the bushes.

'Don't chase after him, Guy,' begged Phillipa. 'We can leave all until morning.' She smiled through her tears. 'He's hardly likely to go far without his breeches!'

From her vantage point amidst some bushes, Mother Saxton was convulsed with silent laughter. The Banks whelp had been well and truly thrashed, and humiliated into the bargain. Revenge was sweet indeed. It had all worked out better than she could ever have imagined.

Chapter 7

Kill the Witch!

'Wake up, doctor!' urged John Bradedge, shaking his master the next morning. 'You must come at once. There's murder afoot.'

Simon blinked confusedly and sat up. 'What is it? What do you mean?'

'It seems half the town is off to Mother Saxton's cottage with mayhem in mind. Dr Hugh's already ridden over to Sir Arthur Clarington's estate to ask him to go there at once, bringing the Justice with him. He says will you follow the crowd and do all in your power to calm them.'

Simon got out of bed at once. 'I'll certainly do as he asks, but I doubt anyone will listen to me.' He thought a moment. 'Will you go and find Master Page and beg him to come with us? He may be able to knock a bit of sense into them; at least they know him and many respect his abilities.'

Ten minutes later, all three men were mounted and on their way. 'What's brought this to a head?' Simon asked Andrew Page as they turned on to the lane going down to the old woman's cottage.

'Cuddy Banks, who else?' the schoolmaster replied. 'He appeared in the early morning without his breeches and with the stripes of a beating on his backside, claiming that Mother Saxton had put a spell on him, as a result of which he was drawn into the wood last night, came across Phillipa Carter at the stile by the peasefield and attempted to rape her.'

'But that's preposterous!' Simon exploded. 'Surely no one can possibly believe it, coming from a lout like that?'

'Did he say the witch had enticed him out of his breeches or gave him the stripes on his backside?' John chuckled.

'His story is that he had Phillipa Carter up against a tree – solely through the influence of the old woman, of course – when of a sudden Guy Somerton appeared and gave him the thrashing of his life.'

'Now that I *do* believe,' grinned Simon, 'but as for the rest it seems hardly credible that it's sufficient to rouse a mob.'

Andrew Page looked grim. 'It was merely the tinder that set them aflame.'

'Then God send we get there in time.'

It did not take long to catch up with the stragglers, while the sound of an angry mob could clearly be heard in the distance. The three men increased their speed and soon came abreast of townsfolk carrying a motley collection of weapons – billhooks, cudgels and pitchforks, while one old fellow even clutched a rusty musket to his chest. By the time they reached the cottage it was already ringed with people. They dismounted, secured their horses and pushed their way through the crowd to stand with their backs to the door. If Mother Saxton was inside, she gave no sign of it, and no smoke rose from her chimney. Immediately outside the door was a wooden tub and without more ado Page turned it over, then stood on top of it.

'Have you all taken leave of your senses?' he bawled over the noise of the mob. 'You know very well that Sir Arthur Clarington's coming this morning, bringing with him a Justice of the Peace. They are even now on their way. Go back at once to your homes and leave the law to him.'

But this only served to enrage the townsfolk more and he was shouted down by cries of, 'Go home yourself!' and,

'Go teach yourself, schoolteacher! and, 'Get out of the way if you want to keep a whole skin.'

Page bravely stood his ground. 'What good do you imagine your action will achieve?' he bellowed.

'It'll rid the world of a witch,' cried one man. 'Therefore move out of the way so we can string her up.'

'Burn her, better,' screamed another. 'That's the best way with witches.'

Page tried once more. 'Take the law into your own hands and you'll hang too. Murder is murder, no matter what the reason for it.'

It was old Banks who first thrust his way towards the door. 'After how she bewitched my son, I'm willing to take that chance. Now I'll tell the three of you one last time: get out of our way or take the consequences.'

At least twenty men followed him, and even John did not see how three could triumph against so many. Reluctantly they moved aside. Banks and his followers elbowed them out of the way, kicked open the door and marched inside. There was a short silence and then they reappeared.

'It's empty,' Banks called out to the rest of the mob. 'The old bitch must have flown off on her broomstick.'

'We'll fetch her then,' shouted a voice, and a young fellow ran round the side of the house towards the crowd, a piece of burning thatch in his hand. There was a cheer.

'Now what?' demanded Simon.

'We're bringing the witch,' called out Cuddy Banks. 'They say that if you fire a witch's thatch, she'll come running.'

'If you fire a thatch, then anyone will come running, fool!' bellowed Page.

For a few minutes nothing happened, and the thatch had burned itself out when there was a roar from the crowd; they fell back of a sudden as Mother Saxton herself appeared from the wood, panting for breath.

'The Plague and all the Devil's curses fall on you,' she shrieked when finally she was able to speak. 'What do you want with me?'

'So there you are, you old whore,' shouted Cuddy's father. 'Have we fetched you with fire in your tail?'

'Beat her, kick her, hang her, burn her!' yelled the crowd, then fell to chanting, 'Kill the witch! Kill the witch! Kill the witch!'

To the immense relief of the three men, suddenly above the racket came the sound of horses ridden hard, followed almost at once by an authoritative voice shouting: 'Get back! Get back at once, do you hear?' Three horsemen rode straight into the middle of the mob forcing it to part, the foremost of them, a handsome man of middle years, laying about him with his riding whip. At first the people muttered loudly, several still seeming inclined to argue, but finally they all fell back.

'Make one more move,' the man continued, 'any of you, and I'll have you in the town gaol *and* whipped at the cart's tail.' A sullen silence fell. 'If any among you don't know me,' he continued, 'I am Sir Arthur Clarington and this man here,' he pointed to a soberly dressed grey-haired man who was now at his side, 'is Sir Edward Ratcliffe, a Justice of the Peace. Dr Hugh Brett, you already know.' He then looked over the heads of the crowd, obviously puzzling who Simon might be.

'That is my colleague, Dr Forman, of whom I spoke,' Hugh told him, following his glance, 'and with him his man and our schoolmaster, Master Page. I imagine we have them to thank that matters have not got even more out of hand.'

'Thank God you are here,' Simon called to him, 'for we were quite unable to hold them any longer.'

'You – take our horses while Sir Edward and I see to this,' Clarington ordered John Bradedge. The three men dismounted and strode over to the old woman.

'Witch or no,' the Justice reassured her, 'I will see the law is obeyed. In the meantime remain where you are.' Then he turned to the mob.

'Of what do you accuse this woman?' he shouted out,

swiftly adding: 'God's Breath, don't all speak at once,' as a veritable torrent of accusations of curses, illnesses, sick cows and spoiled crops poured out, a torrent which was only contained when Clarington again threatened to go in among them with his whip.

'She bewitched my son into trying to force a young woman,' asserted Banks when he could finally make himself heard above the rest. 'And her curse was on me even this morning, for when I went to fetch my horse to ride here, it was sick with the glanders while last night she was quite healthy. I'll take my oath on it, all this against my family is along of this witch here, Mother Saxton.'

'I found my wife and a serving man from the town thrashing together in my barn,' complained another, 'the kind of thrashing which has no need of corn, and when I asked my polecat why she'd betrayed me, she swore on her conscience and with many tears that she was bewitched. And if that's so, what other witch do we have hereabouts but this one here?' His question met with a roar of approval.

'And how about me?' cried the old man with the rusty musket, pushing his way to the front. 'I have a dun cow tied up in my backyard and as my neighbours here will tell you, I am now in so bad a state that ten times an hour I have to run to her and kiss – saving your reverence – her backside. The whole town of Pinner has bepissed themselves with laughing me to scorn!'

In spite of himself Ratcliffe burst out laughing at this. 'And you expect me not only to believe this, but that it is due to this woman here?'

'Who else? For would any man make such an ass of himself, were he not bewitched?'

'This is getting us nowhere,' grumbled the second man. 'Unless you rid the town of her, our wives will do nothing else but dance around other men's maypoles.'

'Aye,' quavered he with the musket, 'our cattle will fall, our wives will fall, our daughters will fall – and how will we be able to stand against such evil?'

Seeing the Justice's difficulty in speaking over the heads of the crowd, John picked up the tub vacated by Page and pushed through the crowd to put it before Ratcliffe, who thanked him then clambered up onto it.

'Listen to me now, all of you,' he said authoritatively. 'You will return at once to the town . . .' His voice was drowned out by the ensuing noise. 'I tell you, you *will* return to your homes. This is an order,' he shouted at the top of his voice 'and anyone not obeying will be taken in charge and summoned before the Bench for causing a breach of the Queen's peace. This afternoon I shall sit in Pinner, and all those who wish to accuse this woman can come one at a time and tell me on what grounds they do so. If I consider you have a case, only then shall I have the woman arrested. But not before.'

'I still say kill the witch!' yelled the zealot. 'Listen to him and she may yet escape burning. Hang her now, I say.' His words aroused the crowd once more, and they again began to chant, 'Kill the witch! Kill the witch!' making no move to go.

'Have we no constable here?' roared Clarington. 'Is there no rule of law in these parts? Where is he?'

The constable, who had been lurking at the back of the crowd, unwilling to intervene, was pushed to the front. 'Go back now with these people,' Clarington commanded him, 'and take note of any who attempt to disobey. The Justice and I will see they are brought before him and tried this very afternoon. Also see to the setting up of a room where the accusations can be heard, and find a scrivener to set them down.' Slowly at first, then with gathering speed, the crowd finally began to disperse, muttering discontentedly.

The old woman had been wrapped in a tattered shawl all the while; now she let it slip. As she did so, she turned and looked at Clarington for the first time. A strange expression crossed her face, a look he returned with a mixture of both dislike and recognition.

'Look, doctor,' whispered John. 'It's as if he knows her from some other time or place.'

Ratcliffe, obviously unaware of such an undercurrent, addressed himself to Mother Saxton. 'Your name is . . .?'

'Lizzie Saxton. Some call me Old Mother Saxton.'

'Tell me then, Mother Saxton, the man who spoke first – Banks, is it? – seems to have a particular grievance against you. What is it?'

'He has persecuted me this long while,' she replied. 'These two gentlemen here,' she pointed to Hugh and Simon, 'will tell you it's only a few weeks since they came on his son and other fellows beating me for picking up firewood.'

'That's true,' Hugh agreed. 'We ourselves sent them packing.'

Ratcliffe nodded. 'I see. Well now, seeing how matters stand with you, will you answer some questions for me?'

'What kind of questions?' she replied suspiciously.

'Of a mild nature and thus requiring mild answers. First, tell us honestly and with a free confession, are you in truth a witch? If you are, and honestly repent your wrongdoing, I'll do my best to see that you are weaned from it – no,' he added, seeing her expression, 'not by violent means, for I see little point in that. I am not of the persuasion who consider the way to cure witchcraft is to drown or burn a witch, unless it is proved beyond all possible doubt and the witch refuses to repent.'

Mother Saxton seemed to accept that. 'Then I will tell you truly, sir, I am not, in truth I am not.'

'Beware of her, Sir Edward,' broke in Clarington, 'for she is much accused.'

His intervention surprised the Justice. 'I'd thought you as sceptical as I am myself, Sir Arthur,' he said. 'Indeed, you told me the reason for you calling me in on this matter was to calm feelings and prevent violence.'

'Aye,' commented Andrew Page, 'I'd thought you had

no truck with all this, which is why you sent the mob packing in so forthright a manner.'

Clarington looked uneasy. 'I sent them away because I didn't want a riot on my hands, not because I thought there was no truth in it,' he blustered, 'for since I first sent word to you, Sir Edward, I've heard she freely claims to be a witch whatever she might say now.'

'If you had been beaten and abused as I have,' the woman cried, 'daily reviled and spat on, then you might say such things to frighten folk off.'

'She has a point,' Ratcliffe agreed.

'They also say now that she's sold her soul to the Devil and has signed a pact in blood,' Clarington continued.

'God's Death, man!' Page burst out. 'This is no tale from the *Faust Book*. We are ordinary folk here in Pinner, not actors in a play at the Rose Theatre!'

'Mind your manners, schoolmaster,' returned Clarington, 'in the presence of your betters.'

'What do you say to that grave charge, Mother Saxton?' asked Ratcliffe.

Lizzie Saxton leant against the wall of her house and swivelled her good eye around to face Clarington again. 'That many folk sell their souls to the Devil for many reasons, and that it doesn't have to be by pacts signed in blood. Men as well as women. Men who covet wealth, ambitious men who hunger for preferment above all else. There are many who consider themselves our betters, who have fine clothes, are laden with titles and honours and great estates, who are far more crooked and twisted in their souls than am I in my body. If what I am makes me a witch, then so also are they.'

Clarington's face was suffused with fury. 'Why should we stand here any longer listening to this, Sir Edward. Let her be taken into the town now while her accusers lay their complaints.'

Mother Saxton looked at him once again. 'If you would know more of witches, then let me tell you of them. Real witches, painted whores who loll in princes' courts, upon whose eyelids lust sits, blowing fires to burn men's souls. Women who exchange what should be their duty to their husbands for coaches, gowns and jewels. Haven't such sold their souls to Satan? And what of those *male* witches, who, with golden hooks, entice maids to give themselves then, once they have achieved their ends, put them aside as dross.'

She obviously made Clarington deeply uneasy, and when she had finished speaking, he seemed visibly relieved. Certainly, thought Simon, agreeing with John, there was more between those two than met the eye. He wondered if Ratcliffe was aware of it?

Of a sudden, Clarington turned away and marched over to his horse, snatching the reins from John Bradedge's hands.

'I've no more time to waste standing here listening to this,' he muttered. 'I leave the matter now in your hands, Sir Edward. I said nothing of it until I was sure the situation here was under control, but before we were called out this morning I received a message from home calling me back at once on urgent business. Should you need me again, Sir Edward, please send me word.' Whereupon without further explanation, he mounted and rode swiftly off the way he had come, leaving the Justice gazing after him open-mouthed and Lizzie Saxton laughing derisively.

'A somewhat precipitate departure,' commented Simon.

'I understand he's a man of a hasty and choleric temperament,' said Hugh, 'prone to going his own way.'

'It seems the witch got the better of him,' remarked John.

Simon agreed. 'So I thought also. I wonder why? Could it be she has some prior knowledge of him?'

'It's clear to me they've met before,' agreed Page. He turned to the Justice. 'So what do you make of what this woman says, sir?'

The Justice regarded Mother Saxton for a moment in

silence. 'I am inclined to believe her,' he said at length, 'though,' he continued sternly, 'that's not to say you haven't made a deal of mischief pretending you are what you are not. Well, I'll hear their accusations this afternoon, but unless there is something new which convinces me otherwise, I shall take no further action. However, if I find there *is* a case to answer, then you will be duly charged.' He paused. 'But even if I find in your favour I think you'd be wise to leave this place as soon as possible, mistress, for there is no way of guarding your safety day and night. Is there anywhere you can go?'

'I was born and bred near to St Albans, sir, so I suppose I could make my way back there, though whether there is any who would take me in or even let me be in peace, I don't know. However, I will do as you say.'

Ratcliffe looked relieved. He had no desire for a witch-hunt followed by the scaffold or the pyre. 'Then let me give you some more advice. Don't meddle again in such matters. Go home, mend your life and pray!'

The old woman nodded, then turned and disappeared into the cottage.

'What now?' asked Hugh.

'We must go into Pinner,' said Ratcliffe, 'and if you'll accompany me, gentlemen, I'll be glad of it after Sir Arthur's strange departure.'

They began to walk over to their horses. Then a thought struck John Bradedge. 'Do you think it might be a good idea if I rode back through the woods, sirs, in case any of those you sent away are now lurking there ready to come back and do mischief?'

'A good point,' agreed Ratcliffe. 'Are you agreeable, doctor? Or do you think it unwise, your man being on his own?'

Simon smiled at his servant. 'I can vouch that John is well able to look after himself in most circumstances. Also, he is on horseback and the rabble on foot. But in any event, I imagine most of them are now trudging into town with the constable.'

As his servant prepared to depart, Simon went over to him and commented quietly: 'A strange business, John. I could bear to know just what the relationship is or was between our choleric squire and the old woman.'

'Whatever it is, he was obviously frightened she'd come out with it.'

'I see you read my mind,' said Simon. 'Well, off you go.' He slapped the horse's rump. 'Take care of yourself! I want you back all in one piece,' he called out.

If there were stragglers in the wood then John saw no sign of them. In fact, after all the noise and hubbub of the last hours, all seemed very quiet apart from the soft sound of his horse's hoofs on the narrow pathway and the odd call of a bird. Then he thought he heard a noise and at first wondered if it was merely his imagination, but hearing it again he reined in his horse. Was it the sound of a trapped animal or a human voice calling for help?

'Is anyone there?' he called.

This time there was an immediate response. It was quite definitely a voice crying for help. Warily, John turned his horse in its direction. Was this the way the robbers had tricked the two injured men found so recently near the wood? Nothing easier than to fool some traveller by pretending to be in distress. He made sure his dagger was loose in its sheath, then plunged off the path and into the thick woodland beyond. Again the voice called out: he must now be almost upon it. The trees parted suddenly in front of him and he found himself in a small dell.

'Here, over here – thank God you've found me!'

Sitting with his back against a tree, his hands tied behind him, was Harry Thornton. John at once dismounted and went over to him. The young man was pale and shivering and bleeding sluggishly from a wound on his thigh.

'Untie me,' he begged hoarsely. 'I've rubbed my wrists raw trying to work loose.'

'You seem to have made a fair job of it too,' said John, bending over to cut him free. 'You'd almost succeeded; a little more and you'd have done it without my help. There now.' His dagger sliced through the rope. 'What happened?'

Harry rubbed his wrists and painfully flexed his arms. 'Robbers. Sweet Jesu, how I wish I'd listened to your advice! They took Susan.' He struggled to stand, wincing at the pain from his leg wound, but was unable to do so. 'I beseech you, leave me and go and see if you can find her. I've called and called but to no avail.'

'I will indeed,' said John, 'but first let me see to your injury as best I can. How many of them were there?'

'Three, possibly more – ouch!' Harry grimaced as John prodded his leg. 'Leave me, please, I'll be all right. We must find my wife.'

In answer John took out a none-too-clean kerchief from his pocket and used it to bandage the wound. 'There,' he said, securing the knot. 'That should do until Dr Hugh or my master sees you. Do you think you can stand now?'

Clinging onto his arm, Harry levered himself upright but with difficulty. 'Susan . . .' he began again.

'I'll go and look for her now, but first tell me what happened so that I've some idea where to look.'

'They came on us suddenly out of a thicket. One pulled Susan off the pillion and held a knife to her throat until Francis and I dismounted too.'

The mention of Wynfred jogged John's memory. Of course, Francis had also been of the party. So where was he?

'We gave them all the money and jewellery we had on us,' Thornton continued, 'hoping they'd go away. But instead they dragged both Susan and Francis off down there.' He pointed to a narrow pathway through the trees. 'One stayed behind, whether to guard me or murder me, I don't know. I pushed him aside and rushed after the others but he caught hold of me. I got this wound fighting him off. Then I was hit on the head and remember no more until I woke here, where you found me.' He stared around and frowned. 'Have I been here long?'

'Twenty-four hours at least,' replied John. 'So now we must see if we can find your wife and Master Wynfred.'

They set off in the direction Thornton indicated, the young man trying his best to keep up with John in spite of his bad leg. In one place the ground was much trodden and there were many overlapping footprints. 'It looks as if you're right,' said John, 'and they did come this way.' They both began calling out Susan's name, but there was no response; meanwhile, Harry was finding walking more and more difficult.

'You wait here,' John told him. 'I'll go on a little further but if there's still no sign of her then it's best I take you back to town with me and we raise a proper search party.' Harry shook his head but had to hang onto a tree to stay upright. Scarcely a hundred yards further on, John stumbled over something. It was a woman's cloak. He picked it up. On the left side were ominous smears. He touched them gently with a finger which came away sticky.

Then he saw her. She was lying on her back in a clearing, her arms outflung. He knelt down beside her and put his head to her breast, already certain help had come too late. The front of her bodice was drenched in blood. He put his hand under her shoulders and tried to lift her a little. She was stiff and cold.

'You've found her then,' called Harry, who had somehow found the strength to limp after John. 'Thank God! Is she in a swoon? Is she harmed?'

John sat back. 'It's best you see for yourself, Master Thornton.'

Harry struggled slowly towards them. 'Susan, Susan, my dear heart, I'm here,' he called out. Then he saw her and the full horror dawned on him. He flung himself down on the ground beside her with a strangled cry.

'Your wife's dead,' said John, 'stabbed through the heart.' A watery ray of sunshine lit up her white face.

'Oh God. Oh Hell!' Harry threw himself across his wife's

body, kissing her cold cheeks, tears pouring from his eyes. 'Oh Susan, Susan,' he sobbed, 'why did I bring you this way? It's my fault, it's all my fault.'

John was suddenly full of misgiving. For of Francis Wynfred, there was no sign.

Chapter 8

Murder Most Foul

John regarded the scene: the blood-stained body of the girl, the young man cradling her in his arms, tears streaming down his face. Even as he felt sorry for Harry it did cross his mind that some at least of the young man's anguish must be due to guilt for having so obviously neglected his young bride during the past weeks. What, he thought, should he do now? Help Thornton back to the Manor, then send a party to bring home the corpse? No, that wouldn't do. There was always the chance that a wandering fox or some other vermin would find the body first. So should he tell Harry to stay where he was beside his young wife, while he went for help by himself?

It was then, to his immense relief, that he heard the sound of voices not far away. Going to the edge of the clearing he shouted for help as loudly as he could. It had an immediate effect, for the voices fell silent. 'Here, over here!' he called out again.

Feet came trampling through the dry leaves and within minutes Jack Page appeared. 'Oh, it's you, Master Bradedge,' he said in some surprise then, as his eyes took in what lay before him, he stopped short. 'God's Death, what's here?' he exclaimed as the rest of the morris men crowded behind him. He came slowly over to John, his companions close at his heels. 'Who did this? Is she dead?'

John nodded. 'Most certainly – and for some hours. The death stiffening is far advanced.'

'Who did this?' repeated one of the young men, his eyes staring in shock. 'So foul a deed! Was it the robbers?'

Harry looked up swollen-eyed from his dead wife. 'We were set on near to this spot. There were three of them. I was taking the middle track as I knew it to be the shortest cut through the wood . . .' His voice trembled and he broke down again. 'Sweet Jesu, how could I have been such a fool! Why did I not heed the advice to keep to the main highway? I knew as well as any that there have been robberies here of late, men assaulted, yet I wouldn't listen.'

'What do you think we should do, Master Bradedge?' whispered Jack.

'I've been asking myself the same thing,' replied John. 'But now there are so many of you here, I think it best we try to find some means of carrying this poor young woman home; also Master Thornton has a nasty leg wound which needs attention. Once we reach the town, you must raise as many fit men as possible and return here with them to scour the woods to see if you can find these villains. Matters will not improve till they're safely hanged.'

The young men agreed that seemed sensible. As to carrying Susan home, one of them recalled having seen some new hurdles lying beside a path a little way back, presumably having been made for a nearby farmer. 'One of you come with me and fetch one,' he said, 'then between us we can carry the young mistress back to Pinner on it.' At once another youth came forward and the two plunged back into the wood the way they had come.

As Jack looked after them, his expression suddenly changed. 'Wynfred!' he exclaimed. 'Where's he got to?' He turned to Harry. 'He was riding with you when you left, wasn't he? Supposedly for at least part of the way.'

'The robbers took him as well when they dragged Susan off,' said Harry numbly.

'And what were you doing while all this was going on?' enquired Jack curiously.

'One of the robbers remained behind to guard me and

110

so I grappled with him, but then I was knocked on the head and remember nothing more. When I awoke I was tied up close to the path as Master Bradedge saw for himself. I was still struggling to break free when he found me, and it was he who discovered Susan, did you not?' he concluded, turning to John, his face still full of horror. John nodded in agreement.

'But no sign of Wynfred?' Jack persisted.

John shook his head. 'I'd a brief look around after finding the girl but didn't like to leave them for long. For all I know, Wynfred might well be lying dead or seriously wounded somewhere between here and the edge of the wood. Either that or . . .' He gave Jack a significant look.

'Or he managed to escape. Is that what you think?'

'If Francis had escaped, he'd immediately have come back in search of us,' Harry broke in, suddenly roused. 'It'd be the first thing he'd think of.'

Jack looked unconvinced. 'Would you recognise any of the men again?'

Harry looked doubtful. 'I'd never seen the one closest to me before, so far as I'm aware, while the other two wore visors over their faces.'

No more was said, for at that point the two young men returned, bringing with them a stout hurdle. 'There was no one about to ask if we could borrow it,' said one, 'but we'll bring it back afterwards – and if anyone objects we'll explain why it was needed.'

It took some time for the party to get back onto the highway again, for it proved difficult to negotiate the hurdle through the trees and thick shrubs. John went in front on foot leading his horse, Harry having been helped into the saddle for it was clear that he was in no fit state to walk home.

As the sad little procession reached the outskirts of the town it occurred to John that the immediate events had caused him to forget entirely the real reason for his going into the wood in the first place: to see if there were any

111

troublemakers lurking there, determined to wreak vengeance on the witch no matter what Sir Edward Ratcliffe had said.

'So,' he said as Jack caught up with him on the road and walked beside him, 'why were you in the wood?'

'For yet another practice of our morris,' the young man returned.

'You were not part of that mob outside Mother Saxton's cottage then?'

Jack shook his head. 'Certainly not. Even had I wanted to be – which I didn't – Father wouldn't have stood for it. We'd planned two days ago where to rehearse some new business to surprise folk the next time we perform, and that is what we did – all but for Cuddy Banks. No doubt you've heard what's happened to him.'

'I'm told he tried to force this young woman's sister, and her a maid, then blamed it on being bewitched when he was caught. He was in the forefront of the mob yelling his head off.'

Jack sighed. 'That's his way. Blame others for his own faults, never himself, then try to bluster his way out of trouble. A foolish hothead. I'm surprised, though, that he should have behaved in such a way towards Phillipa Carter, however much he might fancy her. She's no light wench to tease and murmur, "No, sir", while giggling and making come-hither eyes! I wouldn't like to have been in Cuddy's shoes had he succeeded in his attempt, nor to lay bets on whether it would be her father or Somerton who administered summary justice first!'

The streets of Pinner were busy when they arrived bearing their sad burden, for the events of the day had stirred up much interest. As was usual in such circumstances, people had sought out friends and relations to exchange views and gossip and there was much to discuss, not only the attack on Mother Saxton but the attempted rape of the respectable daughter of a substantial local farmer. Further excitement was stimulated when a notice

112

appeared on the door of the market house advising readers that Sir Edward Ratcliffe, Her Majesty's Justice of the Peace, would be sitting all afternoon to hear accusations against one, Elizabeth Saxton, accused of witchcraft.

The arrival of so sombre a party, however, caused all to stop what they were doing and a sudden silence fell as the makeshift bier was set down outside the schoolmaster's house.

'What's this?' Page called from his doorstep. 'Has there been an accident?' He came forward, stopping in surprise at the sight of Harry Thornton slumped on John's horse. 'How now? I thought you were in London?'

'You'd best take a look at this, Master Page,' said John, motioning towards the bier. 'Then perhaps you can put her somewhere seemly while her father is fetched. Meanwhile I'll go and seek out my master and Dr Brett.'

Page bent over the bier, several interested citizens jostling him from behind as he did so. 'God's Blood!' he burst out. 'What villainy have we here? Poor, poor girl! What will this do to her family?' He turned to his son. 'Jack, run to the Manor and tell them what has happened. Ask them to bring a cart so that she can be taken home. In the meantime, she can be carried into the courtyard of our house. And you,' he said to one of the bystanders, 'fetch Sir Edward Ratcliffe here at once; he needs to know of this. The rest of you go about your business. You'll hear all, soon enough.'

Within minutes, Susan Thornton had been placed in Page's back yard, while John immediately went across the street to Hugh Brett's house to inform both doctors of his discovery. He was met by the housekeeper who told him that Dr Brett was out, but he would find Dr Forman in the parlour reading over some of her master's notes. As succinctly as possible, John explained the train of events to him.

'God's Beard!' Simon exclaimed on hearing the tale. 'Do you think I should go over there or wait until Hugh returns? He could be some time.'

'I think you should come and see it all for yourself, doctor,' John advised. 'There are things about this killing which puzzle me.'

'Are you suggesting young Thornton's not telling the truth, or at least not all the truth?' asked Simon, immediately picking up what his servant had left unspoken.

'Well, doctor, let's just say I find it very strange that there's no sign whatsoever of the man Wynfred. According to Thornton, the robbers took him away with his wife, but if they did, why didn't they kill him too?'

Simon shrugged. 'Maybe he escaped.'

'Maybe,' John agreed, 'but Thornton insists that had his dear Francis got away, he would have come looking for them as soon as it was safe, given their devoted friendship.'

'It's not unknown for friendship, however devoted, to fly out of the window when it's a matter of self-preservation,' commented Simon wryly. 'We'll talk of this again when I've seen the situation for myself. You say Thornton's wounded?'

'A gash on the leg, which I bound up as best I could, and he also claims he was hit over the head.'

'Then I'll take my bag with me. It might be useful.'

The picture that confronted them had changed little since John had left, except that Sir Edward was now present and Harry Thornton once again sat mourning over the body of his wife which was now decently covered by one of Mistress Page's sheets.

'A bad business, Dr Forman,' Sir Edward said heavily to him by way of greeting. 'It seems your witch isn't the only hazard in these parts, for I'm told this is one of a number of recent attacks made on travellers in or near to the woods. Of the two, I tell you now I consider this of more importance than whether or not some old woman is said to practise the Black Arts. There must be an inquest, of course, and I've already sent word to the Coroner. In the meantime, I suggest a party of responsible fellows be sent out to search for any signs of these rogues and also for the third member of the party who, I understand, is still missing. Francis Wynfred, isn't it?' He sighed. 'I fear, given the circumstances, that all we're likely to find are his remains.'

'I'll go with any such party,' John volunteered. 'If young Page comes with me, then between us I'm sure we can find again the exact spot where I came on Thornton, then his wife's body.'

There was a clatter of hoofs in the street, the sound of a voice loudly calling for Master Page, followed by the bustle of dismounting and a woman's softer tone, then Master Carter and Phillipa came swiftly into the yard. Both halted when they saw the sheeted body on the makeshift bier. Saul Carter looked round the circle of sorrowful faces. 'My daughter?' he choked out.

'I'm so sorry,' said Page quietly.

The farmer went over and knelt beside her and carefully drew back the sheet. All present fell silent as he did so. 'Dear God in Heaven!' he whispered as he saw his daughter's still face. He laid his hand on her brow and flinched at its coldness. Then he turned on Harry a face so contorted by fury that the young man cowered in front of him. Carter rose to his feet.

'This, sir,' he raged, 'is all your doing. We warned you of the hazards of travelling through the wood carrying full saddlebags with you but you wouldn't be told, would you? Oh no, not you. And now my darling daughter is dead – while you still live and breathe, damn you!' He looked around wildly. 'And where's that mincing fellow Wynfred you took along with you, he who boasted he could fight his corner should need arise? Ran off, did he, at the first sign of trouble?'

'The robbers took him away when they carried off Susan,' Harry replied wretchedly, 'and you don't need to tell me I should have heeded the advice I was given. Don't you think I've agonised over my foolhardiness ever since this happened?'

115

Carter dismissed this with a wave of his arm. 'I should never have listened to your father's persuasion or Susan's pleas that you should wed her,' he said bitterly. 'Had she married Somerton as I'd wished, this would never have happened. *You've lost me my daughter, Harry Thornton!*' he roared.

Phillipa, who had stood by white-faced and stunned throughout, went over now and caught her father by the arm. 'Now now, Father, not here. We must see to Susan first. There'll be time enough for blame afterwards.'

Her quiet common sense calmed her father and he turned aside, struggling to hide his tears. There came the rumble of a cart from outside and two or three servants from the Manor appeared and stood awkwardly at the opening to the yard.

'Here is the body of my sister,' Phillipa told them. 'Let us place her in the cart and then you must bear her swiftly away. We don't want to make any more public show than can be helped.' The cart was backed towards the yard and willing hands lifted the bier gently into it. As it drove it away, Phillipa thanked the Pages for their kindness. 'My father and I must leave now to make sure all's ready to receive my sister.' Her voice broke. 'She must be washed and laid out in seemly fashion. Then we must see to her burial.'

Harry Thornton struggled to his feet. 'What about me?'

'Find him a horse, someone, and he can ride with us,' Carter responded impatiently. 'I trust your father will demand a proper explanation from you for all this,' he added with a look of disgust. Then he caught sight of Simon. 'I don't see the need for you to be here, doctor, there's nothing for you to do.'

'I understand the young man has a leg wound,' Simon replied, 'so I thought I might ride over to the Manor and see to it properly since Dr Brett will not be back for some time. An untreated wound may well lead to fever after a night in the open.' He cleared his throat and moved closer.

'Also, if you will allow it, I should like to examine your daughter's injuries. It might be of use to know exactly how they were inflicted in the event of her assailants being caught. It could help to prove their guilt.'

Carter was about to demur but Sir Edward stopped him. 'I agree with Dr Forman,' he said. 'I have myself sat on cases where such knowledge has proved invaluable.'

There being no more to be done, the small crowd which had observed the events slowly dispersed. 'First we'll snatch some bread and cheese,' said Simon to John as they left the Pages' yard, 'then you must set off with this search party while I go to the Manor, though I have doubts of my reception there.'

'What do you want me to look for in the woods, apart from Wynfred?' John asked.

'Oh, you're experienced enough now to know what interests me. See what signs these fellows have left, if any. Look for the weapon with which the girl was stabbed, for it might well lead us eventually to its owner. It could have been thrown into a bush somewhere near by. But yes, above all, look for Wynfred.'

Later, as he rode towards the Manor, Simon thought again of the strange relationship between Thornton and the missing man. Why had the robbers separated them, dragging Susan and Wynfred away and leaving Thornton behind? Was there, *could* there, be any collusion between the robbers and that strange young man?

He arrived at the Manor to find a grief-stricken household. Susan had only been mistress there for a short while, but she had been much liked by the servants, many of whom felt sorry, even indignant, over the way their young master had treated his bride, neglecting her and openly preferring the company of his friend. Simon was greeted at the door by Phillipa, still dry-eyed and in deep shock.

'We are presently laying out my sister,' she told him, 'and when all is done, my father has agreed to let you see her. In the meantime, perhaps you would look at Harry's wound as it seems to be causing him increasing pain. He's in the kitchen.'

Poor girl, thought Simon, first to suffer near-rape, then the murder of her sister. Another thought struck him. Could there be any connection between the two events? Yet again Cuddy Banks had been in the woods at the same time. Was there a real possibility he might be in league with the robbers? As Phillipa mounted the stairs, Harry appeared in the hall, clinging to the doorpost. 'Let me go to her now,' he pleaded.

Phillipa stopped. 'I'll tell you when she's fit to be seen. Go back to the kitchen now with Dr Forman and let him see to your injury.' As she looked at him, her tears finally began to flow. 'Susan wanted your love and attention throughout all these weeks, Harry, but you spurned her, lavishing all your attention on Francis instead of your bride. Not now she's dead. You must excuse my lack of sympathy for your grief.' Her voice choked on sobs and she ran quickly up the staircase.

Harry swayed, his face even whiter. Simon went over to him. 'Come on now, Thornton, leave her to do what has to be done. It's only sensible I see to your wound.'

They went into the kitchen, stepping aside to allow a tearful maid to pass on her way upstairs, bearing a bowl of water and some cloths. Harry sighed and sat down heavily on a wooden bench, extending his leg for Simon to examine it. Untying the kerchief with which his servant had bound it, Simon felt a certain amount of satisfaction at how much John had learned during the last years. The wound he exposed was as John had described it to him – long, shallow and disabling, but not life-threatening. It was clean, if somewhat red and angry along the edges. Simon bent over and sniffed.

'You're lucky. It's a little inflamed but there's no sign of putrefaction. It's as well my servant found you when he did. I'll treat it with a salve I have with me, then you must ask your father to send one of the servants into town to the apothecary for certain herbs.' He paused. It occurred to him that he had seen no sign of the master of the house since his arrival. 'I take it your father's here and knows what's happened?'

'He's upstairs with Carter,' Harry informed him. 'I'm surprised you haven't heard them railing at each other.'

'I see. Well, I'll write a note for the apothecary for the herbs, also for the ingredients for a physic to allay any possible fever that may arise.' He examined the wound again. 'It seems an odd place to have such a slash. I'd have imagined an assailant to have aimed first at your body if he chose to use a knife.'

'We were grappling with each other close,' Harry explained, 'it was catch as catch can. He was trying to stab me with a knife and I was doing all I could to ward him off. Then I slipped and we wrestled each other to the ground. It was then I took the wound as I tried to struggle to my feet, after which I was hit on the head and knew no more.'

'Did one of the other fellows return to help his confederate then, or do you think there was a fourth man you didn't see?'

Harry shook his head. 'I don't know. I simply don't know.'

Simon took a pot of salve out of his bag, applied it to the wound, then asked a kitchenmaid to fetch him a clean piece of cloth to use as a bandage. He stood up. 'And now I'll look at your head. Whereabouts were you hit?'

Harry patted the back of his head gingerly. 'Here. You can feel the lump.'

Simon did so. 'Hm, I see.' He prodded it gently and Harry winced. 'It's not as large as I would have expected, but blows to the head are strange things. Sometimes the smallest can cause unconsciousness while a greater has little or no effect. A simple cold compress is the best cure for that. Well,' he concluded gravely, 'it's a wonder you weren't murdered as well as your wife, particularly if, as

I'm told, you saw the face of one of the fellows. He must be fearful you will recognise him again.'

He was knotting the bandage on Harry's thigh when the maid reappeared. 'Mistress Phillipa says you can go up now, sir, but don't stay too long.' Harry at once struggled to his feet. 'No, not you, Master Harry,' she told him firmly. 'She says she'll send for you after the doctor's seen her sister.'

Susan's body lay on the marital bed. It had been washed and dressed in a fine white shift, her bloodstained clothing lying in a heap on the floor. Her long hair, lovingly combed out, lay in a cloud around her. Saul Carter and Adam Thornton were standing side by side gazing out of the window. The tension between them was palpable. Saul turned as Simon entered.

'Now I hear even more bitter news,' he grated. 'Phillipa tells me Susan was with child. Why did she say nothing of it to me?'

Simon was taken aback. If, as was so widely thought, the marriage had come about so rapidly because of the bride's condition, then how was it possible Saul should not have known of it before the marriage took place? What other reason could there be for so much haste? And Adam too. And even if, for some unimaginable reason, Carter had *not* been aware of his daughter's pregnancy, then he would surely have guessed by now, some two months after the wedding? Simon did a swift calculation in his head.

To be reasonably certain she was with child before the marriage, the girl must have missed her courses at least twice, which would make her now over four months forward. Her gowns might have concealed it from the casual observer, but surely not from those who lived with her or knew her from childhood.

He made no comment, however, merely asking Phillipa quietly if he might now be allowed to examine her sister's wounds. She nodded and turned aside as he gently untied the ribbons that fastened the girl's shift. The death stiffening had almost gone. He bent over and looked closely at her chest. To his surprise he saw she had received but one blow and that, most accurately, into the heart.

'This is the only wound?' he enquired. 'From the state of her gown, I'd thought she'd been stabbed many times.'

Phillipa shook her head. 'There was no other. It was enough.'

'It was certainly enough,' Simon agreed grimly. 'All that can be said by way of comfort is that death must have been instantaneous and that she felt no pain.' He hesitated before asking the next question. 'There was no . . . no sign of violation?'

The girl gave him a level look. 'No, doctor. It seems we've both been spared that.'

Cautiously, with a backward glance at the two men who had resumed staring out of the window, he opened the girl's shift a little more to see her abdomen, then drew back in surprise. He had expected to see the noticeable swelling of a woman almost halfway through her term, instead of which he could see no signs of a child, apart from a possible enlargement of the breasts. He looked up at Phillipa and frowned.

'You say your sister was with child. Are you certain? There are no outward signs of it.'

'She was barely two months forward,' replied Phillipa. 'She told me she must have conceived on her wedding night or very near to it. But she was quite certain. She had missed her courses twice and besides was sick of a morning.'

'And she told no one but you? Why was that?'

'Apparently,' broke in Carter, overhearing this, 'her father-in-law didn't know either – and he was living in the same house as my girl. That is, if he's to be believed!'

Adam began an angry reply but Phillipa at once sternly intervened. 'Remember where you are. If you wish to quarrel then do so downstairs, not in front of Susan's body.'

121

Simon turned to her again. 'Did your sister explain why she wanted only you to know? Surely it's usual for such glad tidings to be shared? Or was it because neither of you now have a mother and Master Thornton's wife too is dead? Or even perhaps because she feared she might miscarry the child if she talked of it too early? Some women are superstitious that way.'

Phillipa shook her head. 'No, or at least not exactly. She wanted all to know of her joy, but said Harry had told her she must keep the news to herself for the time being. When she asked him why, he told her it was for fear Old Mother Saxton would hear of it and bewitch her so that she either lost the child or delivered one that was stillborn or hare-shotten. I told her that was nonsense, but she wouldn't go against her husband. Before she left for London, though, she told me that he had promised she might tell everyone on their return.'

There seemed little more to say. Simon carefully retied the ribbon on the shift and then crossed the arms over the breast. As he left Phillipa went over and bound up the jaw with a cerecloth and placed coins on her sister's eyes.

The two men followed him out of the room. 'We must leave no stone unturned to bring these villains to justice,' said Adam Thornton gruffly as they reached the hall.

'Had your precious son listened to reason, my daughter would not be lying up there now,' raged Carter in reply. 'But no, he was determined to ride through the wood – and as for that creature he took with him . . .' Words failed him.

'Did you know young Wynfred before?' Simon asked Thornton.

He shook his head. 'No, never. I was as puzzled as anyone else that my son should have so close a friend yet I know nothing of it. But he's always been one for keeping some matters to himself.'

Simon left them to their mutual recriminations and mounted his horse, his head seething. Again and again he returned to the question of Susan's pregnancy. Had she thought she was with child when they were wed, but then discovered she was not? Had she been so besotted by Harry Thornton that she had encouraged him to make love to her then lied to him to ensure he married her? Had she, perish the thought, given herself to someone else, who had then refused to marry her and therefore she had prevailed on Harry to do so? If any of those reasons obtained then it might go some way to explaining Harry's coolness towards his young bride, if not to excuse it.

Chapter 9

Place of Murder

Simon was surprised to discover on returning to Hugh's house that John Bradedge was still there. He found him sitting with Dr Brett in the parlour informing him of the day's dramatic events.

'What's happened to your search party?' enquired Simon.

'You might well ask,' fumed John. 'First there was an argument as to who should go, then some of those chosen also wished to give evidence against the witch to the Justice and insisted on doing so before leaving – and so it's dragged on and on. I've left them to it after telling them that by the time they make their minds up, the robbers will be safely in London spending their ill-gotten gains, if they aren't there already.'

'I share John's frustration,' Hugh agreed, 'but it's always so in small communities – self-importance, who-does-what, feelings of slight can all take precedence over common sense. Sir Edward isn't going to go away. Those with something to tell him could have done so when they came back. I'm sure John's right – the culprits will be well away by now. A more rational reason for delay is that a jury must be selected for tomorrow's inquest. It's best it's conducted swiftly so that burial can take place and the grief of the families concerned is not made worse.'

John stood up. 'Now you're back, doctor, I'll go over to

Master Page's and see what's to do. Surely they must have agreed to set off by now.'

'I had been hoping to return to London tomorrow,' Simon told Hugh as John left. 'Sadly, I cannot stay here much longer as there are pressing affairs to see to at home. But I feel I must remain a little while longer, for there is something about this business that worries me. First, there is the complete disappearance of Francis Wynfred though this search party, when it finally organises itself, might well find his body and that would explain it. Nor am I entirely satisfied with young Thornton's account of events. Then there's the question of Susan having been with child when she died.'

'That can hardly come as a surprise,' commented Hugh, dryly. 'Half the town were convinced it was the sole reason for so hasty a marriage.'

'Then it may startle you as much as it did me to learn, when I examined the body fully expecting to see all the signs of a young woman by now more or less halfway through her term, to find no obvious evidence of it at all. When I queried this, Phillipa assured me her sister had indeed been with child, though only some two months forward.'

Hugh frowned. 'That does indeed come as a surprise. What does her father say about it?'

'That he didn't even know of it.'

'What!' exclaimed Hugh. 'He must have done.'

'According to Phillipa, who Susan insisted on telling, she and Susan were sworn to secrecy by Harry Thornton on the grounds that if it were known Susan was carrying a child, then she stood in jeopardy of being bewitched by Mother Saxton, with dire results. Phillipa did not believe such stuff but Thornton certainly convinced her sister. It therefore seems clear the child was conceived in wedlock.'

Hugh looked nonplussed. 'I'm at a loss to know what to make of it all. The speed of the betrothal and wedding certainly suggested otherwise and so set tongues clacking.

Do you think she was mistaken beforehand or perhaps lost the first child after the wedding had been arranged? The latter might explain why she did as her husband told her, fearful it might happen again.'

'There seem to me to be a number of possibilities,' Simon began and was about to launch into them when they were interrupted by John Bradedge.

'We're off at last,' he said. 'Do you want to come with us, doctor?'

Simon thought for a moment. 'Very well. If you'll excuse me, Hugh, I think I will. Saddle my horse for me again, will you, John?'

A few minutes later they were riding along a route which was becoming all too familiar, past the gate of the Manor, a little way further on, then right into the wood. The group was led by Jack Page, who reckoned he could remember exactly where he had come on John and the wounded Harry, and was soon proved right for within twenty minutes or so he had guided them to it. All dismounted.

'Can you show us where you found Thornton this morning, Master Bradedge?' asked the leader of the party, a burly farmer by the name of Sam Jukes.

John looked around then pointed to a place beneath a tree. 'That's where I found him. His hands were tied behind him and he'd been trying to work them free.' He bent down. 'Look, here's the rope with which he was tied. You can see where I cut it through, though he had almost managed to free himself by the time I came on the scene.' He pointed towards the path leading away opposite. 'And it was down there I discovered the body of the poor young woman.'

'What do you think we should do now, doctor?' asked Jukes. 'My own feeling is that we should spread out and search the area as well as we can, though I can't really believe the robbers are still hereabouts.'

'We can at least see if they've left any traces,' replied

127

Simon, 'places where they might have tied up horses, tracks leading off in any particular direction. And, of course, we need to look for Francis Wynfred's body and the knife or dagger with which Susan Thornton was killed. Will you see what you can find on the paths leading away from here? Meanwhile John and I will examine the place where the body was found. It might tell us something.'

He turned to John. 'Show me, if you can, exactly where you found the body.'

John led the way and within a few minutes had reached the place. 'You can see there was something lying here,' he pointed out, 'and some of these footmarks around about are those of the men who put her onto the hurdle, plus Thornton's and my own, of course.'

Simon sighed. 'It would certainly be impossible by now given the number of folk who tramped up and down around here to find any useful traces of what might have happened. Unless, of course, she was killed somewhere else. Thornton says she and Wynfred were dragged away. Perhaps there was an attempt at rape, a struggle and the girl was killed by mistake and the body dumped back here. Let's go on a little further.'

As usual the wood proved confusing for there were at least three paths leading away from them now, the first one obviously well used by both riders and those on foot, the other two less so. The prints of deer on the middle one suggested it was mostly the preserve of wild creatures. They therefore took the third path and soon found themselves in luck, for within fifty yards John pointed to a small piece of yellow cloth caught on a briar; a couple of feet further along was another. 'The girl's gown was that colour,' he said. 'She must have either been taken through here or brought back this way.'

Simon bent over to look. 'And here's another. Now that's odd.' John looked at him enquiringly. 'See now, from where we are standing the brambles on which they're caught are pulled forward.'

'So she was killed down here somewhere then carried back.'

Simon shook his head. 'I don't think so. Look, there's another fragment, back the way we've come.' He reached down for it. 'And there's something else too. Let's see . . . a woman's black travelling hat.' He lifted it up. 'The pin's still in it and some long hairs. It looks as if it was pulled off forcibly rather than having fallen off.' He paused. 'I don't think she was brought back this way dead, I think she was alive and running. Let's go back the way we came and this time we'll look more carefully.'

They retraced their steps and were rewarded by the discovery of several more scraps of yellow wool along with a small piece of petticoat lace. 'Now,' said Simon when they arrived back where they started, 'let's see if there's anything here.'

The leaves had blown steadily off the trees during the last few days and the floor of the clearing was thickly carpeted with them. But finally they found a place where the ground underneath had obviously been disturbed. Simon knelt down and cleared away the leaves with his hand. 'See, there are some marks here though they are not very clear. But surely this small footprint is that of a woman?' He frowned. 'That's strange. There's another small print here as well but the two are not alike. The rest of the ground is much churned up.' He put his hand down on the ground to steady himself and then drew back. 'What's this?'

'It looks like blood,' said John

Simon scooped away the leaves. 'There's quite a lot of it. And something else.' It was an ornate dagger sheath made of leather banded with chased metal. 'A handsome piece for a footpad,' he remarked grimly, handing it up to John.

John examined it. 'What do you think, doctor?' he asked as Simon rose to his feet.

Simon looked thoughtful. 'I'm not sure. I believe Susan

129

Thornton was killed here, where we're standing. That before that, she ran *into* this clearing, not away from it and then, after her death, she was taken to where we found her. But why? Thornton insists she and Wynfred were taken away almost immediately and he left behind here in this very spot – yet if that was the case, she must have been killed in front of him.'

'He *was* knocked unconscious,' John reminded his master.

'Even so, why take his wife's body away? There was nothing he could do; the girl was already dead and he securely tied up. Oh dear, I thought we might learn something by coming here, not confuse ourselves even more.'

There was a soft rustle among the bushes and suddenly Mother Saxton appeared, apparently from out of nowhere, the black dog at her heels. John at once jumped back as if stung. She looked at him with amusement.

'So while they were all railing at me and threatening me with the scaffold there was murder afoot in the woods,' she said. 'I warned you of it. I said there'd be death.'

'What do you know about it then?' John asked, feeling deeply uneasy. 'It's occurred to me before that you might well be in league with the villains who haunt this place. Do you give them notice of travellers who might be in or near the wood in exchange for gold or other goods?'

She turned to face him with her good eye. 'Since you also think I can raise Satan and cast spells, why should I bother with mere mortal cut-throats? Surely I can also conjure up fairy gold?'

John was about to come back at her but Simon motioned him to be quiet. 'Do you know anything of what happened hereabouts recently, Mother Saxton? This is where John found Harry Thornton this morning, bound and wounded, his wife stabbed to death close by. Is it possible you can help us? I must tell you that the reason my servant was in the wood was to try to prevent any of the rioters from creeping back to your home and taking matters into their own hands. You owe him your thanks.'

'If you were aware of any men lurking about in the wood,' added John, 'can you tell us the direction in which they went? Or if you have seen anything of the young man who was travelling with the Thorntons at the time?'

Mother Saxton gave this some thought then slowly shook her head. 'I've seen nothing of any young man nor have I seen or heard anything of any strangers hereabouts over the last two or three days, though as a rule I know if there are folk in the wood even if they avoid me, as they mostly do. But I will tell you what I did see early yesterday morning, though whether it has any bearing on the matter, I cannot say.'

'Tell us then,' growled John.

'You say these folk set out on their journey yesterday morning? Well, at dawn I left my house to gather sticks and pick mushrooms before others were up and about, and I went some good distance along the roadway for the best mushrooms grow in several places on the verges. By chance I happened to come on young Master Thornton and the man, Guy Somerton, close to the Manor gates, deep in a quarrel.' She paused to see what impression she was making, saw she had their attention and continued.

'I may be half blind but there's nothing amiss with my hearing, and anyway they were both shouting. Somerton was telling Thornton that he was treating his wife shamefully, preferring his friend to the woman he had only just promised before God to love and honour. Thornton demanded what it was to him since he had so swiftly switched his affections to his wife's sister, to which Somerton replied that he had every right, both as the accepted suitor of Phillipa Carter, who was made most unhappy by his behaviour, and because of his past love for her sister. I didn't catch what Thornton said next but it enraged Somerton and he accused someone . . . Francis, was it? . . . of being Thornton's catamite, at which the two would have fallen to blows had not some farm labourers appeared, at which point they obviously thought better of it.

'So they parted, Thornton shouting as he left that he would call Somerton out and fight him when he returned from London, whereupon Somerton yelled after him that he'd settle the matter before that. Somerton remained for some time after Thornton left, pacing up and down in fury. What he did next, I don't know for I went back to my house for my breakfast, along with my familiar here.' She bent down and patted the dog which licked her hand.

It was an interesting tale, thought Simon. He recalled Somerton's anger at Susan's wedding. Obviously his feelings against Thornton still ran deep. Was it possible, in spite of his professed feelings for her sister, that he was still consumed with jealousy towards Harry Thornton?

He thanked the old woman. 'Whether or not what you saw has anything to do with what happened later, only time will tell. At present we are still seeking for robbers though I myself am not so sure, and I believe you when you say you weren't aware of anyone hiding out here yesterday.'

'I swear to you I was not. Nor does it make sense, for weren't they being sought for the attack on the two men on the highway? They'd be fools to set on another party again so soon after. For all they knew, there could have been men posted in the wood waiting for them to strike.' Even John had to agree that her words did indeed make sense.

Simon touched her hand gently. 'And now I think you should take the Justice's advice and pack up and leave this place. Whatever the outcome of his enquiries, I fear for your safety. You'll never sleep quietly again.'

Lizzie Saxton gave a weary smile. 'I would that I could. But now there's more to prevent me.'

Simon was about to ask what she meant when they heard Jukes calling out for them. 'We must go back to the rest of the men,' Simon told her. 'It's best you aren't seen.' Without another word Mother Saxton vanished as quietly as she had come, just as the rest of the men reappeared.

'I see you've had more luck than we have,' commented Jukes, seeing the hat in John's hand.

'And we found this too,' he replied, holding out the dagger sheath. 'Do any of you recognise it?'

Jack Page came and took it from him but shook his head. 'It's a fine piece of work, though – hardly likely to be the property of a common robber.'

'Unless he stole it from one of his victims,' commented Jukes. The sheath was handed round the group but no one claimed to have seen it before. 'Where did you find it, Dr Forman?' asked the farmer.

'Right here. Which makes the matter even more baffling.' He did not elaborate, contenting himself with remarking that he presumed they had found nothing.

Jukes sighed and shook his head. 'Nothing at all. We've searched around as well as we could, looking among the briars and in the bushes to see if Wynfred had been left dying or dead, hidden out of sight, but there's no sign of him.' He glanced at Susan's hat. 'Not even his hat, which you might have expected to fall off during any struggle. Nor did we find any traces of men either having hidden out or made off in a hurry.' He turned to his party. 'Well, lads, it'll soon be dark. We'll make our way home and find out what's toward there. What with witchcraft and murders and now an inquest . . .'

The men mounted their horses and picked their way carefully along the path until they reached the highway and could ride freely. 'Do you think this fellow Wynfred could be in league with the robbers?' asked Jukes as he fell in beside Simon.

'I've certainly considered it,' the doctor confessed, 'but he seems an unlikely member of such a band. We're talking of rough and violent cut-throats, possibly disaffected ex-soldiers or masterless men. Wynfred was obviously well brought up, softly spoken and very much the gentleman, though I suppose his involvement can't be ruled out. Perhaps he promised to run away and say nothing in exchange for his life.'

Jukes nodded. They had reached the end of a lane. 'My farm lies up yonder,' he said, 'and I'm one called to sit on the jury at the Crowner's 'Quest which is likely to be tomorrow. Will you be there? Your man is to be called since he found the body.'

'Then I will be there, Master Jukes.'

Simon was just about to spur his horse when they heard galloping hoofs on the road behind them and a horse and rider came into sight. The horseman, seeing the party, pulled up his mount. 'Good day, gentlemen,' he said. 'Do any of you happen to be Sir Edward Ratcliffe?'

'Sir Edward's in Pinner, hearing accusations of witch-craft,' Jukes replied. 'Have you come from the Coroner? I know Sir Edward's sent for him.'

The man looked mystified. 'I know nothing of any Coroner. I've come to find Sir Edward in his capacity as a Justice to say we have three stout rogues in custody who have committed highway robbery hereabouts. I was told he was either in Pinner or on his way there.'

'You have caught our robbers?' broke in one of the men. 'That's fine news indeed. We've just been out searching the woods for them. How did you catch them and where?'

'They were caught red-handed on common land outside Edmonton,' the man replied. 'One of the villains, trying to save his own skin, told us that they'd also attacked and robbed travellers in and around these woods. I am sent as messenger to tell Sir Edward so that he might know they've been taken and to see if he wishes to question them also.'

'God be praised!' responded Jukes. 'It seems we have our murderers, lads!'

'Murderers?' repeated the messenger doubtfully. 'The rascals said nothing of murder, though they've admitted dealing harshly with their victims.'

'Harshly? Is that what they call it? If it is the same fellows, they injured a man some two months back so badly that he died, left two others for dead beside this very road three days ago, and only yesterday morning murdered a young woman and wounded her husband.'

The messenger looked puzzled. 'It seems very likely these same men are responsible for the first two crimes, but as to the murder of the young woman, that cannot be. For by dawn yesterday we had them safe in custody. I fear you must look elsewhere for your murderer.'

'So now where do we look?'

Simon set down his wine cup. He and Hugh had talked long over supper, for there was much to discuss. Pinner was in turmoil. The Coroner was arriving first thing in the morning and the inquest was to be held at eleven o'clock in the Crown Inn. The number of those wishing to lay accusations against Lizzie Saxton had dropped off somewhat once news had got around about Susan's murder, but Sir Edward had still sat late into the afternoon.

Also it had proved no easy task to gather together fifteen good men and true for the inquest jury at such short notice, as well as trying to ensure all the relevant witnesses would be present. As to the inquest itself, Hugh told Simon it was expected to be a mere formality, the verdict being that Susan Thornton had been foully murdered by robbers who had waylaid the party on its way through the woods. Indeed, arrangements for Susan's burial had already been made for the same afternoon.

'I admit it seems strange there could be two sets of robbers in the woods,' said Hugh when he was told of the recent arrest, 'but how else can it be explained? Harry Thornton is adamant that they were set on by a band of violent men. Surely you aren't accusing him of lying?'

Simon sighed. 'I simply don't know. I agree he seemed to be telling the truth, but there are things in his story that don't hang together. Which brings me again to Wynfred.

135

Do you think he was privy to some altogether different plot and that he and the men in the wood were accomplices to it?'

'To what end?' queried Hugh.

'I told you I'd heard Thornton quarrelled bitterly with Somerton shortly before he and his party set off for London. Also what Somerton said of Wynfred. Suppose he was right, that the young man *was* Thornton's catamite, lover – call him what you will. I saw for myself how shocked Wynfred was when he learned of Thornton's marriage. Is it possible that he planned the whole thing, that these men, friends of his, paid assassins even, should set on them on their way to London and kill the girl? Her death would allow him to continue his intrigue with Thornton without let or hindrance.'

Hugh looked most doubtful. 'You describe something that sounds like a scenario for the playhouse. Even if you're right, surely Thornton would have realised what was happening? Or are you suggesting he was so besotted that he agreed to it, or at the very least is prepared to shield the man?'

Simon looked rueful. 'I don't know. But you must admit it's strange that there's no sign of Wynfred at all. Even if he's completely innocent of any wrongdoing, you'd have thought he'd have gone back to aid his friends, had he managed to escape, not just leave them to their fate to save his own skin.

'Then to return again to Somerton and the quarrel between him and Thornton, I myself heard him talking wildly of revenge at the wedding. But I ask myself what he could possibly gain from killing Susan when he's planning to marry her sister? As to Harry, he was already threatening Somerton with a duel, so why invent tales of visor-clad robbers if it *was* Somerton? He would surely be shouting the name of the murderer from the rooftops, eager to see him hang.'

'Well, I can't make head nor tail of any of it,' said Hugh.

136

He yawned. 'I'm for my bed. What a day! First a witchhunt, then I am called out to some poor soul who has suffered an apoplexy miles away, only to return to find we are in the midst of a murder. Whatever next?'

Simon was following him up the stairs when there came a banging on the front door. 'Oh no,' moaned Hugh.

'I'll open it,' said Simon. 'No doubt your housekeeper's abed.'

'Tell them that unless it's a matter of life and death, it must wait until morning,' said Hugh and disappeared into his bedchamber.

The unwelcome visitor was a breathless servant from the Manor who had obviously been running. 'It's Master Harry,' he gasped. 'He's taken really bad. He has a fever.'

'That's hardly surprising,' said Simon, 'it often happens in such cases. Has he taken the medicine I prescribed?'

The servant shook his head. 'He's refused all aid since you left, sir, but just keeps weeping and blaming himself for the young mistress's death, and now he's claiming to see a black dog in the room.'

'Then see to it that he takes his draught whether he will or no,' Simon told him firmly. 'Inform your household that either I or Dr Brett will come and see young Master Thornton in the morning. The wound will heal and the fever will pass. Now be off with you for I, too, am going to bed.' And with that he closed the door and shot home the bolts.

Chapter 10

The Woman in Black

As soon as they had breakfasted, both Hugh and Simon set off for the Manor, for Simon wanted Hugh to see Harry Thornton's wound for himself as well as to check on his fever. While they were eating, Andrew Page had called to tell them that Susan's body was to be brought to the church to enable the jury to see it, rather than be placed in an outhouse at the Crown, and that the burial would take place that afternoon following the inquest; meanwhile John Bradedge had been served with an official summons to attend as witness to the discovery of the body.

They were greeted at the Manor door by a distraught housekeeper. 'Your servant came last night and spoke with Dr Forman about young Master Thornton's fever,' Hugh told her, 'so now we have come as promised.'

The woman looked uncertain. 'They will shortly be here to take the young mistress's body to the church,' she said, tears welling up in her eyes. 'As to seeing the young master . . .'

'What is it, Nell?' Harry's father appeared behind her, his face showing clearly the effect of the last two days.

'We are here to see your son. I brought Dr Forman with me as he treated him yesterday in my absence.'

'You'd best come in then.' Adam motioned them inside. 'Though whether you can do any good, I don't know. Come upstairs quietly and then keep out of the way. Susan

139

is coffined and will be taken from here any time and I don't want Harry to know. He will only try to go with her, and there is no question of his being fit enough to attend the inquest or her burial. Never have I seen such grief!'

The two doctors looked at each other at this but said nothing, merely following Thornton up the wide staircase. Harry lay twisting from side to side in his bed, his face flushed with fever. Hugh felt his forehead and then his pulse, then pulled aside the bedclothes. The bandaging on his thigh was quite clean, no blood had seeped through it. Nor, when he peered under its edges, was there any sign of growing inflammation. Like Simon before him, he sniffed the area but there was no smell of decay.

'I find it hard to understand why he should be in this state,' he said to Adam finally. 'Except that Dr Forman was told last night that he had refused to take the draught prescribed for allaying any fever.'

Adam sighed. 'Harry said it would be useless. We all tried to make him take it, but he refused. He was ever wilful.'

That much was certain, thought Simon. Then he looked over to a corner of the room and to his amazement saw two full saddlebags propped against the wall.

'What are those?' he enquired. 'The dark blue cloth bag looks like the one I saw attached to your son's saddle when they were setting off for London.'

'It is indeed that very bag,' said Adam. 'Early this morning a farmer from Oxhey called here, bringing with him the bags in his cart. He said he'd found them on the verge beside the road to London. It seems the scoundrels must have taken flight as they did after the last attack and dropped them.'

'Whoever put them where they were found, it was not the same robbers who set on the two men so recently attacked on the highway,' said Simon and explained to Thornton how those particular men had been safely in custody when his daughter-in-law was killed.

140

'Well, there must be others lurking out there in the woods,' returned Adam crossly. 'But what of it? I thought you were here to treat my son?'

'And so we are,' soothed Hugh, 'but surely you want his attackers to be caught and punished? Have you examined the bags?' Adam shook his head. 'Then might it not be wise to do so in a little while? The villains could have left some clue behind which might help them to be traced. Jewellery stolen and later offered for sale, for example.'

There was a groan from the bed as Harry thrashed about even more wildly. 'What's this?' he whimpered, clutching at the sheet. 'A winding sheet?' He shrieked and sat bolt upright, bringing his father to the bedside.

'What ails you now, son? Here's Dr Brett come to see you, and Dr Forman.'

Harry's cries brought Phillipa speeding into the room. 'Here is the draught Dr Forman prescribed for him yesterday, and Nell has also heated up the posset.' From below came the sound of movement and tramping feet. She motioned Adam over to her and said softly, 'My father's below with the cart ready to take Susan to the church. Best you go now and help him – and let there be no more quarreling between you. Think how great our loss is compared to yours! I will see to Harry and then follow you to the Crowner's 'Quest. There's plenty of time.' Adam patted her arm then went without another word.

'Come now, Harry,' said Phillipa as soon as Thornton had departed, 'cease this foolishness. You are working yourself into a worse fever. Take the draught and you will soon feel better.'

'Yes, do,' urged Hugh, 'for like Dr Forman I can see no reason now why your wound should not heal quickly and well.'

Harry stared at them with unseeing eyes. 'Francis? Where's Francis? He came here last night when all were abed. Where is he now? Francis! Francis?'

141

'Wynfred's not here,' said Phillipa impatiently. 'He's not been seen since you were attacked – no one knows where he is. How could he visit you last night?'

Harry looked round wildly. 'He *was* here, I tell you. The back door was unlatched and he came in.' He gave them a cunning look. 'He's clever, is Francis. He said he'd told a fellow outside he was my horse-boy come to tell me he'd found my mare, so that he could visit me in my sickness.'

'It's but a dream,' Phillipa remonstrated, laying her hand on his arm, 'a fancy caused by fever, no more.'

'No, no, it's true.' Harry pushed her hand away. 'He said he'd haunt me now for I'd plucked down thunder on his head.' He frowned. 'Why him and not Susan?'

'This is madness, brain fever,' muttered Hugh.

Then Harry cried out again and pointed to a corner of the room. 'The black dog,' he yelled, 'the old witch's black dog! Surely you can all see it? Look, see how it prowls up and down. And now it's coming towards the bed.' He pressed himself up against the bed head, covering his eyes with his hands. 'Don't let it touch me!' he shrieked. 'See how I'm bewitched! Kill the witch, kill the witch!'

'There is *no* black dog here, Harry,' shouted Hugh, and slapped him hard across the face. 'Enough of these hysterics. If you don't stop this raving then for your own good you must needs be tied hand and foot and put in some dark place until you come to your senses. Simon, hold his head back and I will tip this draught down his throat.' Harry struggled at first but finally let them do it. 'And I've also brought with me some poppy syrup. You must swallow this too. Then you will sleep off your fever.'

This time Harry took his medicine quietly and within minutes, obviously exhausted, he fell into a deep sleep.

'Well, that was most strange,' commented Hugh, 'but then the brain can be affected by most odd fancies with high fever. But he still doesn't appear sick enough to me for so violent a fit.'

'Certainly this fever seems out of all proportion to his

142

injury,' Simon agreed, and would have gone further but was suddenly aware that the dead girl's sister was still present.

'We must leave him now, Mistress Phillipa, and you, no doubt, will wish to make ready for the inquest – and what comes after.' Hugh took her hand to comfort her. 'You are welcome to come with us and wait in my house if you wish.'

Phillipa shook her head. 'Thank you, Dr Brett, but I have things to do here. I doubt I will be visiting the Manor much in future.' Her eyes travelled to the saddlebags. 'It was strange, their being found by the roadside like that. One would have thought the thieves would have stowed them away out of sight against their return. I pray to God they're caught.'

Simon and Hugh exchanged looks. 'Perhaps you haven't heard, mistress, that the robbers who have been plaguing us of late have been taken,' said Simon, 'but you must also know that they did not kill your sister for they were already in gaol.'

Phillipa looked bewildered. 'So there must be more of them then. Is no one out searching the woods?'

'My servant and I joined a party ourselves yesterday,' Simon continued, 'and looked high and low but could find no traces of anyone at all.' He decided, for the time being, to make no mention of the hat and dagger sheath, or his growing certainty that Susan had been running *towards* the place where she was killed, not dragged away from it. 'I dislike asking you this,' he continued hesitantly, 'but had your sister or her husband any enemies that you know of?'

'No,' she replied with certainty. 'There has been, well, argument between Harry and Guy Somerton and that is well known, but as to murder . . . No, most definitely not.'

Simon thanked her. 'Perhaps later you could look in the saddlebags and see what, if anything, might have been taken; jewellery belonging to your sister, perhaps? Particularly any that could be traced back to her, as Hugh suggested. Or anything else that is of interest.'

'I'll do that,' she said, 'and if I find anything amiss, I promise I'll let you know.'

The two doctors went down the stairs and out into the forecourt. The cart was ahead of them, both Adam and Saul riding at its side. Phillipa was about to go back downstairs when on an impulse she went over to the saddlebags and knelt down beside them. She opened her sister's first. In it Susan had crammed the two gowns they had chosen together, another shift, two pairs of stockings, one of silk, gloves, a lace cap and at the bottom a small leather case. Phillipa lifted the lid and saw that her sister's jewellery was still there, including the pearl necklace which was her father's wedding present, the garnet earrings that had belonged to their mother, the brooch curiously formed in the shape of a butterfly which Harry had given her on their betrothal, and the comb for her hair set with semi-precious gems.

She sat back on her heels. Why hadn't the thieves at least taken the jewellery? The little case would easily have slipped into a doublet. Her interest now thoroughly aroused, she turned her attention to Harry's leather bag and undid the straps. Here again there were clothes, along with a change of linen, a book, a gold chain in a small case and at the bottom some kind of parcel, wrapped in cloth. She rooted down and pulled it out of the bag. As she did so the wrappings fell away and she looked in horror at the long thin dagger that fell out onto the floor.

The benches set out for the public at the inquest were, not surprisingly, crowded. News was only just getting around that the footpads responsible for the previous violent robbery, and who it had been assumed were also responsible for the murder, were already in gaol before the last attack took place. This was causing much noisy speculation in the makeshift courtroom.

The Coroner, Sir Robert Baldwyn, appeared sharp on

eleven o'clock, preceded by the constable and followed by the Clerk of the Court bearing rolls of parchment, an inkpot and several quill pens. All rose and the room fell silent.

'This Inquisition,' intoned the Clerk, 'is held today to enquire into the circumstances surrounding the death of Susannah Mary Thornton of the Manor, Pinner, the proceedings being before Robert Baldwyn, Coroner to this district. It is called here in Pinner in the county of Middlesex this 28th day of October 1592 in the thirty-fourth year of the reign of Elizabeth, by the Grace of God, Queen of England, France and Ireland, Defender of the Faith, in the presence of the said Robert Baldwyn, upon the view of Susan Thornton here lying dead and slain. The jury will now take the oath.'

There was a shuffling of feet as the fifteen members of the jury entered, each in turn swearing the oath on the Bible placed before them by the Clerk. Simon noticed Sam Jukes among them.

'You have viewed the body?' enquired the Coroner.

'We have, your honour,' they chorused.

'Have you elected one among you to be foreman?'

'We have decided it should be Samuel Jukes,' replied their spokesman.

The Coroner thanked them and asked the Clerk to read the indictment which he did, stating that on the morning of 24 October, the dead woman, her husband and a friend had been riding through the woods on their way to London when they were set on by footpads. According to the word of Harry Thornton, these footpads forcibly took away his wife and friend, wounding him in his attempt to come to their aid. The body of Mistress Susan Thornton was found the following day. She had been stabbed through the heart.

'Is Harry Thornton present?' asked the Coroner.

The Clerk shook his head. 'No, sir, I am told he is too sick to appear.'

Baldwyn frowned. 'I see. Then call the first witness.'

First to take the oath was John Bradedge who explained how, on the request of Sir Edward Ratcliffe, he had made his way through the woods with orders to deter any hotheads who might decide to return to the cottage of Elizabeth Saxton where there had been trouble earlier.

Baldwyn acknowledged that he had heard as much and asked John how he had come to find Susan's body.

'First I came on Master Harry Thornton, his hands bound behind him, and so searched near by to see if I could find his wife, which I did, sir. But she was past all human aid.'

'Did you find any weapon lying near by?'

John shook his head. 'I looked then and my master, Dr Forman, and I returned again yesterday to seek further but there was no sign of any weapon that we could see.'

'So what did you do after you found the body?'

'Informed Master Thornton and then, God be praised, I heard voices and called out and some young men from the town came to my aid.'

'You are sure they were men from the town? Did you recognise any of them?'

'Oh yes, sir. One was Jack Page, the schoolmaster's boy, and I knew several others by sight. They are morris men and had been practising their mystery in the wood – they took no part in the morning's affray.'

Baldwyn thanked him and John, wiping the sweat from his brow, stood down.

Next came the constable, who described the state of the body when he saw it first, told the Coroner of the sending out of a search party, and informed him that word had then come that the men under most suspicion for the crime had been apprehended before it had taken place.

Although the Coroner had already been informed of this fact by Sir Edward Ratcliffe, he was obviously puzzled. 'Your woodland is substantial but hardly a forest. Is it not strange that two such bands of villains should be operating within it at the same time?'

The constable had to agree that this was so. 'And the young man who survived the attack, he is certain that he was set upon by footpads?'

Again the constable agreed.

'I understand the young man's father is here,' said the Coroner. 'Would he be willing to come before us?'

Adam Thornton stood up from his place on one of the public benches to growing mutterings from the onlookers.

'You must be silent,' ordered the Coroner, 'or I will have to clear you from this place. Now, Master Thornton, can you tell us how your son described his attackers?'

Thornton repeated the story Harry had told John: of how he had fought with a man he had never seen before while his two companions had their faces concealed. This latter appeared to interest the Coroner.

'Could it be that these assailants were no ordinary robbers?' Without waiting for a reply and unconsciously echoing Simon's question to Phillipa, he added, 'Does your son have any enemies?'

Thornton paused at this. 'Well,' he said awkwardly, 'not an enemy exactly . . .'

'What do you mean by that?'

'Guy Somerton of Blackgates Hall was to have been betrothed to my son's wife, but she changed her mind and married my son instead. Somerton had much to say on the matter at first, indeed threatening both of them. But it's said he's now to marry Susan's sister, Phillipa. I had thought the ill-feeling between the two was over, but my son told me that just before he left for London they had quarrelled again, and that he was threatening to call Somerton out when he returned. However, Harry can often be rash in his behaviour and I doubt it would have come to that.'

'Do you know on what grounds they quarrelled?'

Thornton swallowed. 'It seems Somerton accused my son of neglecting his wife in favour of a friend, Francis Wynfred, who arrived at my house shortly after the

147

wedding and remained with us until two days ago.'

'Wasn't this Wynfred one of the party riding through the woods?' Thornton agreed that he was. 'So what happened to him?'

'We don't know, sir. There has been no sign of him since, although the woodland near by was thoroughly searched yesterday. It may be he escaped or that his body lies hidden elsewhere.'

The Coroner thanked Adam Thornton, dismissed him, then turned to the jury. 'You have heard the evidence given to this inquest. You may consider your verdict but it seems to me there is little choice as to what it should be. Do you wish to retire?'

Jukes looked round at the jurors, who all shook their heads. 'If we may confer quietly a moment?' he asked.

The Coroner nodded and the men went into a conclave in the corner while the noise on the public seats rose considerably. Some muttered that drastic action against footpads should have been taken long ago, except that those who had most to say in the town were either too cowardly or too lazy to act, while others claimed that they'd always thought Somerton was too big for his boots. 'Putting on airs like a lord's son,' said one woman, 'and his father only a country squire.'

This provoked an argument with her neighbour who defended Somerton, saying that she had always found him most civil and straightforward, and that though one shouldn't speak ill of the dead, that Susan Thornton had led him a fine dance, minx that she was, and no doubt had she lived, the reason for her hasty marriage to Harry would soon have become obvious to all. In her opinion, Somerton had had a lucky escape. At this her neighbour, who had brought her knitting with her, waved her needles vigorously and pointed out that all these troubles had only come to the town since Old Mother Saxton got up to her mischief: the sooner Sir Edward had her under lock and key the better. They then fell silent as the jury reassembled.

Baldwyn looked at them gravely. 'Members of the jury, have you considered your verdict?'

Jukes stepped forward. 'We have, sir.'

'And what judgement have you reached?'

'That Susan Thornton was most foully murdered by person or persons unknown.'

'Thank you,' said Baldwyn. 'I can but agree with you. But I would like to add two things. First, that every effort should be made to clear the area of these rogues, and second, that there are many aspects of this affair that I still find puzzling. It might be well if further enquiries are made.'

'Hardly satisfactory,' commented Hugh as his house-keeper served them their dinner a little while later.

'But all that could be expected in the circumstances.' The reference to Somerton had made Simon uneasy in view of what he had heard from Lizzie Saxton, and now it was common knowledge that the two men had fallen out as late as the very morning Thornton set off for London. Yet for the life of him he could not imagine that Somerton was in any way involved.

But the day had still one more surprise in store. Shortly after two o'clock in the afternoon the great bell of St Luke's Church began to toll, six taylors for the death of a woman, followed by nineteen strokes for the years of her age, then a continual solemn tolling as the mourners went into the church – the coffin, of course, having been carried there before them.

Simon had slipped into the church after the inquest with no very clear notion in mind, just as the carpenter and his boy were about to nail the lid down on the coffin. 'We'd thought her husband might have come for one last look,' the man remarked, 'but we're told he's grievous sick.'

'In mind, if not in body,' Simon agreed. He took one last look at the waxen face of the murdered girl. Already the first faint signs of putrefaction were beginning to stain

149

under her eyes and at her throat.

'There was one came to look though,' said the carpenter's boy. 'A lady, all in black. Did you know who she was, Joe?'

The carpenter shrugged. 'Never seen her before, so far as I know. Some cousin or friend from outside the parish, I imagine.' There was no more to be gained from staring at the corpse and Simon bade them good-day and returned to Hugh's house.

Now he stood towards the back of the church which was crowded with members of the two families concerned, their friends and neighbours and those who were there because they enjoyed a good funeral, not to mention the ghouls who fed on the circumstances surrounding the death. Simon noted that Guy Somerton stood close beside Phillipa throughout.

The service was brief, although Hugh's zealous parson, Wytherley, while praying that strength be given to all who mourned, robustly ordered the Lord to smite down those whose hands were stained with the blood of the innocent, as He'd done to the Babylonians and the Assyrians – with the rider that their carcases be thrown to the dogs. There was a slight noise behind him and Simon turned and saw that a woman had dropped her prayer book and was stooping to pick it up. She was all in black and heavily veiled, but as if feeling his eyes upon her, she looked across at him as she stood up. He could not make out her features through the black lace but she gave the appearance of being young. This, then, must have been the boy's lady in black.

The service came to an end and the parson led the mourners out of the church. Outside, the skies were grey and a faint drizzle was falling, bringing a chill to the air.

'I am the Resurrection and the Life, saith the Lord . . .' intoned the parson, and the mourners followed him to the newly dug grave. The well-known words continued beside it, ending finally with: 'For as much as it hath pleased God in His great mercy to take to Himself the soul of our dear sister, Susannah Mary here departed, we herewith commit her body to the ground. Earth to earth, ashes to ashes, dust to dust.'

Saul Carter stepped forward and threw the first handful of earth on the coffin, followed by Adam. Phillipa came next, and as well as the earth, she also threw down a piece of rosemary for remembrance and a bunch of late flowers. The rain began to fall more heavily and the crowd soon dispersed, Carter walking to his horse between Phillipa and Somerton, while Thornton waited by the gate of the church talking to some of the mourners, among whom were the Page family. As the two doctors made their way down the path Thornton beckoned Hugh over as if to ask him something and Simon fell back, glad to allow the rest to go before him.

He was content to linger awhile. The previous day's discoveries were leading him with ever more certainty to the conclusion that whoever had murdered Susan Thornton, it was not opportunist thieves and that this burial was not the end of the matter. The rain fell even harder and he sought shelter under a stout yew, noticing that the grave-diggers, sacks over their heads, were standing inside the church porch waiting for the rain to stop so that they could fill in the grave. Then he saw her.

It was the woman in black, her veil clinging to her face with the rain. She walked slowly up to the open grave, bent down, picked up a handful of earth and threw it down onto the coffin. She stood by the grave for several minutes, the rain soaking her clothing. Then, abruptly, she turned away and walked swiftly past him towards the path to the back of the church and so out through the other gate.

151

Chapter 11

The Search for Francis Wynfred

Towards the end of the afternoon a message came from the Manor begging Dr Brett to visit his patient once again. Hugh sighed. 'I simply can't believe that Harry is as sick as they seem to think. But I suppose I must go. One would have thought an inquest, followed by a burial, would have been more than sufficient to keep the family occupied without worrying themselves unnecessarily over a healthy young man who has little wrong with him other than a cut leg and some fever. I'm sure the root cause of his anguish is his grief at the violent loss of his wife, and for the assuaging of that he should turn to God. I shall tell them it would be best they send for Parson Wytherley to help him bear his loss with fortitude, rather than a doctor.'

'I will come partway with you if I may,' said Simon. 'I would like another word with our witch.'

Hugh looked startled. 'Do you consider Harry Thornton might be right then when he raves on about her?'

Simon shook his head. 'No, I don't. But given that now it's beginning to occur to everyone that there must be more to this attack in the woods than simply an assault by robbers, there are other matters about which I would like to question her.'

'Do you think she saw more than she said?'

'Possibly, but I now wonder if the roots of all this lie somewhere else all together. Consider what has happened. Harry Thornton returns from Sir Arthur Clarington's

153

estate in Hertfordshire and is almost immediately betrothed. The reason given out for this is that the couple's
respective fathers are old friends and much desired the
match, added to which the young people are madly
in love. But it was also common knowledge that the
Thorntons were in dire straits and that Carter's money
was more than welcome to put matters right.

'The speed with which the wedding followed led many
to believe, including you and me, that the young couple
had anticipated matters with the obvious result, none of
which was surprising if the two had felt so deeply for each
other. Yet the way Harry behaved after his marriage hardly
suggests that was the case on his part.

'Somewhat later it is announced that the same Sir
Arthur Clarington is to visit his estate near by, following
appeals for his assistance from some of his tenants who
complain that a witch is causing havoc hereabouts. So
down he comes, bringing with him a Justice to judge the
situation and decide whether or not to sit and hear any
accusations that might be made. Events, however, take
over and by the time the two arrive at Mother Saxton's
door, the house is already surrounded by an angry mob.'

Hugh was puzzled. 'I can't see where this is leading.
Surely Clarington did the right thing, dispersed the mob
and put Sir Edward in charge?'

'Think back to that confrontation. You must have been
aware, as I was, that Clarington was surprised, even shaken,
when he saw who it was with whom he had to deal. It was
obvious he and Lizzie Saxton had met before; indeed, he
told Sir Edward that before the present trouble "she had
been much accused". That in turn led her to make strange
counter-accusations.

'As well as listing those women who used their arts to
gain wealth or a place in the bed of a powerful protector,
she also spoke of "male witches", men who lured innocent
young girls into their beds with glittering promises then
abandoned them to their fate. Whereupon Clarington, who

behaved at first like a sensible man seeking the truth of the matter, suddenly recollected that he had pressing business which called him home without delay. Had there not been so many other happenings since, I would have paid more heed to it before now. So I propose asking the old woman what it was all about.'

'And you think it has relevance?'

'I don't know, but it seems all roads lead back to Clarington or Clarington's other estate, not least the trouble caused to the young couple by the arrival so soon after the wedding of yet another former Clarington servant who has now disappeared.'

The two men rode together to the Manor gates, Hugh warning Simon to be careful on the road as dusk was falling rapidly and it would be dark when he came home. It took Simon some time to raise Mother Saxton, though smoke from the crude chimney and a dim light through a wooden shutter showed that she was at home. Finally she opened the door a fraction and peered out.

'What are you doing here?' she demanded. 'I sent for no doctor, though . . .' She left the rest of the sentence unspoken.

'I mean no harm,' Simon assured her. 'I've come to ask you again for your help and advice.'

She opened the door an inch or so more and regarded him. 'Very well, you can come in and since you're here, you can give me yours in exchange, though I think it unlikely it will be of much use. Do you agree that's a fair bargain?'

Simon agreed and she let him in. The room was full of smoke from a fire of green wood which had driven the black dog into a far corner. Simon noted with some surprise that there were still no signs of imminent departure. She motioned him to a rickety stool by a makeshift table and sat heavily down on the only chair.

'Well, doctor, so what is it I can do for you?'

'I've come to ask you what you know of Sir Arthur Clarington.'

He was unprepared for her reaction. She rose to her feet and looked at him open-mouthed. 'It seems I'm not the only one here with the second sight! Have you been casting horoscopes or conversing with spirits?'

'No,' Simon assured her, 'there is no witchery involved. It is just that I'd like to know more of him. Since we met yesterday I've learned that the robbers suspected of attacking Thornton and his wife were already in gaol when the assault took place. I believe you, whatever Harry Thornton might assert to the contrary, when you say you are almost certain there were no other strangers hiding out in the woods. Therefore we must needs look elsewhere for Susan Thornton's murderer.'

The old woman regarded him shrewdly. 'But why do you ask of Clarington?'

Whatever her outward appearance and her reputation, Simon was aware not for the first time that Lizzie Saxton was far from slow-witted. Born into better circumstances she might have done well, despite being half blind. He explained his reasoning, adding, 'I might well be chasing after hares but I have this feeling that young Thornton's relationship with Clarington has some part to play in this business. What I would know is, what is it you hold against him? It was obvious to me that there was already some matter of contention between you which had nothing to do with what happened the other morning.'

In answer, she stood up and made her way to the far end of the room where, in a dark corner, was a straw mattress on which lay a figure covered with old pieces of blanket and rags. At her head was the stub of a candle stuck onto a piece of broken pot. The old woman bent down and picked it up then held it over the figure in the bed.

'This is my daughter. Is she not a pretty sight, doctor?'

Simon's eyes took in the bald head, the sores around the mouth, the feverish eyes and the spasms of pain. He recognised immediately that the sick woman was not long for this world.

'The pox?' he said in a low, compassionate voice.

'Most certainly.'

'Have you treated her at all?'

'I put a salve of soapwort on the sores and have purged her.'

'You have no guaiacum to infuse?'

She gave a bitter laugh. 'No, doctor. Nor plates of fine lead to lay on her kidneys.'

'You seem well versed in these matters,' Simon said, surprised, for this was a treatment for the disease rarely used by other than qualified physicians.

'Years ago and even for a while when I was first here, folk sought me out to help cure their sickness, not to blame me for it,' Lizzie Saxton told him. 'What I have is countrywoman's lore, but I don't deny that of late I've found much pleasure in pretending to be what they say I am. Though had I really such powers, do they think I'd be living in this hovel, hard-pressed to find the next crust and with only rags to my back? As to guaiacum, how would I buy it, poor as I am? You see how I live. I survive because sometimes, even now, a man or woman who thinks I've helped them will bring me some eggs or vegetables or a rabbit.' The woman on the bed stirred and moaned.

'What brought her to this?'

She spat onto the floor. 'You asked me of Clarington. You want to know the matter between us? Well then, here it is before you. My daughter Nan here was a kitchenmaid in Clarington's fine house at Ware. She was a plain girl but at least she wasn't ugly with a wall eye like her mother, and although I knew Clarington to be a lecher I didn't think she had sufficient looks to catch his eye. Mind, he'll have any woman prepared to lift her shift for him, and if persuasion won't do it then he'll use force.

'Not that he needed to force this poor fool, she was so overcome with the "honour". Truly believed she would at the very least be his official mistress, riding about in a carriage decked out in silks and satins. Of course, within a few weeks he'd turned to another and soon after that she found she was with child. She could have stayed with me, it would have made no odds, but what must she do but run away with another servant and I heard or saw nothing of her for a long time.

'I went then to Clarington and cursed him for what he'd done to my darling. He merely laughed at me and told me to mind my tongue or I'd lose my cottage, but I didn't do as he asked and some time later he turned me out. I wandered the roads for a while then came on this place. Its owner had long since died, and as you can see, it's falling down but it was a roof and so I stayed here. When Nan finally returned to our old home, already sick, she found me gone and it took her some time to seek me out. She was half-dead when she turned up here. When I asked where she'd been and what she'd been doing, she said she'd gone to Bristol and earned her bread whoring with the sailors. As to the child? Delivered in a ditch somewhere, alive or dead, she doesn't know.'

The old woman stopped, and passed a hand over her eyes. Then: 'I asked her for news from our old neighbourhood and she told me there was, as usual, much talk of Sir Arthur. It's said he's shortly to marry, but rumour has it that a young maid in his household from a decent home has long been his mistress; this girl had told several people that he was intending to make *her* his wife. Whatever the truth of the matter, she left shortly after the announcement of his betrothal and hasn't been seen since.'

Simon knelt down beside the dying woman and felt her brow and pulse. 'How long has she been like this?' he murmured.

'The night before we met in the wood I heard a scratching at the door and she dragged herself in just as you see her now.' Lizzie sighed wearily. 'I had decided to take the Justice's advice and go away, but how can I leave my daughter?'

Simon rose to his feet. 'You must know as well as I do

that it can't be long now. I have nothing with me to give you, apart from a little poppy syrup which you can have willingly. Your daughter is in God's hands, and will soon be at peace. And then for God's sake go from here while you still can.'

At the Manor, Hugh found Harry Thornton little better than he had been the day before. Interludes of torpor were interrupted by bouts of extreme restlessness, when he muttered again of black dogs and witches and beseeched both Wynfred and Susan to come to him. Hugh admitted frankly to Master Thornton that his son's condition was a mystery.

'All I can suggest,' he said, 'is that you keep him quiet and let the fever pass. When he seems rational, keep telling him his mind is racked by fancies, nothing more. As soon as he shows the slightest sign of improvement, make him get out of bed. It will do him no good to lie there.'

When he went downstairs to take his leave, Dr Brett was surprised to find Phillipa still at the Manor. He greeted her warmly then told her he had thought she was going home.

'I shall go in the morning,' she replied. 'Although I've little love for Harry, it's hard for Master Thornton with no wife and only servants to turn to in times of sickness.' Her face hardened. 'Do you know what they are saying now? That it was *Guy* who set on Harry and Susan! That he courted me only to stay close to her, that after the quarrel with Harry he lay in wait for them in the forest and tried to force Susan to leave Harry and come with him.'

Hugh sought to reassure her. 'No one with any sense could believe that. He was very distressed at first when your sister said she'd not marry him, and no doubt he said things he now regrets, but he's no rash fool. Nor is he an abductor. Where do these gossips imagine he would take her, for he could scarcely live in his own home after such a scandal! Above all, why *kill* Susan?'

'They have an answer for that too: that if he couldn't have her, then neither should Harry.'

'And where was Wynfred all this time then? Sitting idly by?'

'No. They would have him run away, poor pretty boy that he is.' Her eyes filled with tears. 'We were scarce out of the churchyard when the tattle started. Even Master Thornton is tainted with it, shakes his head and mutters, "no smoke without fire". Yet it's only days since they were praising Guy to the skies for saving me from ravishment.'

'Have you spoken with Guy?'

'Of course I have, and assured him of my love and belief in him. Sweet Jesu, I pray Father believes him innocent too or we are both lost. But Dr Brett . . .' she paused and a look of fear crossed her face.

Hugh took her hand. 'What is it?'

'I found . . . there's something . . .' She looked round. 'We can't talk here.'

'If you wish to confide in me, rest assured it will go no further.'

She looked at him gratefully. 'I know that.' She paused. 'Let me consider a little while longer – then, if I may, I will come and seek you out, for I fear it bodes nothing but ill.'

Simon and Hugh sat late into the night, drinking wine and going over the events of the crowded day. Phillipa had given Hugh no clue as to the reason for the fear she had expressed and he was unable to conjecture what it might be.

'It could be no more than that she believes Harry is lying about the attack,' Simon commented, 'but fears that if she says as much, it will throw even more suspicion on to Somerton. I was never happy about his story, and after my own discoveries in the wood yesterday I was convinced he wasn't telling the truth, even before we learned that the robbers had been captured.'

'Could it be,' Hugh said tentatively, 'that it was Wynfred who stabbed Susan? That there was some furious quarrel between him and Harry, during which it became obvious even to Susan that they had long been lovers. Perhaps she tried to intervene and in doing so was killed by tragic accident.'

Simon agreed. 'I've thought along those lines myself, or that Wynfred, possibly fearing the loss of his lover after Harry and Susan returned to London, became overcome with jealousy and murdered his rival in a fit of passion.'

'Perhaps he had just learned Susan was with child,' Hugh suggested.

Simon looked at his friend. 'I think you may have scored a hit, Hugh. Indeed, that could very well be it.' He came to a decision. 'I'm now determined to go into Hertfordshire and try to discover what is known of this Wynfred locally around Sir Arthur Clarington's estate. It might well be the two men were a talking point there too.'

'Has this notion come about because of what Lizzie Saxton told you?'

'Not entirely. As you know, I was already thinking along the lines that what's happened here is rooted in events elsewhere of which we know nothing. Certainly Clarington and Mistress Saxton are old enemies. She's still consumed with hatred over his treatment of her daughter and she has some justice on her side. There is nothing to be done for the girl, indeed she may already be dead, but it would please me, Hugh, if you would go up there and take with you a flask of my poppy syrup to help ease her passing.'

Hugh gave his assent, then added, 'When do you intend to go?'

'Tomorrow, though I must first send a message to Anna Bradedge to tell her I will be delayed a little longer. I'd told her we'd be back about now.'

John Bradedge was exceedingly put out when informed that he would not be accompanying his master to Ware but was to remain in Pinner to keep an eye on matters there. He enquired somewhat acidly whether the good doctor were planning to make use of the famous Great

Bed of Ware while in the neighbourhood. This massive piece of furniture had been constructed for the owner of Ware Hall, but rumour had it that he had fallen on hard times and that the Great Bed was to be had for hire for special occasions.

Simon ignored this. 'I might well be going on a wild goose-chase and so need someone to be my eyes and ears while I'm gone. Pay particular attention to Phillipa Carter, for Hugh tells me she has something on her mind that worries her, aside from the gossip about Somerton. Whatever it is she knows may place her in jeopardy. Apart from that you've my blessing to follow up anything you feel might need looking into.'

The morning was chilly but dry when Simon set off. In spite of the fact that he was now convinced there were no more robbers lurking in the wood he made a detour around it, after which he made good progress. He stopped at noon in St Albans to break his fast, and there he was in luck for a fellow traveller knew Clarington's estate well and told him the nearest village to it was Datchworth, to the north-west of Ware; the village boasted a passable inn called the Plough which Simon could not miss for it faced out over the village green.

It was dusk by the time Simon reached Datchworth and he saw little point in pursuing his enquiries further until the morning. Indeed, he was glad of a period of quiet as he'd yet to decide exactly how to proceed. One way might be to go boldly up to the door of Clarington's house and ask to see him – but what then? What excuse would he have for questioning so choleric a man about a mere secretary called Harry Thornton no longer in his employ, let alone Wynfred about whom he knew nothing at all. For the first time it occurred to Simon to wonder exactly what kind of position Wynfred had held in the Clarington household.

Yet whatever it was, Clarington must know something of Wynfred's background. He must have been taken on either with a recommendation from someone of substance or because he was already known to Clarington. So wealthy a man must have much of value in his house, and it was unlikely even a serving wench or groom would be employed without some enquiry as to their honesty.

Later, sitting over an excellent pigeon pie, he asked his hostess if he was right in thinking Sir Arthur Clarington lived hereabouts. Certainly, she told him, the Hall was but a short ride from the village.

'Do you know him then?' she enquired.

'I've met him once,' Simon replied carefully, 'for I've been visiting a friend in Pinner where, as you must know, he has another property. Indeed, he's been there only recently having had complaints from tenants about an old woman they claim is a witch.'

The woman gave him a shrewd look. 'Would that be Lizzie Saxton?'

Simon was surprised. 'Has word got back here then?'

She nodded. 'We had a peddler here some months back who spoke of the witch near Pinner who held everyone in fear, and when I asked her name he told me it was Mother Saxton. You see, she used to live hereabouts and an ugly thing she was too, with her wall eye and withered arm, but while there were some who muttered "witch", she was more generally thought of as a wise woman who charmed warts, sold love potions and gave young wives possets of raspberry leaf or horehound to ease childbirth.' Her voice sank to a whisper. 'Sir Arthur put her daughter in the family way as he's done many others, and 'tis said she laid a black curse on him and so he had her turned out of her house. I wonder, did he know it was Lizzie Saxton there in Pinner?'

'No,' said Simon, 'I don't reckon he did, for I was there when they met and he seemed much taken aback.'

'Do you think she *is* a witch?' the hostess asked curiously, raising her voice back to normal again.

Simon sighed. 'No, I don't, but there's no doubt she's

163

pretended to be one, having been much persecuted. I think she saw it as a way of keeping a gang of lads from harming her, but I fear that in doing so she has caused half the town to believe that she has sold her soul to the Devil in exchange for knowledge of the Black Arts. It's got quite out of hand, and now any mishap for miles around is blamed on her. The Justice has been listening to accusations against her but I have no knowledge of the conclusion he's reached. His advice to her was to return whence she came as quickly as possible and to pray for her soul.'

The landlady nodded. 'I seem to remember she had some family out near St Albans. She'd best go there, for she'll need to keep out of Sir Arthur's way. If she comes here it will be out of the frying pan and into the fire, though he's much to occupy him for he is to be married come November. Perhaps a very young wife will keep him from lusting after others, at least for a while.'

Simon woke the next morning still unsure what to do next. Having found his hostess of a chatty disposition he asked her if she had ever come across a young man called Harry Thornton who, he understood, had been secretary to Sir Arthur. Yes, she told him, a very pleasant young man who had taken food and drink in her inn a number of times. However, she understood he had left Sir Arthur's employment some time ago on his marriage. And another, of the name of Francis Wynfred? She looked puzzled. No, she knew of none nor had seen Harry with a young man fitting the description Simon gave her.

He decided that he should at least take a look at Clarington's property and, as his landlady had told him, it was easy to find. The fine stone house faced out over parkland; a drive led up from the road, beside which was a small lodgekeeper's cottage. Simon dismounted and was about to walk up to the gate when suddenly a small child dashed out in front of him, tripped, measured its length on the ground and immediately commenced roaring loudly.

Simon went over and picked it up. Dressed as it was in

skirts and with uncut hair it was hard to tell its sex, but he was soon to be informed for almost immediately a young woman appeared from out of the lodge door shouting for 'Johnny' to come back at once. She stopped short when she saw Simon with the child in his arms.

'Your son's taken a tumble, nothing more,' he told her.

She ran her hand through her hair and came over to him, holding her arms out for the boy. 'Come here, you devil's sprat!' she admonished him. 'I'm sorry, sir, he seems to have muddied your coat,' she said, turning to Simon, speaking as loudly as she could through the din.

'It's nothing that won't brush off,' Simon reassured her. 'Let me see if there's any damage.' The woman raised the child's frock to reveal two chubby knees, one of which was grazed and bleeding slightly. 'You see? Nothing of any note. They fall easily at this age.'

She smiled. 'Will you come in and take a tankard of ale, sir? And let me clean your coat.'

He was about to refuse when it struck him that she might well be able to give him some useful information and so, after tying up his horse and unstrapping the small bag he almost always carried with him, he followed her into the house. He divested himself of his doublet and handed it to the woman, then set Johnny on a convenient stool.

'Now, young master,' he said, 'stop this noise while I mend your leg for it gives me a pain in the head. You sound like the bull caught in a gate!'

Addressed in such a robust manner, Johnny stopped short, his roars turning to hiccups. Simon again uncovered the knee and took from his bag a pot of salve. 'It's merely calendula ointment, made from marigolds,' he told the child's mother, adding, 'I am a physician. Dr Simon Forman at your service.'

The woman looked somewhat awestruck. 'Then it's even kinder of you, for you must have many calls on your time.'

'Not at present, for I'm but passing through.'

Her name, she told him, was Alice Collins, wife to Samuel, who was at present up at the Hall seeing to various matters for his master.

'Sir Arthur Clarington's at home?' enquired Simon.

She shook her head. 'There's soon to be a wedding at the Hall and he's away visiting his betrothed over the other side of Ware. Mistress Anne Basset is I think but fifteen or sixteen years old, no more, and a considerable heiress so she's a good catch, though he's more than old enough to be her father.' She finished cleaning the mud off his doublet and gave it back to him, then went out into her scullery to fetch the ale which she handed to him in her best pewter tankard. 'You're a stranger in these parts then, sir?'

Simon explained that he had been spending a few days out of London and had hoped to renew his acquaintance with a young man by the name of Harry Thornton who he understood was Sir Arthur's secretary.

'Then you will be disappointed, sir, for Harry Thornton left Sir Arthur's household some time ago,' she told him. 'He has a new secretary now.'

'Ah well, it seems I'm out of luck,' said Simon easily. 'But when I met young Thornton he had with him a close friend called Francis Wynfred who was also in Sir Arthur's employ. Is he still, do you know?'

She considered this. 'I don't recall anyone of that name up at the Hall. Do you know the nature of his employment?' Simon admitted that he did not. She gave the matter some thought but finally shook her head. 'No, I can think of no young man with a name like that up at the Hall, either now or while we've been here in the lodge. It could be, I suppose, he was only there for a little while . . .' She brightened up. 'Or perhaps you misheard and he wasn't a servant at all but one of the many guests Sir Arthur invites here for the hunting or a ball. If that was the case then he could have met with Harry then.'

Simon had to agree this was a distinct possibility, though

166

if that was indeed the case, why had he claimed to have been a mere servant? Was he a young man of position who thought it best to pretend to be other than he was? There came the sound of a door being opened at the back of the house and almost at once a tall young man entered, clad in leather breeches and jerkin. He looked somewhat taken aback at the sight of Simon.

'This is Dr Forman,' Alice told him. 'Your eel of a son ran out of my arms and straight into the road, where he fell over. The doctor picked him up and see, he has treated his knee with salve! And stopped him roaring. He gave me a rare fright.'

Collins swept his son up into his arms, causing the child to break into a wide grin. 'You young imp,' he said. 'What do you mean, frightening your mother so? You deserve a whipping!' Obviously this grave threat had been made before without being carried out, for young Johnny now chuckled merrily and poked his father in the chest.

'We do spoil him,' Alice admitted. 'It was four years before I conceived, so we'd almost given up all hope. Yet already now I'm three months forward again.'

'He'll be less spoiled when he has a stout brother or pretty sister to share the attention with him,' commented his father. 'Fetch me some ale too, will you, Alice? I've been sawing wood and stacking it against the winter all morning and with little help, for everything's upside down with preparations for the wedding.'

'Dr Forman was asking after young Harry Thornton. I told him he'd left Sir Arthur some time back.'

'A friend of yours?' asked Collins.

'No, more an acquaintance through one who is my friend,' replied Simon with truth, 'but since I was passing near by on my way back to London, I thought I'd look him up.'

'Thornton left quite suddenly,' said Collins. 'So far as I'm aware he went home to see his father and sent word to Sir Arthur to say he wasn't coming back. I thought him rather a weak lad, myself.'

'Dr Forman also asked after another young man he said was friend to Thornton,' Alice told her husband, 'and who he thought had also been a servant at the Hall. Francis . . . what was it? I told him I knew of none such.'

'Francis Wynfred,' said Simon.

Collins frowned. 'Nor do I.'

'Yet I was sure he'd told me himself he was employed here,' Simon persisted.

'Then he told you wrong for had he been so, I would have known him, for I have worked at the Hall since I was a lad.'

'I told Dr Forman that it might be he was a guest of Sir Arthur.'

Collins shrugged. The subject was obviously of little interest to him. Talk turned again to the subject of the wedding and Simon, having drawn a blank, was content to sit and listen. The girl's family had insisted on a tightly drawn-up marriage contract and the lawyers were still arguing over the final details. Since the bride was so much younger than the groom, provision had to be set out for her and any children she might have in the event of Sir Arthur's demise.

'I'm glad neither of us were rich and had such stuff to consider,' laughed Collins, putting his arm round his wife. 'All I had to do was speak to her father and arrange for the banns to be called out in church.'

'It's to be hoped he'll stay faithful to her,' declared Alice, 'though I doubt it, once the excitement of a young virgin bride has passed.'

'I fear the servants up there agree with you, wife,' Collins told her. 'They are already taking wagers on how long it will be before he takes a mistress!'

Alice had to smile. 'Do you remember that young woman who was there for a while last winter? The grammar schoolmaster's daughter from Ware? Sir Arthur seemed very smitten with her, so much so there was talk of marriage, though it came to nothing, her having no money. Some said *she'd* become Sir Arthur's mistress,' Alice explained to Simon, 'but I think in her case it was just talk, for she was most quiet and respectable. She told me once her family had fallen on hard times through sickness and she was at the Hall for a little while to assist the house-keeper with the linen and such like.'

Right, thought Simon, a grammar schoolteacher's daughter in Ware shouldn't be all that hard to find. Perhaps she would be able to tell him more. He rose and thanked the Collinses for their hospitality. Alice stood in the doorway to wave Godspeed with Johnny in her arms as her husband walked over with Simon to where he had left his horse.

'You've set me puzzling now,' Collins told him. 'Francis Wynfred, you say? There is something familiar about the name, but for the life of me I can't think what it is.' He shook his head. 'No, it's gone. I'll probably recall what it was as soon as you've ridden away!'

Chapter 12

Devil's Work

Cuddy Banks was not a happy young man. It was with the greatest reluctance that his erstwhile friends had been persuaded to let him join them at all at their last rehearsal before performing their morris on Saturday before all the town. In vain did he declare that he was irreplaceable, that without him the entertainment would be nothing. His behaviour, he was informed, had put him beyond the pale. Drunkenness, fighting and hurling insults might all be overlooked – albeit with difficulty – in order to keep the team together, although opinions were divided as to the rights and wrongs of attacking Mother Saxton's cottage, but attempted ravishment . . .

He tried to defend himself, firstly by saying that he had been bewitched and had acted under a spell laid on him by Mother Saxton and then, when he found this cut little ice, claiming that Phillipa Carter had enticed him on, only to change her mind at the last moment. This last was greeted with derision and disbelief, the general opinion being that he was lucky to have suffered as little damage as he had at the hands of Guy Somerton. 'Will you believe the word of a possible murderer rather than me?' he raged self-righteously.

'No one has yet convinced me that Guy Somerton murdered Susan Thornton,' declared Jack Page firmly. 'It's nothing but tittle-tattle. I wouldn't wonder if you and your family hadn't started the tale going to take attention away from your own misdeeds. I should mind your tongue, Cuddy,' he threatened, 'or when Somerton hears the slander he may well try to murder *you*!'

Cuddy was about to reply with information gleaned from his father to the effect that Sir Edward Ratcliffe was most likely going to issue a warrant against Mother Saxton for witchcraft and that Guy Somerton was to be questioned regarding certain accusations made against him, but decided for once to bide his time. When Lizzie Saxton was tried as a witch and hanged or burned, and Guy Somerton went to the scaffold, think how red-faced they would be, how they would beg his pardon. Just wait and see!

Now free from immediate fear of robbers, the band of morris men set off for the woods on the afternoon of the day Simon rode to Datchworth, giving Mother Saxton's cottage a wide berth. Most of them carried bread, cheese and a bottle of ale for refreshment but Cuddy secretly carried in his bag a bottle of sack taken from the cellar, along with a flask of *aqua vitae* purloined from the small cask his father kept hidden at the back of a cupboard.

As he trudged along behind the others, very obviously excluded from their laughter and conversation, he paused every now and then to take a swig of sack. He had eaten little over the last couple of days as well as passing several sleepless nights, and he was already light-headed. By the time the dancers arrived at a suitable spot he was becoming unsteady on his feet. Preparations for the rehearsal began. One of the band took from his bag his tabor and pipe, another tuned his fiddle while Jack Page assembled the hobby horse.

'Isn't this the spot, or near to it, that we found the young maid's body?' enquired a youth as he strapped his bells onto his calves. A slight shudder went through the group and they all looked at one another. It was a dull afternoon, and in the gloom one clearing looked very like the next. 'You went back again afterwards, Jack. Is it the same?'

'I don't think so,' he replied, 'though it's quite near, I believe.' He looked round again. 'No, I don't recollect that great tree there. But if you're frightened of ghosts and spirits then all the more reason for making our dances as loud and lively as we can to drive them away. So step out bravely, lads!'

Cuddy, his head now beginning to swim, held onto a sapling and squinted across the clearing. Through the trees he saw a slight movement and was sure he could discern a figure. 'Look,' he shouted, 'look over there! That woman all in black – it's Susan Thornton's ghost!'

All turned as one to where he was pointing but there was nothing to be seen.

'I did see her, I did,' he babbled. 'She's gone now but she was there, I swear it.'

Jack came over to Cuddy, sniffed and stood back. 'God's Breath, man, you stink of sack! You saw no woman in black, it's all in your head.' He looked him up and down. 'I doubt you're even fit to dance.'

Cuddy steadied himself and informed him with drunken dignity that he was quite capable of holding his own with the best, as he would prove. So the rehearsal began. It was soon obvious that Cuddy had been far too optimistic as to his capabilities. At first he was just slow and uncertain and had to be pushed and shoved into the right place, but as time went on and he became hot and thirsty, he applied himself once again to his sack bottle with predictable results.

The next dance was that in which stout staves were used, the men hitting them against each other in a variety of different ways. Cuddy, by now falling over his own feet and mumbling incoherently, managed to smack his stave against his partner's knuckles, causing the other to drop his own stick and dance wildly about swearing and sucking his hand. At this point, the rest of the team, thoroughly fed up and determined to get to the end of their programme before dark fell, marched Cuddy off to the foot of the

173

aforementioned tree, set his back against it and told him to stay where he was if he valued his skin. Within minutes he was snoring.

The rest quickly ate their bread and cheese, had a swig of ale, and continued dancing until they reached their finale. By the time they finished, the light was going rapidly and they realised it would soon be dark. It was while they were putting away their gear that one of the number, looking across at the recumbent Cuddy, suggested that it would be a good joke to pretend to be fairies and elves and give him a good fright. No sooner said than done. Jack donned the hobby-horse costume, decorated it with bits of bracken and bound two forked twigs to his head, while the rest pulled their shirts over their heads to pass as ghosts. Then the tabor-player banged on his drum, all rattled their bells and a great shout was raised.

Thus Cuddy, struggling awake, found himself surrounded by ghostly white figures led by a devil with horns. 'Help!' he shouted then quavered, 'Where am I, what's this?'

'You have strayed into the realm of the Queen of the Fairies,' intoned Jack Page in a stern voice, at which the white ghostly figures cackled. 'Cuddy Banks, we are here to take you to the fairy realm where you will be made to serve our Queen for seven years for trespassing on her very own fairy ring,' he concluded to a chorus of shrieks and groans which soon collapsed into laughter.

In spite of his confusion Cuddy recognised the voice. 'You whoreson knaves, you rooting hogs!' he shrieked. 'Fairy Queen, is it? You wait, Jack Page, I'll get my own back for the way you've all treated me. I won't stand any more of it, do you hear?'

'Stand any more? You can't even stand *up*!' called out one wag.

There was more laughter as the young men tidied their clothing, finally packed their bags and prepared to go. 'You'd best come with us even so, Cuddy,' relented Jack, 'for you're hardly in a fit state to find your way home alone.'

'Sneck off!' snarled Cuddy. 'I'd rather go alone than with a parcel of rogues like you.'

'Suit yourself,' retorted Jack. 'And if you plan to join us on Saturday then you'd best be clean, sober and have your wits about you. There's still time to replace you with someone else,' on which salutary note he slung his bag over his shoulder and walked off with the rest.

Cuddy regretted his decision not to accompany them almost as soon as the sound of their voices had died away. It was now almost dark and he had no idea where he was. He cursed himself for drinking on his way through the wood instead of noting where he was going and, worse still, he found when he did begin to walk that he was still unsteady on his feet. However, for a good half hour he tried to find his way out onto the road but without success, and soon concluded that he must be going round in circles. The moon had still not risen and he had no light to guide him so finally, coming on a small sheltered dell, he sat down and huddled his jacket around him. He felt in his bag and took out the bottle of sack only to discover that he had drunk the lot. Then his fingers closed on the flask. Well, he thought, if I have to stay here until the moon is up I might as well be warm and so, having come to this decision, he removed the cork from the flask and took two mighty swigs.

Unused to fierce spirit, it made his eyes water but it was certainly warming. Emboldened, he finished the whole lot then, quite overcome with drink, weariness and rage, he lay down and once again fell into a heavy if disturbed sleep. His last thoughts before he slipped away were that come the morning, he would start planning the destruction of his enemies. He would personally see to it that Mother Saxton was hanged and that beforehand she publicly confessed to bewitching him, innocent that he was, into attempting to rape Phillipa Carter. Also that Guy

Somerton paid for his assault on him, if not with his life (as he hoped) after being found guilty of Susan's murder, then at least with some dire consequences which would include his publicly begging Cuddy's pardon on his knees. Then there was Jack Page . . . he snored and fell into a deep sleep.

He woke suddenly some hours later from an unpleasant dream, prompted no doubt by the *aqua vitae*, in which he again thought he saw the ghost of Susan Carter, not veiled in black but standing beside her open grave in a light gown with a great stain on it. The moon, still almost full, was now high above him, lighting all around with an eerie white light. Close by, he heard the rustling sounds of animals going about their nocturnal business while from the trees above came the hooting of owls hunting prey. He shivered in the night chill and rose to his feet. His head was pounding and he felt nauseous but he must get himself home.

It was at that moment he became aware of something strange. From away in front of him there came a noise as of pattering feet, next the ground below his feet began to vibrate, then, without warning a monstrous black hound leapt into the clearing, followed by a host of figures from out of a nightmare.

Some of those on foot were white-faced with streaming hair, others had the heads of animals, while behind them came other ghastly figures on spectral horses through the sides of which Cuddy could clearly see their skeletons. All were lit by a hideous greenish-white glow. At their head rode a huge glittering figure crowned with mighty antlers. These were no town lads playing goblins.

Stories of a once enjoyably frightening kind, told by the fireside of a winter evening when he was a child, came flooding back to him. Oh God, he thought, it's Herne the Hunter. I've raised the Wild Hunt. Sweet Jesu, save me!

The noise of their shrieks and yells was augmented by loud and discordant music. Cuddy fell on his knees, frozen, unable to move hand or foot. The music reached its climax and the spectral horde shouted even louder then all turned away from him and looked upwards to where, suddenly, there arose a great wheel of fire which began to spin, in the midst of which, stark and black against the red and orange, was a monstrous horned figure.

'Our Father Who art in heaven,' babbled Cuddy, then, reverting to an older faith, crossed himself half a dozen times. Church had meant little to him and he'd even had difficulty learning his catechism sufficiently for confirmation. Now snatches of prayers came to him that had meant nothing before. 'Oh Lord,' he begged, 'keep me from the noonday demon and the peril that walks by night! I'll be good, I swear I'll never drink again. I'll stand outside church in a white sheet as a penitent for what I tried to do to Phillipa, but don't let them take me to Hell. Please God, *don't let them take me to Hell!*'

There came a final crash and a blinding light and afterwards he swore he saw a vision of Susan Thornton, pressing her hands over the wound in her breast, crying out, 'Help me, help me!' to two dark figures close by, one of whom appeared to remonstrate with the other who remained unmoved. Then all went black and he fell into a swoon only yards from the spot where Susan had indeed met her death.

At the end of the same afternoon Hugh's elderly housekeeper opened the door to Phillipa Carter, who informed her that she had urgent business with Dr Brett. He came at once and ushered her into his parlour, asking the woman to bring them some refreshment. Phillipa took off her cloak and put down the bag that she was carrying. It was obvious she was much distressed.

'Would you like me to fetch my friend from across the road?' he asked gently. 'She is kind and discreet – in fact, you can be the first to know that we're shortly to be married.'

177

Phillipa smiled at that. 'Then you have all my good wishes, Dr Brett, but I prefer this to be between just you and me, though I'm sure Mistress Morrell will make you an excellent wife.'

'Thank you, my dear. It was only finally agreed between us this afternoon and I'm looking forward to telling Dr Forman the good news when he returns.'

'He's gone back to London? I thought I saw his servant here just now.'

'He's gone into Hertfordshire,' Hugh explained, 'to see what he can discover that might help solve this mystery, not least what is known of Francis Wynfred, for if he too was in Sir Arthur Clarington's employ at Ware there must be many on the estate or in the neighbourhood who knew him.'

At the mention of Wynfred, Phillipa paled. 'It is about the killing of my sister that I've come,' she began hesitantly. 'You did say that if I felt able to tell you what was concerning me, to come to you and you would hear me out?'

The housekeeper knocked, then brought in a tray on which was a bottle of canary wine, two wine cups and some sweetmeats. Hugh thanked her then dismissed her. 'I can see you find this difficult, my dear. You're quite sure you wouldn't like me to fetch Jessica?'

Phillipa paused for a moment then gulped, 'No, doctor. I think the fewer who hear what I have to say, the better.' She reached into her bag and brought out a bundle of cloth. She handled it with obvious repugnance, but making a visible effort, began to unwrap it. However, before she finally revealed what lay inside, she turned to Hugh again.

'When you and Dr Forman came to see Harry, you remarked on the saddlebags and I explained that a farmer had found them beside the London road. With all that was going on – the inquest, my sister's burial and Harry's illness – they were not given the attention they deserved, but after you both left I thought I should take your advice

178

and see what, if anything, might have been taken, most especially with my sister's jewellery in mind.

'I discovered almost at once that whoever had taken the bags did not have robbery in mind, for my sister's bag was exactly as we had packed it together; nothing was missing even though she had taken her best jewellery, including the pearls Father gave her on her wedding day. Then I looked in Harry's . . . and at the bottom found *this*.' She shook the last piece of wrapping free and exposed the silver dagger. 'As you see, it's quite clean and so is most of the wrapping, though I fear these small spots are my sister's blood.' Her voice trembled as she said the last few words.

'Is this Harry's?' asked Hugh in consternation.

'No. I'm almost certain it's Wynfred's. See, it has a chased hilt. But I can't be quite sure because he wore his dagger always in its sheath. That I would recognise, for it was of curious workmanship and very fine.'

Hugh rose to his feet and went over to a small cupboard to fetch out the dagger sheath Simon had found in the wood. 'Would this be it?' he asked.

'Yes,' she whispered. 'Yes.' She picked up the dagger and put it into the sheath. 'See – it fits. There is now no doubt. Where did you find this?'

'Dr Forman unearthed it in the woods when he went out with the search party. The Justice has told him to keep it safe. It was discovered close to where your sister died.'

Phillipa nodded. 'I thought as much. It's what I feared.'

'Are you trying to tell me then that Wynfred might have murdered your sister?'

Her eyes filled with tears. 'What else can I think? But what's even worse, if that's so then surely Harry Thornton must have colluded with him, even going so far as to conceal the dagger.'

Hugh was puzzled. 'But why keep it and conceal it? Why not just throw it into a bush like the sheath?'

'It must be that he knew it would be recognised and lead to Wynfred's being accused of murder, and so took it on himself to conceal it. Perhaps he intended disposing of it well away from where my sister died but was overcome with fever before he could do so.' She paused. 'Though why should Wynfred remove the sheath from his belt?'

'There is another explanation, of course,' suggested Hugh. 'Wynfred may have stabbed Susan, injured Harry in a subsequent struggle and somehow managed to knock him unconscious, then rode off taking Harry's horse with him, deliberately leaving the saddlebags where they would be found, after hiding the dagger in Harry's so as to throw suspicion on him for murdering his own wife.'

Phillipa agreed that this was possible, 'But what reason could Francis Wynfred possibly have to hate Susan so much?'

Hugh poured out the wine. 'Dry your tears now and drink this,' he said, handing a cup to her. 'You've been through much during the last few days, but you've been brave enough to come here and tell me your fears, and you were right to do so. Now let's see if we can take this matter forward, for if we're right in what we suspect we have a true villain on our hands.'

Phillipa wiped her eyes, tried to smile and drank from the cup. 'I must be sensible,' she agreed, 'and already I feel some relief at having shared my fears with you.'

'Was there any open quarrel between your sister and Wynfred before they set off for London?' Hugh enquired next.

'No,' she replied, 'not that I'm aware of, though it was always an uneasy situation. At first Susan welcomed Francis as Harry's friend, but when he showed no signs of leaving the Manor and the two spent so much time together, then naturally she became upset. I tried my best to persuade her to have it out with Harry and tell him that it was not reasonable and he must send the man away. I was even more forthright on the subject when people began to talk, as you must know they did.' She paused and coloured slightly. 'Do you think that what was between

Harry and Francis was unnatural? That they loved after the fashion of men and women?'

'I must admit to thinking that might be the case,' Hugh admitted. 'Such things are not unknown, though rarely brought into the open in such a way.'

'But it's a mortal sin,' she argued.

'I doubt much thought is given to that by those in the grip of passion, and if Harry and Wynfred *had* been all in all to each other when in Sir Arthur Clarington's employ, then Wynfred might well have felt towards your sister as would a rival mistress who had been publicly spurned.'

'My sister said Harry was much shocked when Francis arrived at the Manor. Francis was obviously distressed and took him to task in front of everyone for not telling him of the wedding or inviting him to it.'

'Let us suppose then,' said Hugh, 'that while they were passing through the woods a quarrel broke out. Perhaps Wynfred changed his mind and said he would like to accompany Harry and Susan to London and your sister objected. So they get down from their horses, Harry lifting your sister off the pillion, and have it out. Wynfred persists and Harry finally puts his foot down and says he must now put his wife first, for she is with child.'

'And that enraged Wynfred to the point of killing her?' queried Phillipa.

'It would be sufficient reason for an unbalanced young man, mad with jealousy, given the circumstances. Possibly Harry does his best to protect his wife and is wounded in the leg; he falls down, whereupon Wynfred hits him hard on the head, maybe with the hilt of this very dagger. He then turns on your sister, stabs her through the heart, and makes his escape. When Harry comes to, he's alone and at first doesn't realise what's happened. Then Susan's body is found and his worst fears are realised. Yet, in spite of all, he still loves his friend and invents the tale of the robbers. Had it not turned out that those felons had already been caught, no doubt he would still be believed.'

Phillipa was quiet as she sat and thought through all the implications. 'It would explain Harry's strange fever and his mad ramblings: his guilt over the murder of his wife set against his passion for his friend.' She stopped. 'What do you think we should do now?'

Hugh thought for a moment. 'If you are strong enough, I think we should go and find Sir Edward at the Crown, where he is putting up tonight, and tell him what we have discovered and what we think happened. I'll explain that Dr Forman has already gone into Hertfordshire to see what he can find out about Wynfred because his disappearance had already aroused our suspicions. Simon might even find him, for he must have fled somewhere after the murder and would surely be most likely to make for a place he knows.'

Half an hour later they were sitting in a private parlour at the Crown telling Sir Edward of their fears and showing him the knife Phillipa had found. He heard them out to the end, only interrupting once or twice to ask relevant questions then he sat back in his chair.

'If what you say is true, then this young man's a positive fiend.'

Hugh agreed. 'It's damnable. Yet to look at him you would never guess. He's too effeminate for my taste but most definitely handsome and quietly spoken, with excellent manners.'

'Not all those who sell their souls to the Devil are malformed and ugly like Mother Saxton,' Ratcliffe commented. 'Don't they say that Lucifer, who fell from Heaven, was beautiful as a Son of the Morning?' He thought for a moment. 'I think what is best is that I issue warrants for the bringing in of this young man – one to allow for a search locally and another to be sent into Hertfordshire. I understand Dr Forman's servant remains with you. Do you think he will be able to find his master?'

'He can but try,' Hugh told him, 'though I fear they might miss each other and Simon arrive back here while his servant seeks him there. However, it's a risk we'll have to take for there's no time to be lost.'

John Bradedge learned of the decision while he was sitting in the taproom over a quart of ale, wondering how much longer they would be staying in a place which offered no bear pits or playhouses, only a handful of inns and taverns and where the next major event was *morris dancing* – young men prancing around with bells on their legs and flowers in their hats, banging sticks and generally making fools of themselves.

So the news that he was to ride after his master bearing a warrant for the arrest of Francis Wynfred delighted him though he was not optimistic as to whether he would be able to track the good doctor down. 'Once he gets some maggot in his brain and rushes off after it, there's no telling where it may take him,' he grumbled to Hugh. 'For all I know, he's on his way to the other side of the country by now. But I'll do my best, if someone can tell me where this Sir Arthur has his property.'

He was up at the crack of dawn the next morning, had his horse saddled and was leading it into the street when he saw a bizarre figure approaching. It was waving its hands and shouting loud enough to raise bedchamber windows and bring people out of their houses. As it drew nearer he saw it was Cuddy Banks, mired of face, briars and burrs clinging to his torn clothing. In no time at all he had collected a small crowd and John, having first glanced at the church clock, could not resist going over to find out what it was all about.

Cuddy was completely incoherent. At first all he could do was gasp out bits and pieces of prayers, uncommon enough in itself, while the crowd surrounding him grew and the questions rained on him. Finally, drawing breath, he began a disjointed tale in which there figured practical jokes played on him by his companions, ghoulish hob-goblins, spectral horsemen, black dogs, Herne the Hunter, rings of fire and Satan himself. It was early on in this narrative that his father arrived on the scene; his mother having woken to find her darling boy was not in his bed, she had immediately despatched her husband into town to see if the Pages knew where he had got to.

'Herne the Hunter, is it?' roared Banks, pushing his way to the front of the crowd. 'Black dogs and rings of fire, eh? It's *aqua vitae*, not Black Magic that's addling your brain, lackwit. Don't think I didn't see my cask had been half emptied, nor that a bottle of my best sack was missing from my cellar!'

The crowd roared with laughter, one wag asking Cuddy if His Satanic Majesty had offered him any bargains in the way of sacks of gold or troops of beautiful women.

'But I did see it,' pleaded Cuddy, 'I really did. It wasn't the drink.'

But the crowd was breaking up, the good burghers returning to their homes and work while Banks, still furious, marched his son up the street to where he had left his horse. 'And you, you scurvy-valiant ass, can run behind – and the first thing I'll do when we get home is put your head under the pump. I give you fair warning now: one more piece of misbehaviour and I'll whip you, big as you are!'

Chuckling like the rest, John Bradedge remounted his horse and with the warrant safely inside his doublet, set off as fast as he could for Hertfordshire.

Chapter 13

The Entry in the Church Book

Ware was a sizeable town but it did not take Simon too long to track down the home of the grammar schoolmaster whose daughter had been in the employ of Sir Arthur Clarington. An elderly master at the school informed him that John Aldersey had, unhappily, died some six months previously, having ailed for some time before that but his widow, Anne, lived only a few minutes' walk away in a small house on the corner of that very street. He obviously disapproved of married schoolmasters, informing Simon with a sniff that, 'As to the daughter, so far as I know she does not live here any more. There was talk of her having married but I cannot say how true that is. I fear there has been some falling out, for her mother never mentions her when we meet.'

The woman who opened the door to Simon was of middle age and had the faded looks of one who had once been pretty. He wondered if her daughter took after her.

'Mistress Aldersey?' enquired Simon. She nodded. 'I wonder if I could ask you for the direction of your daughter, for I wish to consult her on an urgent matter.'

She was obviously taken aback. 'What matter? And who are you?' she added suspiciously.

'I am Dr Simon Forman from London and the matter about which I wish to speak to your daughter concerns the time she spent in the employ of Sir Arthur Clarington.'

At this Mistress Aldersey looked even more suspicious.

185

'A doctor? What does my daughter need with a doctor? And what did she do at Sir Arthur Clarington's that you need to speak to her of it?'

'So far as I know, your daughter has no need of a doctor,' Simon soothed, 'and what I wish to ask her has nothing directly to do with her, but concerns a young man I'm urgently seeking who might have been in Sir Arthur's employ at the same time. I was hoping she might be able to help me find him.'

This appeared to mollify her somewhat but she remained cool. 'I see. Well, Dr Forman, I'm afraid I can't help you for I don't know where my daughter is. I haven't seen her for over a year. The last time she was here was when I sent to tell her that her father was grievously ill and wanted to see her.' She paused. 'We had heard worrying gossip that she was too familiar with Sir Arthur.'

'There always seems to be gossip about Sir Arthur and any personable young woman,' commented Simon. 'I imagine much of it is exaggerated.'

'Maybe, but it greatly concerned her father in his last illness. However, the upshot was that she and my late husband quarrelled bitterly and she stormed out of the house saying she would never return. Cissy was always a stubborn girl; quiet but stubborn. Since when I've heard nothing. She didn't even come home for her father's burial – if she knew of it, that is.'

So, thought Simon, the trail ends yet again. 'And you've no idea at all where she might be?'

'You could try my sister, Bess,' replied Mistress Aldersey grudgingly. 'She saw Cissy two or three times after we did, and when she visited me not long ago she said she'd heard that she had married. Mind you, though Bess claimed she didn't know where my daughter was living, it could be that she wasn't telling all she knew. Perhaps Cissy had forbidden it, though even if that's so I think Bess wrong to keep it from her own sister.'

Simon's heart sank. This meant yet more time-consuming hunting around strange territory in search of Mistress Aldersey's sister, but here he was in luck for to his relief it transpired that the sister lived just outside Datchworth. Mistress Aldersey gave him her direction. 'She is called Bess Coughton and her husband is a wheelwright. You'll have no trouble seeking her out, I'm sure.' She hesitated. 'If you do find my daughter, will you tell her that her mother wishes to see her, married or not, whatever she's done, even if the gossip about her and Sir Arthur was true.'

It was growing dark by the time Simon returned to Datchworth and the Plough, and he decided before starting his search to call in for refreshment and also enquire of the hostess as to the whereabouts of the Coughtons. So it was, with some surprise, that he entered the taproom to find John Bradedge there before him, a foaming pint of ale in his hand.

'God's Wounds! What are *you* doing here?' he demanded. 'I thought I'd said you were to stay close in Pinner. And how did you find me?'

'I found you because I came here to Datchworth, saw this fine inn and asked the hostess if she knew of a Dr Forman who might have visited the village, you being what you are when you set off on these mad chases. To my relief, she told me you were actually staying here and were expected back tonight. As to leaving Pinner, doctor, things have moved on since you left.' And John brought his master up to date with the discovery of Francis Wynfred's dagger and the subsequent issuing of the warrant for his arrest.

Simon listened with grave attention. 'Matters are indeed serious,' he said, 'but trying to serve that warrant is not going to be easy, for no one around here seems to have heard of Wynfred, not even the lodgekeeper on Sir Arthur's estate, so we can hardly go to the authorities and ask that he be taken into custody.'

'I said we should have gone home days ago,' grumbled John. 'You've enough to do without playing at being a constable or a sheriff's officer.'

'However,' continued Simon, ignoring this, 'I have been on the trail of a young woman, Cissy Aldersey, who was in service with Sir Arthur Clarington at the same time Wynfred claimed he was. I thought she might be able to tell me something of him – his background, where he came from, if he had any family . . . even if there had been talk of an improper relationship between him and Thornton when they were all in Clarington's employ in his household.'

He sighed wearily. 'But the girl also seems to have vanished, though I now have hopes of finding out where she might be from her aunt, who lives near by. I've also heard from several quarters that there was talk of something between Cissy Aldersey and Sir Arthur, though it may only be gossip. To listen to the people round here, you'd think no woman between the ages of sixteen and sixty was safe from the man, though I imagine the tales grow in the telling. The girl's mother says that she thinks her daughter might have married, and if that is the case then we will need to be very discreet if we don't want to avoid raising suspicions in the mind of her husband.'

After joining John in a tankard of ale and ordering supper for later, the two men set out for the home of the wheelwright, having thankfully discovered it was less than half a mile away. The Coughtons lived in a substantial cottage, with outbuildings in which the wheelwright's trade was carried on. A large and rather splendid wheel stood beside the front door of the dwelling proclaiming the nature of the business. Simon rang the bell and the door was opened almost at once.

It was immediately apparent that Mistress Coughton, a plump and talkative lady, was likely to be more forthcoming than her sister. She at once invited them in and insisted on their trying her elderberry wine.

'So you want to find my niece?' she said at length, after chatting on about everything from the weather for the

188

time of year to the price of cambric for shirts. 'Well, I'm not sure I can help you there. It was foolish, not to say lacking in duty, of Cissy to quarrel as she did with her mother and father, particularly when poor John was so sick.'

'Her mother hinted that there had been gossip about her and Sir Arthur Clarington,' prompted Simon, 'and that was the cause of the falling out.'

'I fear there was more than a whiff of truth in it,' the woman replied, 'for when I asked young Cissy about it, although she denied it I had the feeling she wasn't being straight with me. I even wondered, God forgive me, if he had got her with child for she seemed very unhappy as well as being pale and sickly-looking. Then suddenly she was gone and I heard nothing for months, until I was in the market one day when I met up with an old friend I hadn't seen for a long time, and she asked me if I knew my niece was married and living in Knebworth.

'I didn't like to tell her the truth of the matter, and I've been meaning to go over there ever since, but there's much to see to here and what with one thing and another, time has passed too quickly. We've taken on two new apprentices and I'd to see to my own daughter at her lying-in. But if it is the case that Cissy is married and settled, then I can't understand why she hasn't been home to see her mother. Whatever may have been said in the heat of the moment, I'm sure Anne would be only too happy to know she had found herself a decent man.'

'If she was married, I wonder where the marriage took place?' wondered Simon.

'Well, I suppose you'd better try Knebworth first, but there are many little villages around about and she could have married in any of them, or even somewhere altogether different – perhaps in her husband's parish. But if you do find her, please persuade her to visit her mother. Tell her she can come here first if it makes it easier and we will journey to Ware together. Poor Anne has no one at all now

189

John's dead.' The two men thanked Mistress Coughton, complimented her on the elderberry wine, and were shown to the door.

'Just one more thing, mistress,' said Simon. 'Have you ever heard of a young man called Francis Wynfred? He, too, was supposed to have been in Sir Arthur's employ.'

There was no mistaking the shock in her eyes and her rosy complexion paled. Then she recovered herself. 'No, doctor, I know no young man of that name. Of that I can assure you.' They left her staring after them, wide-eyed in surprise.

'Now what do you make of *that*?' whistled John as soon as they were out of earshot.

Simon shook his head. 'I'm completely mystified, but she obviously knows of him, to have reacted that way.'

They returned to the Plough, still mulling over what they had learned. 'Had I not seen the fellow with my own eyes, I'd wonder if it was Wynfred this girl had married, and that her aunt knew it and was keeping quiet about it for some reason,' said John, helping himself to a large portion of excellent stew.

'It's certainly a possibility,' Simon agreed. 'Let's suppose that to be the case. Why should she marry Wynfred, apart from fondness? Say this young woman was with child by Clarington and needed a husband, any husband, and there was Wynfred in Clarington's employ. Could it be that he offered Wynfred money to take her off his hands, avoid a scandal and give the child a name? It has been known, even in the highest circles. If you recollect, even the Queen's own Lord Chamberlain married off his mistress to a Court musician in exchange for a fine dowry when she became with child by him.'

John smiled but said nothing, recollecting how his master had also enjoyed romps with that very same lady.

Simon continued: 'Perhaps that's why he came and stayed so long in Pinner – to avoid having to live with a girl he found uncongenial. Indeed, if his proclivities are what

190

we think they are, then *any* young women would prove uncongenial.' He yawned. 'Well, it's no good thinking any further tonight. Tomorrow we'll go and see what we can find out, after which, successful or no,' he added, seeing John's expression, 'I promise we'll return to Pinner, explain the position to Hugh and Sir Edward Ratcliffe and go home!'

They woke the following morning to fine rain which persisted all the way to Knebworth, by which time Simon was wet, thoroughly fed up and beginning to agree with John that he was on a fool's errand of his own making. Common sense informed him that if the girl was indeed married, what hope had they of tracing her without knowing her married name? They could ask around for a Cissy Aldersey or even, taking a chance, for a Cissy Wynfred – but the chances of finding her, unless luck was on their side, were pretty remote.

He shook himself. He must be practical; the first and most sensible action to take was to ask the parson or churchwarden if they might look in the Church Book of the parish for the record of a wedding of a young woman, a spinster by the name of Aldersey.

Knebworth proved to be a wealthy parish but with an absentee parson and only a curate living in a poor cottage close to the church. The man was elderly and deaf and seemed unsure of the names of any of those married within the last twelve months, but finally he was persuaded to bring out the Church Book for Simon to peruse. He went painstakingly through the births, marriages and deaths of the good people of Knebworth for the last two years, all carefully recorded in a crabbed hand, but without finding the marriage of any woman by the name of Aldersey.

From Knebworth they went on to the next nearest village, where they disturbed that parson as he was getting ready for a day's hunting, the rain having cleared somewhat. He told Simon grandly that he couldn't be expected to remember from one day to the next the names of all the peasants who came and recited their marriage vows in front of him, but if they liked to knock up the church-warden and tell him what they wanted, he'd show them where the Church Book was kept and good luck to them. There came the sound of a hunting horn and with a wave of his hand he was gone. Again Simon turned over the pages but there were even fewer entries for marriages in it than in the Knebworth Church Book and it was quickly apparent that Cissy Aldersey had not married there.

'You're mad,' John protested. 'She could have married *anywhere* – Oxford, Bristol, Carlisle . . . You could spend your whole life looking without success.'

'We'll look in one more place,' Simon replied dispirit-edly. He cast his eyes around and saw by the church wall an ancient milestone with the name *Condicote* engraved on it. 'Come on,' he urged. 'We'll make this the last throw.'

The parson in Condicote was a pleasant man with a friendly wife and several small children and he invited Simon and John into the parsonage parlour while he went and fetched the Book. 'When did you say this young woman was married?' he asked as he returned with it.

'I'm not too sure. I think some time in the last twelve months. I'm looking for her on behalf of her family, for she became estranged from them some time ago and her mother, recently widowed, is anxious to be reconciled.'

The parson began to turn the pages, running his finger down each. Time passed and Simon had given up hope when suddenly he stopped and smiled. 'I believe you're in luck, gentlemen. Yes, now I come to think of it, I remember this marriage for it was by Bishop's Licence, the banns not having been called. The bride was a pretty young thing, as I recall. Here, take a look. You see?'

Simon came over and examined the page. For a moment shock deprived him of speech then he beckoned John to look as well. 'God's Breath!' he exclaimed, then recollecting where he was, added, 'Sorry, parson.'

192

The man looked puzzled. 'You seem astounded, sirs. Is there something wrong?'

'Very wrong,' Simon said soberly. 'Desperately wrong. Sweet Jesu, the poor young woman. We must find her.'

'Is it a true marriage?' John asked as soon as they were outside.

'Most certainly. There's no doubt of that.'

John was aghast. 'The wicked impertinence of the fellow, marrying like that then riding into Pinner as bold as brass as if it had never happened. So what now? Back to Knebworth in search of the girl?'

'Most definitely, if we're not already too late. Then hell-for-leather back to Pinner!'

Armed with their new information, it did not take long for Simon and John to discover where Cissy Aldersey was living. It was a small neat terraced dwelling in a quiet street. There did not seem to be any sign of life but in spite of this Simon knocked loudly on the front door. After a while this brought out a neighbour who informed them that there was no one in. 'That poor young woman,' she sighed. 'She said she'd gone in search of her husband.'

The two men looked at one another. 'Did she say where?' Simon asked. The woman said she did not know, but was obviously disposed to talk. She was also curious as to what the two gentleman wanted with her neighbour. 'I'm here on behalf of her mother,' lied Simon. 'The girl became estranged from her family and now they want reconciliation.'

'I'm glad to hear it,' the woman replied, 'for she had no one to comfort her throughout her trouble.'

'What kind of trouble?' Simon enquired.

The woman settled in for a good gossip. 'You might well ask. They seemed such a pleasant young couple when they came to live here – that would be, oh, six months or more ago. She was already with child and they both seemed very fond, but then about two months ago her husband went away. She said he was visiting relatives but she was near her time and he still didn't come back.'

'And the child?' asked Simon.

The woman shook her head. 'Lived only hours, not even long enough to be christened, and a fine boy too. But she was really bad; the midwife almost despaired of her for she suffered a great flux of blood.' She sighed. 'She was most loyal to her man but still he never came, and finally she told me she was going in search of him. I haven't seen her since.'

They thanked her and went back to their horses. 'We're most certainly too late,' said Simon. 'Two months too late.'

'Do you think she's still alive?' asked John tentatively.

Simon looked grim. 'I cannot say. But knowing what we do, I fear for her. Although it's late, we must set out for Pinner without delay. Sir Edward must be told of all this.'

'You don't think we should look in the back garden for traces of newly dug earth?' John suggested.

'Possibly, if we had more time. But if she is dead, her body could be anywhere. No, I think it best we go back and hand the matter over to the proper authorities.'

They returned to Datchworth and retrieved their belongings, assuring the hostess that only urgent business drove them away that night. 'I fear you'll have a wet ride,' she warned them. 'From the look of the sky there's much rain to come.' For some time they rode together in silence then suddenly Simon reined in his horse, slapped his thigh and turned to John.

'*Of course!* What a fool I am! It's been staring me in the face all the time. I *knew* it didn't sound right.' John gave a heavy sigh. Already heavy spots of rain were beginning to fall and now his master was in the throes of one of his fits.

'Why, celandine and white of egg and a compress of feverfew and comfrey for the belly-ache! It's what a midwife would prescribe for a difficult lying-in.'

★ ★ ★

Phillipa Carter had arrived back at her home fully intending to keep her discoveries to herself. Sir Edward was aware that the news of the warrant for Wynfred's arrest would soon get out, but the longer it took the better in case he was still hiding out somewhere locally.

Also it was thought best Harry Thornton did not immediately hear of it, nor of the discovery of Wynfred's dagger in his saddlebag. It was not outside the bounds of possibility, as Hugh had suggested, that Harry had known the whereabouts of Wynfred all along, and that he might now have recovered sufficiently to send his friend or lover word of what had happened, thus enabling him to escape. It seemed all too likely, seeing how Harry had lied from the first as to the nature of the attack. Therefore the matter was to be kept close.

Phillipa had thought this sensible and did not see why keeping her counsel should be a problem, only to be met by her father who summonsed her into the parlour before she had even had time to take off her cloak, to inform her that if she were still expecting to be betrothed to Guy Somerton, she could forget it. He would never agree to the marriage of his second daughter to the possible murderer of his first.

'But you can't believe that, Father!' exclaimed Phillipa. 'Why are you taking notice of such poisonous gossip, for it's no more than that. What proof is there? Why should Guy do such a thing? Oh, I know the tale that's gone the rounds about his secret and continuing love for Susan and how he was still consumed with jealousy, but I know it's not true. We have spoken of it much together, Guy and I, and he has assured me that he now realises that what he felt for Susan, and which for a long while she encouraged, was but infatuation, while what he feels for me is altogether deeper, more serious and so more lasting.' She looked at her father pleadingly.

'Yes, he was angry with Harry for the way he was treating Susan, so were we all. I tried in vain to persuade her to have the matter out with him, but she refused. Father, you either didn't realise fully what was going on, or wilfully blinded yourself to the scandal of a newlywed husband who spent all his time not with his bride but with a young male stranger. It was on those grounds and those alone that Guy took it on himself to rebuke Harry – an action which resulted in Harry's brazening it out and threatening to call him out in a duel.'

But her father looked at her unmoved and would have walked away. She clutched his arm. 'Think how he saved my honour, our family honour in fact, by defending me against Cuddy Banks's attempted ravishment.'

Carter shook off her hand. 'As to that, why was he so conveniently in the wood when you were attacked?'

'He was sent a message. He told me.'

'Message, pshaw!' grunted Carter. 'He'd been lying low in the wood all day after killing your sister. I'll hear no more. Tomorrow a party of us are going to ask Sir Edward Ratcliffe to issue a warrant for his arrest.'

'Then you will be too late,' cried Phillipa. 'For I can tell you that to my certain knowledge he has already issued a warrant for another, and that even now Dr Forman's servant is riding into Hertfordshire to find the doctor, bearing a copy of it with his authority to ask for assistance in apprehending . . .' She faltered, torn between her love for Guy and her promise to say nothing. 'To apprehend another against whom there is real proof,' she concluded.

Carter stared. 'May I ask why you are party to all this, Phillipa, when solid citizens such as myself are excluded?'

She looked at him levelly. 'Because, by chance, I found that proof and because Dr Brett, who also knows of it as well as Sir Edward, has asked me to keep silent until there is news from Hertfordshire. But unless you lock me in the house and shackle me to my bed,' she continued, with growing courage, 'I shall not stop seeing Guy. I beg you, Father, to believe me and for once listen to what I have to say. It will be known soon enough who murdered Susan, and you'd do well not to ally yourself with those who point the finger at Guy for they will be proved wrong and be made to look extremely foolish in the process.'

Carter considered his daughter in no small amazement. She had always been brighter and more forthright than the gentle Susan, but she had also been a dutiful girl, a constant comfort to him after the death of his wife, and he was unprepared for her resistance to his will. He had never before known her to cross him in such a way.

He sighed. 'I don't know what has brought all this about.' Then, grudgingly, 'Very well then, I'll give it until tomorrow. But unless this Dr Forman arrives back with news of your murderer having been apprehended and safely bestowed, or Sir Edward is willing to confide in me, rather than in my green girl, then I will see that proceedings are started against Guy Somerton without further delay. If he's innocent as you say, he should have no problem proving it.'

Sir Arthur Clarington had almost reached his home after a reasonably satisfactory conclusion to the business side of his coming marriage; the negotiations had taken the best part of the day. That finally out of the way, various other matters occupied his mind as he rode along. He was not a man given to introspection nor to dwelling on his misdeeds with a view to repentance, but there were one or two occasions over the last few days when he had become concerned that his past might well catch up with him or, at the very least, embarrass him at an inconvenient, not to say crucial, time.

He was forty-two and had known for a good while that it was more than time he was married and provided his two estates with an heir, yet he had always resisted the urge to tie himself down to one woman, even if it was a marriage of convenience. He wanted neither years of boredom with a plain and complaisant bore prepared to put up with his infidelities so long as she had every comfort, nor a hot and lusty piece of whom he might soon tire or, perish the thought, who might actually tire of him.

After a severe dressing down from his uncle, his late father's youngest brother, as to his duty to the family name and lands, he had finally agreed that he must take a wife, whereupon his uncle applied himself to the task with diligence, finally finding a girl on whom all parties could agree. Elinor Farmer was the only daughter of a wealthy baronet, indeed his only child, the rest having died in infancy. During her early years she had been over-protected for fear she would follow her brothers and sisters to the graveyard, but she had proved to be a robust child with a sound constitution and had now achieved the age of fifteen in glowing health. She was also a good-looking girl who showed promise of being extremely handsome in the years to come.

Elinor had been the last of the brood and her parents were now elderly and wanted to see her successfully and prudently settled. She had not been particularly enthusiastic at the notion of marrying a man nearly three times her age, but had been somewhat soothed when her nurse pointed out that it might well not be too long before she was a brisk young widow with two fortunes and many happy years ahead of her, hence the wrangling over the terms of the marriage settlement.

In the end, Sir Arthur mused, he had been forced to agree to most of the baronet's terms if he was ever to see the marriage take place. All in all he had not come too badly out of it. While he had been forced to make considerable provision for her in the event of his demise, especially if there were no children, he felt reasonably complacent. He might be well – a little older than she was, but he was in excellent health and saw no reason why he should not live until he was ninety. As to children, there shouldn't be any problem on *that* account. He had proved that all too often.

It was the matter of his illegitimate offspring that had

caused him some concern, for Elinor's father had asked him outright if the rumours he had heard of his behaviour towards women and its consequences were true. He had laughed it off, he hoped to the baronet's satisfaction, by claiming that while he had been no saint, particularly when young and foolish, such tales had grown mightily in the telling. As to bastard children – well, there was a young girl growing up at a farm outside Datchworth whose mother had been a dairymaid on his estate, but that was in the past when he had been young and hotheaded. He wasn't the first and wouldn't be the last to be caught out in such a way. He said nothing of a more recent involvement which was worrying him for, in this particular instance, he had wanted to know of the progress of the child.

He rode into his courtyard and his grooms came running to take his horse. Almost at once his present secretary, a man of middle years, appeared in the doorway and came over to inform him that there was a message from the steward on his other estate at Pinner which demanded his immediate attention. Even now the messenger was awaiting his reply. Sir Arthur growled his annoyance, muttered that he'd better hear what it was all about, then strode off in the direction of the room used as an office for the business of the estate. A young groom, booted and spurred, sprang up from the bench on which he had been sitting as he entered.

'So,' barked Clarington, 'what's this message which won't wait my taking off my boots and having some refreshment?'

The groom gave a nervous smile. 'Your steward sends word to tell you that some days since, your former secretary was set on in a wood near Pinner and his wife murdered.'

'God's Blood!' Sir Arthur paled and sat down suddenly on the bench. 'Are you sure of this?'

'Quite sure, sir. The young woman is already buried.'

'And has the perpetrator of this foul deed been caught?'

The groom shook his head. 'No, sir. At first it was thought to be the result of an attack by the robbers who have harassed the neighbourhood of late, but now it seems not to have been the case.'

'Thornton and his wife were alone at the time? Without even a groom?'

'It seems there was a friend of Thornton's with them,' the young man replied, 'but he's not been seen since. It's not known whether he's dead or alive.'

In answer Sir Arthur stood up. 'Fetch fresh horses for my servant and me,' he commanded, 'and tell him we leave for Pinner at once. Don't stand there staring, do as I say – and get them to send me in some ale while you're about it!'

Chapter 14

The Night Before Hallowe'en

Harry Thornton's feverish ramblings had passed and he now lay in his bed, staring at the ceiling, refusing all offers of comfort. Assured by Hugh Brett that his son's wound was well on the mend and that what was needed now was exercise and fresh air, his father strode into his bedroom and yanked the bedclothes off the bed, urging his son to get up at once, dress himself, and stop behaving like a sick girl.

'All right, so you have lost your wife and suffered a nasty leg wound into the bargain, but lying there all day feeling sorry for yourself won't help anything. It's a pity you didn't feel as much for poor Susan when she was alive. At least, I hope that's what's troubling you. You've rambled on almost as much about Wynfred.' He gave his son a shrewd look. 'Unless you are seen out and about, helping to track down your wife's murderers, the gossip about you and Wynfred will start up all over again, if it hasn't already. Tongues are already wagging because you weren't at the burial; not everyone believes you were sick!'

With extreme reluctance Harry did as he was told while his father stood over him to ensure he did so. He winced as he eased his leg into his breeches for his thigh was still sore then, limping slightly, he made his way downstairs to the kitchen where a maid brought him some breakfast. If he had thought that by doing this his father would now leave him alone, he was mistaken.

201

Adam Thornton did not know of the warrant for Wynfred's arrest but was all too well aware of the talk about his disappearance as well as the gossip concerning Guy Somerton. He sat down heavily opposite his son. 'As you've lain in your bed, much has happened,' he began. 'First and foremost—'

'If you're going to ask me to join a party to track down the robbers then, weak as I am, Father, I'll do so if that's what you want,' Harry broke in quickly. 'Obviously I want them brought to justice as soon as possible.'

'Robbers!' roared Master Thornton, banging the table. 'What robbers?'

'Why, the ones that attacked us,' replied his son in some surprise.

Master Thornton leant across the table. 'See you here, Harry, you'd best know now that no one believes any longer in your tale of robbers.'

Harry was obviously shaken at this but raised to his father a face of injured innocence. 'What do you mean? Of course there were robbers. How else could all this have happened?'

'It's *you* who should be answering that question, as no doubt you will have to, in due time,' responded his father. 'The robbers you assured us had set on you could not possibly have done so, for they were already in custody in Edmonton and have confessed to their previous crimes hereabouts.' Harry swayed on his seat as if he were about to faint. His father looked at him with contempt. 'Pull yourself together, and act like a man, for Jesu's sake! Now both Somerton and your precious friend, Wynfred, are under suspicion for killing Susan and wounding you. Though if it was Somerton, why you should be shielding him defeats me.'

Harry said nothing. 'Come on,' demanded his father, 'let's have some answers, starting first with Somerton. Everyone knows you quarrelled over Susan though he's as good as betrothed to her sister, even that you wanted to fight him when you returned from London. Did he therefore lie in wait for you in the woods and accost you, as some suppose? Declare his undying love for Susan and challenge your right to her in view of the way you were treating her? Was that when violence took place? In such a case it could be that Susan was killed by mistake and you wounded trying to protect her, and if that's what happened, then say so and the matter can be taken from there.'

Harry swallowed. 'I can't tell you,' he replied in a low voice.

'Can't *tell* me?' bellowed Thornton. 'What kind of an answer's that?'

His son looked away. 'I can't remember.'

The older man rose to his feet. 'Can't remember? And you so certain in every detail of an attack that never happened? Very well, so what of Wynfred? Have you forgotten all you said of him too? How he was dragged off by those same robbers, along with your wife? If there were no robbers, then who killed your wife and where is Wynfred?'

'I don't know,' Harry replied again, his voice trembling. 'Would to God I did.'

'There's many feel the same way though not, I imagine, for the same reason,' declared Adam. 'If your friend has nothing to hide and nothing to fear, why hasn't he come forward like an honest fellow?'

'Stop it!' wailed Harry, burying his head in his hands. 'Stop asking me all these questions! My head aches and I'm sick to my stomach.'

Adam came behind his son and yanked his head back by his hair. 'Why did you lie? Tell me. Why did you lie?' Harry looked as if he were about to burst into tears. With a snort of disgust, Thornton released him and made for the door. 'You're not the only one with a turned stomach. Well, for your information I'm told there's now a hue and cry out for Wynfred. Dr Brett's colleague Dr Forman has made it his business to go into Hertfordshire to see what he can find out about the fellow, and whether anyone has seen hide or hair of him since Susan's death. Let's hope he succeeds so that we can finally get to the truth of the matter.' He paused in the doorway. 'Are you sure you have nothing to tell me?' he asked one last time, but Harry appeared bereft of speech and with a further angry exclamation, Thornton left the room.

Harry rose from the table leaving most of his food uneaten, limped into the garden and sat on a bench wishing he had brought his cloak with him, for although the day was fine the wind was chilly to one who had been confined to a sickbed. He leant back against the stone wall behind him and peered dizzily into the pit which now yawned before him.

He knew his mind had been disturbed during the last few days, but there had been lucid moments and he was as certain as he could be of anything that Wynfred really had visited him in the middle of one night, that this was not a dream or a hallucination. If that was so, then he must be hiding out somewhere in the vicinity, but where? He must find out and somehow send him word that he was being accused of Susan's murder. It would be best, thought Harry, if his friend could be persuaded to flee to London where it was easier to disappear into the crowd. At all costs he mustn't either be captured or give himself up.

Harry Thornton was not the only one endlessly reliving recent events. For once Cuddy Banks had had a real fright. Hitherto whatever he had done and whatever the consequences, he could rely on his father to support him – but not this time. Old Banks might well believe Lizzie Saxton to be a witch and would happily see her dead, but he drew the line at drunken ramblings of demons on horseback. His son had made him a laughing stock. When he took part in the morris with the other men on Saturday, or rather *if* he took part, his parents had made it clear to him that it was to be for the last time.

Furious at being disbelieved, determined to try to regain

his former status among the young men of the town, Cuddy fumed and fretted while his father kept him busy with work about the farm. Then he had what seemed to him to be an excellent idea until he voiced it to his father. Banks looked at him in disbelief.

'Go and see the parson?' he echoed. 'That old fool?' He looked his son up and down. 'Are you still out of your head? It's all we can do to get you to church of a Sunday to avoid paying a shilling for you, hempseed. Do you want the congregation to laugh at us every time we go to Sunday service? Get on with your work, there's plenty of it.'

Nothing daunted, however, Cuddy waited until his father had disappeared on some farm business and then, having craftily ordered a simple-minded youth to take over his task, he set off briskly for the parsonage. He knocked on the door and demanded of the young maid who opened it that he be let in at once as he had urgent business to discuss with Parson Wytherley. He could not have chosen a better recipient for what he had to say. The good parson had considered himself slighted ever since the meeting Hugh had held about Mother Saxton, when his sententious pronouncements had been more or less ignored. And what was the result? The decent God-fearing people of the town had been forced to take matters into their own hands to rid the place of the menace that threatened them all, only to be prevented at the last moment by an interfering Justice of the Peace brought along by a wealthy and largely absentee landlord with a doubtful reputation!

It was therefore with the greatest eagerness that he greeted Cuddy, when the youth threw himself dramatically onto his knees and begged for protection against witchcraft, throwing in for good measure that Satan himself had appeared in the nearby woods. Wytherley at once invited Cuddy into his parlour, sat him down and, eyes ablaze, pressed him to explain what this was all about. Flattered by the rapt attention he was receiving, Cuddy embarked on a story that lost nothing in the telling. At one stage he briefly recalled the promises made to the Almighty when he stood in fear of death or worse, how he would lead a better life, stop telling lies, even that he would stand outside the church of a Sunday as a penitent, but he firmly put them aside. After all, anyone would have done the same in the circumstances.

Parson Wytherley listened open-mouthed. This was proof of the evil in their midst beyond his wildest dreams. 'Dear Father in Heaven!' he gasped. 'You say these demonic apparitions appeared from nowhere?'

'There came a great noise as of thunder and a blinding light, and of a sudden, there they were,' Cuddly confirmed. His mouth went dry as he again described them. 'The horses . . . I could see right through them and they glowed in the dark, and there was this figure leading them with antlers growing out of his head. It was Herne the Hunter, I swear it! Then suddenly there came a great ring of fire and . . . and . . . I'd swear Satan himself was in the midst of it.'

'Go on, go on,' urged the parson, quite carried away.

It was here Cuddy departed completely from the truth. 'And Mother Saxton was there too, dancing about in front of him with that black dog of hers, her familiar.'

Wytherley nearly burst with excitement. 'You're certain of this?'

Cuddy crossed his fingers. 'Quite certain. I was as near to her as I am to you now.'

It might be thought that at this stage it would have been as well for Parson Wytherley to seek advice both as to what to do next and also with regard to Cuddy's reputation for veracity. From the legal point of view, Sir Edward was still in town hearing evidence while Cuddy's family and friends would have been quick to point out that his word was notoriously unreliable. Certainly, had he spoken to his known companions and asked what they made of it all, Wytherley would have quickly learned that Cuddy had seen his visions following the drinking of the best part of a pint of sack followed by *aqua vitae*. But he did not. He rubbed his hands in glee. It would surely do him nothing but good with the church authorities to know they had such a stalwart fighter against evil in charge of the parish, a soldier of Christ prepared to bring a servant of Satan to justice. As to the law of the land, Sir Edward Ratcliffe was proving dilatory, sitting about listening to accusations for hours while the witch remained safely where she was, spinning her evil webs.

He turned to Cuddy. 'You are indeed fortunate to have survived. God must have saved you for a purpose.'

'I did pray to Him for help,' asserted Cuddy virtuously.

'See then how He responded to your prayer.' Wytherley struck a dramatic pose. 'There is now a great evil in the woods, a source so baneful that Satan himself manifests his presence. That source must be Mother Saxton, for it was not so before she came here. It must be stopped before even worse befalls; before we know where we are, others will be corrupted into witchcraft.'

'But that's already happened,' cried Cuddy earnestly. 'I heard her shout out that there are now at least three or four other witches in the parish, thanks to her,' and he proceeded to name several people against whom either he or his father had a grudge.

'This witch must be brought in and put securely away,' declared Wytherley, 'after which we must seek out the others who have been corrupted.'

'What about the Justice?' enquired Cuddy. 'Won't we have to ask for his warrant?'

Parson Wytherley brushed this aside. 'He need know nothing until she's brought before him, and when she is I shall tell him that in the opinion of the Church, of which I am the representative, the matter would brook no further delay if we are to prevent the whole town being infected with evil as if with the Plague. Indeed, the Plague would be preferable, for those who die of it might well go to Heaven, but what will be the fate of those infected with witchcraft, come Judgment Day? I will send word to my Bishop at once, telling him what I'm doing. Now, how best to go about it? Can you find sufficient stout fellows, half a dozen should do, who can go with us?'

Cuddy's heart sank. 'Must it be tonight? For this evening the morris is to be performed outside the Crown by torchlight in front of all the townsfolk.'

'All the better,' said Wytherley. 'For while most of the town is so occupied, you and I, accompanied by the men I have asked you to find, will go to Mother Saxton's house and fetch her back here.'

Cuddy began to have doubts as to the wisdom of all this, not to mention his overwhelming disappointment at having to forgo taking part in the night's performance. He tried to make his point again. 'But I'm supposed to be with the morris men – we've been practising for weeks. Can't it wait until tomorrow?'

'Tomorrow? Don't you realise what tomorrow is?' Cuddy shook his head. 'It's All Hallows Night, what many still call Hallowe'en, when witches and warlocks walk abroad unfettered, their powers at their greatest. That's another reason for acting without further delay. As for performing with the morris men, surely God's work comes before what many regard as a pastime we would be better without. What is your hobby horse but a pagan symbol, your Jack-in-the-Green, the Green Man? And such prancing and leaping leads to foolery and lustful thoughts. If I had my way, all such antics would be stopped.' He took on an air of purpose. 'Now I'll get my groom to come with us – that's two – and leave it to you to bring the rest.'

'What happens if she bewitches us all when we get there?' asked Cuddy, the rush of confidence he had experienced while telling his story now rapidly evaporating.

Wytherley dismissed this with an airy wave of his hand. 'We shall go armed with righteousness, secure in the armour of the Lord. Rightly is it written in the Bible that we must not suffer a witch to live. See what has happened by ignoring God's holy will. We will meet here in my house an hour after dark. While your morris men are busy with their so-called entertainment, we will set off for Mother Saxton's.'

Once outside in the street Cuddy, as on all too many previous occasions, cursed himself for his rashness. Now he was faced not only with missing the morris but having to find half a dozen witchhunters besides. How was he going to tell his companions that he would be unable to join them? He decided he would have to send word to them that he had suddenly been taken sick, for if he sought them out himself with an excuse, doubtless Jack Page would run at once to his interfering schoolmaster father to tell him Cuddy Banks was up to no good again. Once more he cursed it being that particular night; had it been any other, he felt sure two or three of the dancers would have been game to come with him, but now he was forced to seek volunteers elsewhere.

His first port of call was to the home of a labourer who sometimes worked for his father. On being told the nature of his business however, the man shook his head.

'Reckon she should be left alone,' he told Cuddy. 'Old Gammer Washbowl cursed her high and low, reckoning she'd caused his sow to cast her pigs a day before she should have farrowed. Yet when they were sent up London to be sold at Bartholomew Fair they got as good a price for excellent pigmeat as ever an ale-wife longed for. He's been praising the old girl to the skies ever since!'

Where do I go next? Cuddy wondered. If he kept knocking on doors asking for men willing to help bring in the witch, word would soon be all over the town and thus reach Sir Edward Ratcliffe at the Crown, and he would certainly consider his authority to have been undermined. Finally he trudged off to a hamlet a mile or so away where he found three unattractive youths hanging around outside the local tavern looking for mischief. The prospect of a witchhunt delighted them and they made so much noise about it that Cuddy had to beg them to stop or the whole plan would go awry. He then swore them to secrecy, telling them that if they spoke of it to anyone the witch would know and put her curse on them. Then he returned home where he found his parents had once again been looking for him.

Clinging onto the door, he told them that he had fallen down in a faint while working outside and had only just regained his wits. In answer to his mother's immediate concern, he told her he had pains in his head and a sick stomach and insisted on going to bed. He then begged his father, in a feeble voice, to send word to Jack Page that he would be unable to take part in the morris that night. This last succeeded in convincing Banks that his son really must be ill, given how much store he had set on taking part in the event during the past weeks.

The rest of the morris men greeted the news with a certain amount of relief: rather no Cuddy than a drunken Cuddy. By seven in the evening a considerable crowd had collected both inside and outside the Crown, eager to forget the events of the past week if only for a little while. Tomorrow, being All Hallows, they would stay home and not venture out after dark, fearful of what they might see or hear.

Cuddy waited until most of the household had taken themselves into town then crept downstairs in his stocking feet, put on his boots and slunk off to the back door of the parsonage where his cohorts were already waiting for him. Parson Wytherley was somewhat disappointed that he had been able to muster so few men, yet had no alternative but to make the best of it. There were, after all, six of them against one old woman. As they left the High Street behind them Cuddy could hear the roar of the crowd as the Fool led the Hobby Horse into the ring and the fiddle struck up. If he'd only held his tongue he'd be among them, showing off and having a good time, not marching off into the woods in the dark to hunt down a witch.

210

On the edge of the crowd watching the morris men, Harry Thornton stood, feeling utterly apart from the general festivities. While several people had asked him how he was and expressed their sympathy over the death of his wife, others had very obviously turned aside when he passed them by, saying nothing. It was as if he were somehow being blamed for Susan's death. He moved further away into the shadows. There had been a time when he had enjoyed watching the morris men but now it seemed a stupid, childish pastime, something fit only for country fools.

He had been racking his brains all day as to how he might discover if anyone had seen Wynfred since the discovery of Susan's body or had an idea where he might be, but there seemed no way of doing so without rousing suspicion. Therefore when one of his old companions, recognising him in spite of the gloom, came over to him then, after asking how he was, brought up Wynfred's name, he thought he might be in luck – though did not hear exactly what was said because of the noise of the crowd and the stamping and banging of the morris men as they clashed their staves together.

'So,' the man continued in a quieter moment, 'you'll now be wanting to know where Wynfred is yourself.'

'Most certainly,' Harry replied eagerly. 'Why, do you know?'

His companion looked at him curiously. 'If I did, I'd not be here now and he'd be safely bestowed.'

Harry stared. 'I don't understand.'

The man looked him up and down. 'I'd heard you'd had a fever, I see now it must be true. You don't know then, that there's a warrant out for his arrest? They're searching hereabouts for him and some fellow's also gone riding off to Hertfordshire with another in case he's taken flight there. When he's found, he's to be brought back here to stand trial. They kept it quiet at first so that if he is somewhere near he wouldn't take fright, but now it's common knowledge.'

Harry paled. 'Warrant? Escaped? From what has Francis need to escape?'

'Where are your wits, man? From the rope, that's what. The noose and the scaffold.' The man gave him an unpleasant look. 'Of course! You swore it was all down to robbers.' He gave him a look of manifest disgust. 'God's Breath, you must have known all along that he murdered your wife!'

Mother Saxton's daughter lay breathing the death-rattle. The old woman bent over and felt first her hand, then her brow; both were chill. She had not been entirely truthful with Simon about what medicaments she had at hand, and as well as using the poppy syrup he had sent to her by Hugh she had added to it some from a hidden store of her own, for she hoped by so doing that her daughter would slip easily out of a life which was now unbearable.

She left the bedside and returned to her stool beside the fire. Had she really the powers attributed to her and which she pretended, she would gladly have sold her soul to cure her only child and to get her revenge on the man whose treatment of Nan had driven the girl into a life which had brought her to this pass. Nor, she thought grimly, was that all he had to answer for.

She had accepted the advice the Justice gave her and would certainly have taken it but for the predicament in which she now found herself. Experience told her that Nan was unlikely to last the night and she had packed her few belongings into a bundle ready for leaving as soon as it was all over. There was nothing more she could do here. As to the other one . . . She glanced over to the shadowy doorway which led to a smaller room at the back. She had done what she could for that one too and it was now out of her hands.

She was weary with watching and in spite of herself began to nod off, hearing nothing until the door was kicked open and the room seemed suddenly to be filled with men, led by a parson in full canonicals holding before him a fine brass cross taken from the church.

'Avaunt, vile servant of Satan!' he cried, raising the cross on high. 'Take her, lads, lay hold of the witch.'

She shrank back. 'Why are you here? Where's the constable? Has the Justice sent you with a warrant?'

'We need no warrant,' cried Cuddy. 'By the time the old Justice had finished, you'd have been clean away.' He pointed to the bundle. 'Look, lads, we're only just in time. A few hours more and we'd have lost her.'

'What this?' asked one of the men, going over to the bed.

'My daughter's dying,' said the old woman. 'She'll be dead before morning.'

The man jumped back as if shot. 'Is it the Plague?'

Lizzie Saxton smiled. 'Would that it were and you'd all catch it! But no, it's the pox. To catch that from her you must needs bed her first. Does the prospect tempt you?'

All the men fell back at this and looked at the parson, waiting for him to tell them what to do next. Wytherley faced something of a dilemma. In normal circumstances he would have asked if the dying woman had been christened, even possibly given it the benefit of the doubt, and thus performed the last rites. But, after all, this was the daughter of a witch. Lizzie Saxton saw what was going through his mind.

'She was baptised and she even had a father who recognised her, though he's long dead. What kind of a Man of God are you that you can't offer her the consolation of your religion even if she's too far gone to know?'

For a moment he hesitated but he had waded too far in. He made up his mind. 'Leave that one where she is,' he told the men, 'for she's but devil's spawn. Two of you bind the witch's hands, the rest search the place to see what else you can find.'

'Where's the black dog, her familiar?' asked Cuddy.

'He's out about his business somewhere in the woods,'

213

the old woman replied, wincing as her hands were tied behind her back. 'He's no more nor less than an ordinary dog and has been my good friend these past months. I pray he'll find another home.'

Wytherley looked across to the door at the other side of the room. 'See if her dog's in there; it will help our case if we can bring her familiar in too. There may also be other things – idols, stuff for spells, evil books and writings . . .'

'Her broomstick?' suggested Cuddy.

The man who had been fearful of the Plague went over to the doorway 'There is something here,' he called back, 'cowering in a corner. Come and see, lads.'

There was the sound of a scuffle and a cry of pain and the man reappeared. 'What do you make of this then?' he asked them all grimly. 'See what I've found.' Whereupon he pushed into the room Francis Wynfred.

Chapter 15

Feverfew and Comfrey

Wytherley could hardly believe his good fortune. 'Tie him up as well,' he ordered. 'I hear there's a warrant out for his arrest – we'll take him back too. They can keep each other company in the town gaol.' He gave a sigh of satisfaction. The discovery and capture of a possible murderer would stop any criticism that there might have been over his setting off a witchhunt when the matter was already in the hands of a Justice of the Peace. Indeed, it would prove how necessary it had been for the witch to be taken in without further delay, since to add to her other crimes, it could be proved that she harboured men on the run from the law.

Francis Wynfred was deathly pale except for a bruise rapidly spreading over one cheek. Normally so immaculate in appearance, his shirt was now dirty and torn and he had obviously lived and slept in his clothes for some days. He looked round at the men encircling him. 'I don't understand,' he said. 'What am I supposed to have done?'

'You know very well,' replied Wytherley, 'it's all over the town. You're wanted in connection with the murder of Susan Thornton.'

'But I can't be. It's not true.' He looked at the parson in horror. 'Who says I did it?' No one answered. 'Not Harry? Surely not Harry?'

Wytherley turned to Lizzie Saxton, still holding the cross firmly between them. 'So as well as dancing with Satan, you hide murderers too, do you, witch?'

'Dancing with Satan?'

'Aye, that young man,' he pointed to Cuddy, 'saw demons here in the wood only a few nights ago and Herne the Hunter then Satan himself in the midst of a fiery ring while you capered about before him.'

'If he saw Satan in the woods then it was he conjured him up,' declared the old woman, 'for I've been here with my sick daughter of nights. As for concealing a murderer, this person is as innocent of Susan Thornton's murder as I am.' She looked at them with contempt. 'You still don't know the truth, do you?'

'Your word counts for nothing,' the parson responded. 'Who will believe *you*?' He looked round the room. 'Let's be off back to town then, we've done what we set out to do and more.'

'And the sick woman?' asked one of the youths. 'You really think we should leave her here alone?'

Wytherley made for the door. 'I've already said my say on that.'

'If your actions make you a Christian,' commented Lizzie Saxton, 'then I'm glad I'm none.'

'Surely you can't leave her to die on her own?' added Wynfred.

'Squeamish, are you now?' laughed one of the men. 'You, who were brave enough to stab an innocent girl to death.'

When they got outside the house they discovered it was pouring with rain and soon they were trudging through pools of water which were rapidly spreading across the road and getting deeper by the minute. It was hardly surprising they encountered no one on their journey. They wasted no time, hustling Lizzie Saxton and Francis Wynfred along as fast as their bonds would allow. As it was, by the time they arrived back in town it was nearly ten o'clock and the morris men were gone, the revellers driven off the streets by the rain. Pinner was deserted.

216

It took some time to knock up the constable as he had already gone to bed, then to persuade him, grumbling steadily, to unlock the gaol. After seeing his prisoners put in the cells, Wytherley went across to the Crown and asked for Sir Edward Ratcliffe. The Justice was also less than pleased at being disturbed as he too was also on the point of retiring. So far as he was concerned, his enquiries into the activities of Lizzie Saxton had proved inconclusive. Certainly she had on occasion laid claim to occult powers, but she had also suffered much abuse at the hands of the local populace which did provide some excuse. He had always been of a sceptical turn of mind about such matters, and found nothing in the catalogue of supposed witchery to change his view.

Young women did miscarry or deliver stillborn babes, cows and horses regularly took sick, people suffered good luck and ill, sometimes in unequal proportions, and all this had been the case since time began. Not to mention the fact that when it came to accusations of witchcraft the loudest voices raised usually came from those who either bore a grudge towards the supposed witch or had scores to settle elsewhere. He had not been persuaded Lizzie Saxton had a case to answer and therefore saw no good reason to issue a warrant for her. In fact, he went further: he hoped she had already taken his good advice and left the district.

So he was extremely angry to learn from Wytherley that the zealous parson had taken matters into his own hands and brought Lizzie Saxton in on his own initiative; his breathless explanation of why this was so urgent, an explanation which involved tales of spectral horsemen and dancing demons, failed to impress Sir Edward in the very least. But the news of the capture of Wynfred was an altogether different matter.

'It seems Dr Forman and his servant will find they have been on a fruitless mission,' he said, 'if Wynfred has been hiding out with Lizzie Saxton all this while. What have you done with him?'

'He's now safe under lock and key,' Wytherley assured him. 'The Constable has put him in the town gaol along with the witch.'

'Then I will come over right away and inform him of the jeopardy in which he stands. However, as to the business of Lizzie Saxton, I must tell you that I am not at all pleased. What point is there in asking a Justice to look into such a matter then acting without his warrant? Do you consider yourself above the law?'

Wytherley stood his ground. 'The law of God is above that of man,' he declared.

'That might well be your belief,' Sir Edward replied sternly, 'but we live in a realm and in a time where justice is administered according to the law of the land – and I am here to see it done!'

Cuddy and his men were still hanging about outside the gaol when the Justice arrived and after thanking them briefly for bringing Wynfred in, he made it clear in no uncertain terms that they had no right to have forcibly removed Lizzie Saxton from her home without his order to do so, whatever their parson might have said. 'I made it clear when first you tried to take the law into your own hands that if witchcraft is suspected, then it must be properly examined with due process and that I would countenance no witchhunts.'

At this point Cuddy seemed prepared to argue but Sir Edward would have none of it. 'Go back to your farm, Banks. You're fortunate you're not sitting where Wynfred is, facing a charge of ravishment!'

The town gaol was a small but secure building boasting two dank cells, each with a grating high up near the roof. It was mostly used as an overnight resting place for the drunk and disorderly, petty thieves and those wanderers described as 'sturdy beggars' before they were brought before a Justice in the morning; it rarely housed those accused of more serious crimes. The cells were dark even in daylight, the straw on the floor rarely changed, the nooks and crevices home to rats and mice.

'Bring me some light,' Sir Edward demanded. 'Two candles at least. I must see what I'm doing.' The constable shuffled off into a cubby hole by the outer door and returned with a piece of candle stuck in an old holder. The Justice took flint and tinder from his pocket and lit it. 'Now go over to the Crown and ask them to let you have another.'

The doors of both inner cells stood open. In the first Mother Saxton leant against the wall, her long grey hair plastered against her face with the rain. In the other, Wynfred sat huddled in a corner. The Justice noted the mark on his face. 'Was he injured when he was taken?' he enquired.

'He has a bruise on his cheek from when he struggled with the men,' Wytherley replied uneasily. They said no more until the constable came back, this time with a tall candle in a candlestick. Ratcliffe went to the door of Wynfred's cell and held it aloft. 'It's no use hiding in a corner. Stand up, if you please, and come over here.'

Wynfred was drenched and shivering with cold, the bruise on his cheek now livid. He looked a sorry sight. Ratcliffe turned to the constable. 'Fetch pallets for them to sleep on and a blanket each. They also need dry clothing if they are to live to stand trial. You, parson!' Wytherley frowned at the mode of address. 'Presumably you have old clothes set aside for the poor, so fetch what you can.

'So,' he said as they were left together, 'you are Francis Wynfred. Then I must inform you that a warrant has been issued for your arrest.'

Wynfred swallowed. 'So they said. On what charge?'

'That of murdering Susan Thornton.'

Wynfred shook his head wildly. 'No,' he said. 'No, no, *no*,' his voice rising with every negative. 'The parson accused me of it just now but I couldn't credit that it was believed. Why should I want to kill Susan Thornton?'

'That's for you to tell us,' said Sir Edward. 'I urge you if

219

you know anything of the business to tell me now.'

'I don't, I can't . . .' he began then shook his head.

Sir Edward sighed. 'This attitude will do you no good at all, young man. I don't know how much you know or what you've heard of what has taken place since you left here with the Thorntons, but I will tell you what is general knowledge. The morning after your departure, Harry Thornton was discovered in the woods, his hands bound, suffering from a knife wound near the thigh and a blow on the head that had rendered him unconscious. A search revealed the body of his wife near by, stabbed through the heart.

'When rescued, he told of a band of robbers who had attacked your party. He described how Susan and yourself were dragged away by some of the men, and that it was in attempting to save you both that he received his leg wound and the blow on his head. He said he knew nothing more until he recovered consciousness, and was found, quite by chance, by Dr Forman's servant John Bradedge. At first he was believed, for as you know there have been several such attacks in recent weeks. Indeed, I'm told you were warned against using the path through the woods before you set off. However, it was quickly shown that his story was untrue, that there were no robbers.'

Wynfred looked bemused. 'So what does Harry say now?'

'Thornton has been suffering from a fever which has caused him to ramble in his mind and there's been no getting any sense out of him until now, but he must be recovered for I saw him myself outside the Crown this evening watching the morris men – though when I approached him, he fled. I intended going to the Manor first thing tomorrow morning to demand a proper account of what happened. Possibly you can save me the trouble.'

The young man looked bleak. 'Do these people with so much to say also explain why I should want to kill Susan Thornton?'

'There are those who say that it was out of jealousy. Surely you must have known that your behaviour towards Harry Thornton and his to you gave rise to gossip? That it was widely rumoured that what was between the two of you was an unnatural friendship?'

'Was it?' Wynfred made a sound almost like a laugh. 'Then I can swear to you here and now that such was not the case.'

Sir Edward became impatient. 'Then if you did not kill Susan Thornton and have nothing to hide, why haven't you come forward before now and told us what did happen? Why lurk in hiding? What have you to say?'

Wynfred looked him squarely in the face. 'Nothing,' he replied quietly.

' "Nothing" is not an answer.'

'It's all I can give you,' said Wynfred.

'Then I trust a night in here, albeit with dry clothing, will cause you to change your mind,' Ratcliffe informed him with a grim expression, 'for I would not want to use the methods that are available to persuade you to speak.'

Almost at once the constable arrived back accompanied by a stableboy from the Crown, carrying between them two straw pallets and a couple of ancient horse blankets. They were followed shortly afterwards by the parson, still smarting from the dressing down he had received from Sir Edward. He flung a bundle on the floor from which he produced a pair of old, but clean, breeches, a coarse thick shirt and jerkin that had seen better days, a flannel petticoat and an ancient shawl.

'Very well,' said the Justice, 'I will come back in the morning, Wynfred, to see if you've changed your mind. Give them the dry clothing, Parson Wytherley.' He looked through the barred door of the other cell, raising his candle again as he did so. 'As for you, Lizzie Saxton, why didn't you take my advice to leave this place and mend your ways?'

'She was nursing her dying daughter,' broke in Wynfred.

'She would have been gone some days but for that.'

'What dying daughter?' Ratcliffe queried.

'She's likely already dead,' said Lizzie Saxton, pressing her face against the bars. 'You can do her no more harm now.'

Sir Edward was taken aback. 'Is this true, Wytherley?'

The parson looked shifty. 'There was a sick woman in the bed there, a whore suffering from the pox the witch claimed was her daughter. She seemed close to death.'

The Justice looked at him coldly. 'It hardly seems a godly act for anyone to allow the woman to die alone, whoever or whatever she might be, let alone a man of the cloth,' he commented. He turned back to the old woman. 'I'll see someone is sent to the house at first light,' he promised quietly, then shook his head. 'I fear there will be little I can do for you now. Had you left when I told you to, you would most likely have been safe. I found no good cause to bring you in but now, well, at the very least you will be charged with harbouring a wanted man.'

The landlady's gloomy forecast of the weather in store for Simon and John had proved all too accurate. The torrential rain that had fallen on Pinner swept north and the night was soon so bad that the two travellers could do nothing else but put up for the night and wait out the storm. Sir Arthur Clarington, on the other hand, had insisted on pressing on in spite of the weather, but did not reach his house until the small hours of the morning, by which time he was wet, exhausted and fit only for his bed.

The rain was over by the time Simon and John finally rode into Pinner the next morning, but the air was chill. Hugh welcomed them warmly and taking them into the house immediately commiserated with them. 'You look tired, both of you, and I imagine you're going to tell me your quest was hopeless, that there was no sign or sound of Wynfred in Hertfordshire.'

'By no means,' Simon assured him. 'Indeed, we bring you news that will amaze you.'

Hugh looked puzzled. 'Of Wynfred?'

'Most assuredly.'

'But he's here – in the town gaol. Parson Wytherley took it into his own hands to raise a bunch of hotheads and take them out to Mother Saxton's cottage to bring her in after that wretched Cuddy Banks spun him some yarn about having seen her dancing with demons in the wood before Satan himself. That was enough for our parson, Justice or no Justice. To cut a long story short, who should they find hiding out in the witch's hovel but Francis Wynfred. Sir Edward saw him last night and is to question him further this morning.'

'Then I must see Sir Edward without delay,' Simon declared, 'for there are things he must know before he takes the matter any further. You'd best come too, Hugh, so that I don't have to tell the same story twice.'

They found the Justice about to go over to the gaol again, and at first he was not disposed to suffer any delay but after Simon had persuaded him of the urgency of the matter, he sat and listened gravely to what he had to tell him. Then he stood up and put his hand to his head. 'But this beggars belief! You are absolutely sure of this?'

'Certain sure.' Simon felt in his doublet and produced a piece of paper. 'Here is the entry as copied from the Church Book.'

'Then it's clear we confront Wynfred with all you have to tell us and, given the circumstances, I think in some place more suitable than the town gaol.'

'You can use my house,' said Hugh. He looked across at Simon. 'Your reputation for finding things out is certainly justified,' he said with admiration. 'Tell me, did you suspect it all the time?'

'I have to admit I did not,' said Simon. 'The entry in the Church Book came as much of a shock to me as it has to you. But later I realised I'd been given one of the clues to it two months ago when I was here last. Do you recall my telling you, Hugh, that when I first met Wynfred he looked to me as if he had recently suffered a severe illness. When I asked him if that was so, he agreed and said that he had suffered from a flux of the bowels. When I pressed him as to the treatment he had received, he spoke of celandine and white wine, comfrey and feverfew. Remember how we were both surprised?'

Hugh thought for a moment then slapped his thigh. 'Of course! But how could we have possibly guessed what was behind it?' Sir Edward looked mystified.

'I'll explain shortly,' Simon told him. 'Now, let's see what Francis Wynfred has to say to us.'

'I'll have him brought over to Dr Brett's house at once,' said the Justice. 'But I can still hardly credit it.' He paused. 'Do you think, if he had not been taken, that there might have been another killing?'

'I do,' replied Simon. 'In fact, I feared it might already have taken place. When a man has killed once to cover up his misdeeds, he can kill again. I was greatly relieved when I was told Wynfred was safely in custody.'

Ten minutes later, Wynfred, white and still shivering, was brought into Hugh's parlour. The large breeches and shirt made him look smaller and thinner. 'You may sit down,' Sir Edward told him. 'Have you had anything to eat or drink?' Wynfred shook his head.

'I'll ask my housekeeper to bring you mulled wine and some food,' said Hugh. 'You're obviously famished and cold to the bone.'

Wynfred looked at him suspiciously. 'I have no appetite.' He was obviously uneasy. 'Why have you brought me here? Surely not to try those methods you were suggesting last night might be used to make me speak? You wouldn't let them put me to the question, would you, Dr Brett?'

'Of course not,' soothed Hugh, 'and now whatever you say I will fetch you a cup of mulled wine and some bread and cheese. Bear with me a moment,' he said to the others,

'I think this will go better if our visitor has sustenance.' He reappeared within minutes with a steaming cup of wine and a plate of food. Wynfred lifted the cup with trembling hands, its rim clattering against his teeth.

'Now,' said Sir Edward, turning to Simon, 'say what you have discovered, Dr Forman.'

Simon looked over at the drooping figure in the chair opposite. 'That the person before you is not Francis Wynfred. Are you, my dear? Nor do I think you murdered Susan Thornton.'

Sir Arthur Clarington slept late and awoke in a rage to find it now well into the morning. He rose at once, roared at his staff for not waking him betimes, had to be persuaded to take any breakfast and before he had finished what was set before him, was shouting for a fresh horse to be saddled for him. Then, accompanied by his weary groom, he set off at a canter for the Manor.

Harry Thornton had suffered a restless night, periods of wakefulness punctuated by violent and frightening dreams. By five o'clock in the morning his mind was going round and round like a rat in a trap. Already unnerved by the deeply unpleasant turn the conversation with his one-time friend had taken, and seeing Sir Edward Ratcliffe coming purposefully towards him, he had turned and run down the nearest alleyway then across the fields to the Manor, careless of the rain that had begun to fall.

He returned to a cold and silent household. His mother had been dead for so long he could hardly remember what it had been like when she was alive, and until he brought Susan home as his bride there had been no woman to take proper charge of household affairs. Housekeepers had come and gone, and for several years the day-to-day running of the place had been left to an elderly retainer determined to do as little as possible, a bad-tempered cook and an assortment of maids. The Thorntons' financial problems had been common knowledge, and servants who knew their worth wanted to be sure of their wages.

But in her brief tenure as mistress of the house, Susan had introduced a breath of fresh air into the place, aided by the practical and strong-minded Phillipa. The latter had brought in servants from home, sacked the cook on her sister's behalf and replaced her with a better one, and saw to it that the maids worked hard but were properly rewarded for so doing. The kitchen was clean, the food wholesome and the bed linen regularly washed and aired. The presence of Phillipa much of the time had added to the general feeling of life and hope.

Susan's dowry settlement had also been put to immediate use. There were fresh tiles on the roof, a number of windows were in the process of being replaced and a sempstress had been employed to make new curtains and hangings. Susan had tried to interest Harry in the changes in the household, not least her plans for the coming child. They could afford a nursemaid, she told him, even a wetnurse, should she find herself unable to feed the child. Only now that it had all gone did Harry realise how much was missing.

Now all was much as it had been before the wedding. The Manor was dark and desolate, without its recent happy bustle of activity. Repairs to the property had ceased, for Susan's father had begun to wrangle with Harry's for a return of at least a proportion of the dowry – a fact Adam Thornton relayed to his son with much bitterness when he arrived back home that evening. For a little while afterwards father and son had sat each side of the smoky fire in the parlour, but finally Harry had been unable to bear it any longer and had taken himself off to bed.

Unsurprisingly, he arose unrefreshed and with the wound on his leg still paining him. He ate a meagre breakfast and was wondering what to do with himself when there was a banging on the front door and he heard a man's voice raised in anger demanding admittance. Before he could go and see the cause for himself, a terrified maid scuttled into the kitchen to tell him that Sir Arthur Clarington was in the hall determined to see him at once and would brook no delay. He limped into the hall and greeted his former employer as normally as he could, expressing his surprise at the visit.

'Surprise? Why should you be surprised, Thornton? I was more than surprised, I was shocked when I was told of the news. God's Blood, why didn't you send word to me at once?'

Harry looked round for his father, praying he was out somewhere, uneasily aware of servants listening behind doors.

He tried to brazen it out. 'Send word of what, Sir Arthur?'

'Of your wife's death. Her *murder*!'

'I don't know ... why...' he stuttered, 'why do you want to know?'

Sir Arthur came over and grabbed him by the front of his doublet, shaking Harry until his teeth rattled. 'You know very well *why*.' He looked around. 'And where's the child? I've heard nothing of the child.'

'What child?' Adam Thornton stood transfixed in the hall doorway. 'Let go of my son at once, Sir Arthur! He's still weak from his sickbed and is suffering from a leg wound.' He came over as the other man released Harry. 'I ask again, what child?'

Sir Arthur slapped his boot with his riding whip. 'Are you all mad here? Or blind or deaf? His wife's child, of course!'

Thornton stared Sir Arthur in the face, then he hissed: 'It's you who are mad, Clarington. Your wits are addled, you have need of a keeper! The Lord only knows what maggot you have in your brain. Certainly my daughter-in-law was *with* child when she died, but only some two months forward. I'd known her since she was a babe herself and I can assure you Susan had no child when she wed Harry.'

227

Sir Arthur stepped back and looked at Thornton in blank astonishment. 'Who's Susan?' he asked.

A somewhat similar scene had taken place in Hugh's study. 'Leave it for a minute or two,' Simon said, 'until the faintness has passed. Take another sip of wine, it will make you feel better.' The figure before him remained silent. 'Now I must tell you that I know exactly who you are and why you concealed your identity as you did – a concealment that might have led to your death had I not discovered the truth. I beg you from now on to be honest with us, my dear.

'You were born Frances Winnifred Aldersey, more usually called Cissy, were you not? And your late father was a schoolmaster at Ware Grammar School?'

She looked at him in wonder. 'How did you know?'

Simon smiled. 'Suffice it to say I made it my business to go into Hertfordshire in search of Francis Wynfred, and was much surprised to find no one seemed to have heard of him. But I was told of a young woman who had been in Sir Arthur Clarington's employ at about the same time, and I thought that if I found her, she might be able to tell me more of this mysterious young man. So I then set about looking for you and eventually found my way to your mother, who told me that you had left home in sad circumstances. Before we go any further I must tell you she is longing to see you, and begs me to say that you will be welcome home whatever your situation.

'She, of course, did not know where you were and so referred me to your aunt, who told me she thought you had married and were living in or near to Knebworth.' He turned to the other two men. 'I thought there must be something very strange about "Francis Wynfred", for when I asked the good lady if she knew anything of a young man of that name she looked alarmed, though she recovered herself very well and told me, most truthfully, that she knew no such young *man*.'

He turned to the young woman with a smile. 'By that time my servant had arrived, bearing with him a warrant for "Wynfred's" arrest and so we set off first for Knebworth, for I thought I might find an entry of your marriage in the Church Book, either there or in the nearby parishes, and that would lead me to you. I even thought you might have *married* Francis Wynfred!'

Cissy went so pale they thought she might faint. 'So you know all?'

'We do,' said Simon. 'I finally traced your marriage to Condicote Church. The parson there found it for me and then said he recollected it, for you were married without banns and by Bishop's Licence. But whatever I might have suspected, it had never even crossed my mind that your husband could be Harry Thornton and that he had married you nearly six months before his bigamous marriage to Susan Carter.'

'It's almost impossible to conceive of such infamy,' said Sir Edward. 'Thornton must be brought to book at once for this. And,' he added significantly, 'much else besides, I imagine.'

'I think Cissy should be left to rest for a little now,' said Simon. 'All this has obviously come as a great shock to her.'

She looked at him gratefully. 'It's a long time since I've been called Cissy. I'm generally known as Winnifred now. That was why I chose to make it my surname.'

'Have you any more suitable clothes?' asked Hugh.

'I had a black gown and veil but they are in Mother Saxton's house.' The mention of the old woman brought her to her feet. 'Please, all of you, believe me, she's not what she's made out to be. And she took me in when I'd nowhere else to go, for she knew me from years ago in Hertfordshire.'

'I'll ask Jessica if she can find you a gown,' said Hugh, 'and also if she'll come over and keep you company for a while. I take it this lady is no longer under arrest?' he said to Sir Edward.

'No. Although when you are recovered I must have the truth from you,' he told her.

'I promise I will do my best,' Winnifred replied, 'though it will be hard in the telling and you still don't know all.'

'I was sorry to hear of the loss of your child,' said Simon, 'but it was then I realised I should have known all along. Do you recall my asking you, when we first met, if you had recently been ill?'

She smiled. 'I do. Also if I'd ever been an actor. That hit home. But I still don't understand.'

'You told me that you had suffered from a flux and that you had been treated with celandine in white wine and a feverfew and comfrey poultice, none of which are used for the flux. But they are the favoured physics of country midwives after a bad childbirth and lying-in!'

Chapter 16

The Two Brides' Tales

The girl who walked into Hugh's parlour later that day, accompanied by his betrothed, looked very different from the sorry spectacle she had presented earlier in the morning. Her dark hair, though short, was now pinned back with a comb, the dress lent to her by Jessica fitted her well and the bruise on her face, while still noticeable, was beginning to fade.

Hugh immediately offered her a chair then asked Jessica if she would be staying with them. She smiled and, after greeting the others, told them that Winnifred would prefer she remained if it was agreeable to them, 'For what she has to say is most distressing.' Sir Edward at once replied that this would be in order then, facing Winnifred, asked her if she would now tell them the whole story as plainly and truthfully as she knew how.

'I will do my best, as I promised,' she replied. 'Dr Forman has uncovered much and might guess more, but there is a great deal you cannot know, including one matter which reflects very badly indeed on me. None of us could possibly have foreseen its outcome but I fear it's at the very root of all that came later.'

It had all begun, Winnifred told them, when her father fell sick. His earnings as a schoolmaster had never been good, and once he was unable to continue in his profession the small amount of savings put by through frugal living had soon dried up. Not only that, as he grew worse he

231

needed visits from the doctor himself, rather than the draughts made up by the local apothecary or, at best, the doctor's man.

It was then an old friend of her mother's, hearing of their plight, wrote to inform Anne Aldersey that she was now in charge of Sir Arthur Clarington's household and that she could use the services of a bright and hard-working young woman to assist her. There had been no question but that Cissy should go. There was no sign of marriage on the horizon for, as a dowerless girl, she fell between two stools. Educated by her father above her station, rough artisans and the sons of ordinary townsfolk in Ware shied away from her as a prospective bride, while those of more financial worth, the small landowners and young men of more substance, wanted girls who would bring money and goods to swell the family coffers.

So she had packed what she could into two large stuff bags and taken the carrier's cart to Datchworth, spent the night with her aunt, and had then been taken on to Sir Arthur's next day by her uncle. She was greeted with warmth by Mistress Margery Dawson, her mother's friend, who first showed her the attic with its two double mattresses that she would share with three other servant girls. Winnifred, an only child who had hitherto had the luxury of a bed and a chamber to herself, ventured to say that she would find this hard, whereupon Mistress Margery, unused to such nice feelings, pointed out that in some households, servant girls slept three to a bed. However, out of friendship for her mother, she would allow Winnifred to use her own small sitting room when she was not needed elsewhere.

Winnifred was soon made aware of her employer's reputation. Stories abounded and grew in the telling, of servant girls put in the family way and dismissed with no money, no employment and nowhere to go. One such, she was told by a wide-eyed kitchenmaid, was the daughter of a witch who had put a curse on him that however many children he might have outside wedlock, no legal eldest son would ever survive.

But at first she had seen little or nothing of the master of the house. She rarely crossed his path and was kept busy with the household tasks allotted to her. Her wages were small but at the end of her first quarter she was allowed to go home for one day to give them to her mother. She returned to the estate with the utmost reluctance, for it was painfully obvious that her father had not long to live.

Shortly afterwards she was given the task of dusting the library, a fine room with shelves on one wall entirely given over to books, a sign of wealth indeed and, having made sure there was no one about, she took several down from the shelves. It was clear from the amount of dust on them that they were rarely read. Among them she found the three recently published volumes of Edmund Spenser's *The Faerie Queene* which she started dipping into with delight, slipping away to continue reading it on every possible occasion; it was here, one late afternoon, that Sir Arthur Clarington found her. It could not be said that he was a reading man. His father had begun to collect books and from time to time he himself purchased those considered fashionable; after all he was a man of substance and they looked very fine on the shelves. Occasionally he would read a little from one or another of them, enough to be able to hold his own in company if the occasion arose. Winnifred had jumped up at once when he found her, curtsied and apologised.

He waved her apologies aside. Certainly so well bred a girl whose father was a graduate of the University of Cambridge must be interested in his books and, so long as it did not interfere with her work and she did not take them out of the library, she was welcome to read them if she liked. Mistress Margery, when told, was not impressed.

'Books, is it?' she exclaimed in scornful tones. 'You watch

233

yourself, young woman. It's not your book-learning that attracts him. Take my advice and keep out of the library, there's plenty for you to do here.' After which piece of advice she did her best to ensure Winnifred was kept busy elsewhere.

Winnifred was finding the shared sleeping arrangements more and more difficult. Her bed companion was a large kitchenmaid who not only snored, but rarely washed and brought with her of a night not only an offensive smell but fleas, while the other two girls talked and giggled into the small hours making it hard for her to get any rest. Once again she pleaded with Mistress Margery to find her somewhere else to sleep, and eventually she was given a tiny chamber in the eaves with just room for a narrow bed and a chest in which to keep her clothes. The move brought friction with her erstwhile companions, who accused her loudly of thinking herself too good for them, which is no doubt how the news of the arrangement reached the ears of Sir Arthur. So it was that in the early hours of one morning she awoke to find him standing beside her bed.

She made no attempt to excuse what happened next. 'He did not force himself on me,' she said frankly, 'and in his own way he was quite kind, considering the stories I had heard about him. I was not happy with the situation but I was flattered and saw it as a way out of the drudgery of endless ironing and mending of linen, of spending my time with girls with whom I had no common interests. Most welcome of all was that he agreed to send an extra sum of money to my parents.'

Not surprisingly, rumours of the new situation soon spread among the rest of the household. At first Winnifred had tried to conceal it, but it was impossible to fool Mistress Margery, who reacted not only with anger but also with distress. 'She wrote then to my parents to tell them that their daughter had become mistress to Sir Arthur, blaming herself for what had happened.'

It was when the third player entered that the scene was set for the coming disaster. Harry Thornton had acted as secretary to Sir Arthur for a period the previous year but had become tired of the occupation and taken himself back to the Manor. However, his father was now so short of money that he forced his son to approach Sir Arthur once again and ask for his old position back. Sir Arthur had graciously agreed.

'Later,' said Winnifred, 'I realised it was during that time that Susan Carter took a fondness for him and their fathers began to plan a match. But he said nothing to me.'

Harry was immediately attracted to the handsome dark-haired girl, so much so that he refused to believe the gossip that she was his employer's mistress. Indeed, when Harry went so far as tentatively to broach the subject with Sir Arthur, the latter had his own reasons for explaining that he found the girl to be so pleasant a companion that he was considering making her his ward. So Harry laid siege to her and, as she told her listeners, 'I had never felt great fondness for a young man before, and very quickly love grew between us.' Soon the young couple became lovers.

'But I had already realised I must be with child,' she continued bitterly, 'and had told Sir Arthur as much, fearful he would turn me out, but to my surprise he assured me he felt a great fondness for me and that we must find some way of ensuring a future for myself and the child. He even told me that had my position in life been different he would have married me, for I was the only woman he had come across with whom he felt he could have lived in some sort of harmony. He promised that whatever happened he would look after me and support the child, but later, when he learned how matters stood between Harry and me, he said he'd a better plan: that I should persuade Harry the child was his and plead with him to marry me.'

That did shock her hearers. 'So you are telling us that you married Harry Thornton, knowingly carrying another man's child?' Sir Edward demanded.

'That was a dreadfully wrong thing to do,' added Hugh, 'don't you agree, Simon?'

'Unwise, at least,' replied Simon briefly.

'I told you I'd much to blame myself with,' she replied, her eyes filling with tears. 'Don't you think I haven't cursed myself over and over again for listening to Sir Arthur? When I argued with him that it wasn't right, he asked me what I thought the alternatives were. I could hardly go home as things stood, with my mother newly widowed. He could hide me away somewhere until the child was born and then find some home for it, but he did not think that would make me happy. This way, all of us would be suited. I would have a husband and father for my child, Harry would have the woman he loved and as for him, the situation would suit him very well. So eventually, with many misgivings, I did as he asked and Harry at once said he would marry me.'

'Does Harry know now that the child was Sir Arthur's?' asked Hugh gently.

She gulped. 'No. I was never able to bring myself to tell him, nor did I think I would ever need to, especially when it did not live.' Because of the estrangement from her family and her condition, Winnifred did not want to marry in her own parish, and therefore assumed she and Harry would wed in Pinner but to her surprise, he was set against it. 'He told me his father would be annoyed at his marrying in such a manner, nor did he want any gossip when the child was born earlier than it should have been.' Therefore there had followed the hasty wedding in Condicote, where neither were known, by Bishop's Licence.

When she told Sir Arthur that Harry was willing to marry her, she was shocked to discover that he expected his own relationship with her to continue much as before. In vain did she argue that this would heap wrong on wrong;

236

he would not have it. 'I dislike sharing you with Thornton,' he told her, 'but you mean a great deal to me and if I am happy with the situation, why shouldn't you be? You say you love him? Oh, he'll make you a good enough husband, but he's a shallow fellow. You'll tire of him, you'll see.' Eventually the only solution against his importuning was to leave his employ and for the couple to set up home outside the estate. For several months, all was well. Harry rode over to attend to his duties each day while Winnifred, no longer looking over her shoulder for Clarington all the time, happily set about housekeeping.

Even so Sir Arthur twice rode over while Harry was kept busy on the estate, pleading with her again to become his mistress, but she fended him off saying it would be unsafe for the child at the present time. As he rode away on the last occasion she determined that as soon as the child was born she would persuade Harry that they must now return to his home in Pinner and that she be admitted to his family. She could not understand why he had not already prepared the ground to do so.

'He paid a number of visits home,' she said, 'and when I asked why he still had not told his father that we were wed and that there was a child coming, he said the time was not right, that it would be better to wait and I, fond fool, believed him. Finally he became cross and irritated every time I asked so I thought it best not to press him.' Then, only a few weeks before the true date on which the child was due to be born, Harry rode off to Pinner and never came back.

' "Who's Susan?" ' echoed Adam Thornton. 'What on earth do you mean?' But before he could take it further, Harry had made a dash for the door, only to be stopped by Clarington who forced him back against the wall. He drew out his dagger and held it to Harry's throat.

'You've done away with Winnifred, haven't you? *Haven't you?*'

'No,' answered Harry, panic-stricken. 'No, I swear that she's alive.'

'And the child?'

'Dead.'

'Prove to me Winnifred's alive!'

'I can't. I don't know where she is.'

Adam looked from one to the other, unable to understand any of it. Then he went to the door and called out into the yard for his servants to come at once. 'I've had enough of this,' he fumed. 'I'll have you thrown off the premises, Clarington. There's nothing you can do to me, I'm no tenant of yours and I will tell the whole world how you burst into my house, threatening the life of my son and demanding to be told of the fate of some unknown woman.' As he finished speaking, half a dozen men entered the hall from outside.

'Are you going of your own accord, Clarington?' Thornton demanded. 'Or do I get my men to send you packing while I lay a whip to your shoulders?'

Clarington did not appear to be listening. 'The child's dead, you say. How? Why?'

Harry ran his tongue over dry lips. 'I don't know – I wasn't there. I've been here these last two months. I imagine it must have been because it came before its time.'

Clarington seemed about to say something then changed his mind and turned to Adam Thornton. 'You can call your dogs off,' he said. 'I'm far from mad and give you fair warning, I intend getting to the bottom of this. But before I leave, tell me – who *is* this Susan?'

Adam looked at him in amazement. 'My son's late wife, of course. Old Saul Carter's daughter. They had been married a bare two months when she was murdered in the woods.'

Clarington threw back his head and laughed, but it was not a pleasant sound. 'His wife, you say? I don't think so.'

'Of course she was,' thundered Thornton. 'Married to my son here in our parish church before all the town.'

Clarington looked across at Harry and nodded as realisation dawned. 'I see all now. God's Blood, what a coil! Master Thornton, your son may well have gone through a form of marriage with a woman called Susan, but it was neither legal nor sanctified by God. For six months ago he married Winnifred Aldersey, one of my servants, in Condicote. Your son's a bigamist.'

Harry slumped down until he was sitting against the wall, his head on his knees. Adam went over to him. 'Is this true?' Harry made no response. His father grabbed him and hauled him to his feet. 'I said – *is this true?*' Harry nodded, unable to speak. Then a sudden and terrible thought struck Adam. 'So what did happen in the woods that day? It was you, wasn't it? Oh my God. *You* killed Susan.'

At first Winnifred simply could not believe that Harry would not return, but as first the days, then weeks passed, by which time she was at her wits' end, she sent urgent word to the estate only to discover that he had left Sir Arthur's employ at the same time as he had left her. Worried to death, she had also feared yet another visit from Sir Arthur but he did not come. 'I assumed, therefore, that he thought Harry had taken me with him.' She determined to go to Pinner in search of him, but before she could do so, she gave birth to the child, almost losing her life in the process.

'As soon as I was recovered I made plans to go at once to Harry's home. The more I thought about it, the more convinced I became that I would find something very badly amiss, and so I decided to go in disguise rather than present myself in a strange town as a wronged wife. It wasn't difficult. I'm tall for a woman and my voice is deeper than some. I simply cut my hair, obtained some men's clothing and with my father's fine dagger on my belt and a horse loaned to me by a friend, I set off and thus it was you met me on the road to Pinner that day, Dr

239

Forman.' She became tearful at the memory. 'In my wildest nightmares it had never occurred to me that Harry had married another woman, only that he might have tired of me.'

So it was that the gross deception began. At first she had wanted to leave immediately but Harry had begged her to stay, promising her that somehow he would resolve matters. 'You see, I still loved him and he assured me he still loved me,' she said, 'though I could see no other way but that he tell the truth: that I was his wife. Believe me, I felt from my heart for Susan, living as she was in a fool's paradise fully believing she was married to Harry.'

For the best part of two months the situation dragged on. 'Then we heard that Sir Arthur was coming here to his other estate and we were both terrified – I that he would see and recognise me, Harry that he would soon learn of his false marriage. He therefore decided that all three of us must leave Pinner immediately, until Sir Arthur's visit was over. Again he promised wildly that he would set matters right and,' her voice broke, 'as God's my witness I truly don't believe he ever intended it would be by . . .' She stopped, unable to carry on.

'Killing Susan Carter?' Simon finished for her.

Harry was already in a bad humour when the three had set off on their fateful journey. He was annoyed that he had been advised against riding through the woods by the mere servant of a London doctor, and he had become increasingly irritable as Susan, riding behind him on the pillion, prattled on of playhouses and visits to the great church of St Paul's and the Tower of London. The third member of the party remained silent throughout. They were well into the wood when Harry's patience finally snapped.

'God's Blood, Susan, can't you keep your tongue still? "Oh, we must see the lions in the Tower"; "Dr Forman says we *must* go to the Rose Theatre"; "Do you know you

240

can climb right up to the top of St Paul's and that folk carve their names there?" and so on and on and on.' He felt her stiffen behind him then begin to quiver with sobs. 'Sweet Jesu, what now?' He reined in the horse and made as if to turn back.

'Why do you stop? What's the matter?' asked Susan, trying to stem her tears.

'Do we go or stay?' Winnifred called out from her place ahead of them.

'God knows.' Harry dismounted and looked up at his wife. 'I've a mind to return to the Manor. Shall we turn back then, Francis?'

Winnifred gave him a long look. 'You can if you wish, Harry. But I shall continue as planned and return home to Knebworth.' She too dismounted, left her horse and came over to face Harry. 'And unless you're prepared to tell her the truth, here and now, you'll never see me again. It's gone on long enough and I can't stand any more.'

'What's he saying?' cried Susan from the pillion. 'Lift me down at once, Harry, and tell me what he means.' He raised his arms and pulled her roughly from her seat, setting her down so carelessly that she cried out: 'For the Lord's sake, Harry remember that I am with child. As for you,' she continued, turning to Winnifred, 'take yourself off to your home. No one wants you here.'

The effect on the person she supposed to be Francis Wynfred was profound. The young woman's eyes widened and her face went deathly white. 'Is this true, Harry? Is she with child?' He made no reply. 'If so, then you have done a double wrong and so, dear Jesu, have I.'

Susan stamped her foot. 'Holy Mother of God, will you tell me what this is all about?' She looked from one to the other. 'I see. They were right, all those that spoke of unnatural love between the pair of you. And when I taxed you with it, Harry, I let you persuade me otherwise. Do you know what he said of you, Francis? That you were Sir

241

Arthur Clarington's most particular servant and that you had forged great bonds of friendship between you when you were both in his employ. Also that he owed you gratitude for some service you had done him.' She laughed bitterly. 'I can see now what it was.'

'I can't bear this any longer,' said Winnifred. 'You are sure you are with child, Susan?'

'As sure as I can be,' replied Susan.

There was a rustling in the bushes and all turned, fearful that while they had been thus engrossed the robbers were about to reveal themselves, but it was only Lizzie Saxton's black dog. There was no sign of its mistress. It looked at them with little interest then lay down and began to wash itself.

Winnifred looked levelly at Harry. 'Why didn't you tell me Susan was with child?' Still he said nothing. 'Then if you won't tell her the truth, I must. Perhaps between us we might even find a way out of this maze, though at present I see none.'

Susan brushed her aside, flew at Harry and began pounding him with her fists. 'Tell me! Tell me what all this means!'

Winnifred caught her by the arm. 'I'm not Francis Wynfred, Susan. My name is Winnifred and I'm as much a woman as you are, and though this will make desperate hearing for you, I'm also Harry's true wife. For he married me in Hertfordshire these six months past.'

'No,' whispered Susan, 'no. Say it's not true, Harry.'

'It's true enough,' he answered brusquely. 'Are you satisfied now?'

She still looked unbelieving. 'Why did you do it? Why did you marry her, and then pretend to marry me?'

'Because I loved her and she was to bear my child. As for marrying you, my father insisted on it as the only means of saving the land and the estate. I dared not tell him I already had a wife.'

Colour swept across Susan's face. 'No,' she said again,

still in the same quiet voice. 'No.' Then she cried out: 'That means that I am . . . my child will be . . . no, no!' She whirled round on Winnifred and of a sudden seized the hilt of the dagger she wore in the sheath at her belt and pulled it free. 'No way out of this maze, is there, Harry?'

Hitherto Susan's life had been the easy and cossetted one of an indulged, younger, motherless daughter. Her pretty looks had guaranteed her plenty of admirers and for a good while she had been happy and flattered at the prospect of marrying the older, handsome and wealthy Guy Somerton. Then her affections had suddenly changed and she was determined to marry Harry, wanted it so desperately that she overrode all her father's objections to his hard-earned money going to swell the coffers of a penniless squire who had squandered what wealth he had. But finally he had given in to her pleas as he always did, and so she had her way and married him. Or so she had thought. Now it had all turned to ashes; the bottom had dropped out of her safe little world. She would be damaged goods, 'wife' to a bigamist, bearing his child – an object both of pity and derision in the place where she had been born and brought up.

She clutched the dagger firmly in her hand. 'If she dies, Harry, here in the woods, who's to know? Mother Saxton's black dog can't tell tales, and coward that you are, you won't say anything. You can tell them it was robbers.'

Harry caught her arm, pulling it downwards. 'Give me that knife. You're not going to kill her, I won't let you.' He wrenched it out of her hand, making her cry out in the process.

She looked at the man she had pleaded with her father to let her marry, and in an instant love turned to loathing. 'No,' she told them, 'I shall go back home. I shall shout out what you've done from the rooftops. You might have made a whore of me and a bastard of our child, but think what this will do to you. Even if you make off now with

243

your stale there, my father will have you hunted down and brought to book. I'll see you in gaol for this.'

She turned from him and began to run wildly back the way they had come, heedless of her gown catching on the briars. It took only minutes for Harry to catch up with her and catch her round the waist. As she turned to face him he plunged the dagger straight into her heart. She gave a little sigh and slipped from him onto the ground. There was surprisingly little blood. At first.

'It was Harry who said we should make it look like an attack by robbers,' Winnifred told the three men. 'He was most cool and calm about it, while I was like one in a dream or rather a nightmare. None of it seemed real. He wiped the knife and pushed it into his saddlebag then told me to throw the sheath away, for its design made it noticeable. Then he dragged Susan's body a little way away. He told me that we must indeed make it look like robbers, that if we were shrewd enough no one would suspect otherwise for if we were caught, I would hang too.

'He said he would give himself a wound to make it look as if there'd been a fight and I must give him a knock on the head to suggest he'd been rendered unconscious. Then I must tie him up in such a way that if he were found it would help allay any possible suspicion, but that the bonds be loose enough to allow him to wriggle free if no one came by. He told me to take the saddlebags and the horses and ride off with them to complete the deception that there'd been a robbery, then to wait for him in our house in Knebworth. And, God pity me, I obeyed him.

'Part of me thought I would awake and find none of it had happened. I was distracted, went as far as the edge of the wood and left the saddlebags there, then wandered about all the rest of the night until Lizzie Saxton took me in. I had not known until then that she was the "witch" they told me of when I was in service. It was she who lent me the black dress when I determined to go to Susan's burial, and it was to her I confessed everything. We had determined that when she left the cottage, I would go myself to you, Sir Edward, and tell you the truth. Now you know all.'

Chapter 17

Black Dog

When Winnifred had finished her story, Sir Edward asked Jessica to take her out of the room while the three men discussed the matter further.

'I wonder if I was right to release her from gaol,' he said as soon as the door had closed behind the women. 'Certainly she was privy to what happened, even going so far as to assist young Thornton in the deception. There are those who would see her on the scaffold beside him.'

'But she has been most candid with us,' argued Simon. 'Most young women would have claimed to have been seduced, even raped, but she has not accused Clarington of either, nor has she justified her becoming his mistress, although I consider he has monstrously abused his position and influence. As to the murder of Susan Thornton, she could, had she wished, refused to say anything at all – for surely a wife cannot be forced to testify against her husband except by those means I cannot imagine you wanting to use, Sir Edward.'

'Nor do we know all the circumstances,' added Hugh. 'It could be that Harry threatened her with a similar fate if she did or said anything untoward. After all, he is still her husband; she's told us she loves him and so did loyally as he asked.'

Sir Edward shook his head. 'I don't know. But it all comes back again to the fact that however much she might claim she loved Thornton, she married him in the full and certain knowledge that she was carrying another man's child.'

'God's Breath!' exclaimed Simon. 'Then Sir Arthur Clarington should stand beside her in any court, for he was the child's father; he it was who persuaded her into this tragic marriage, having faced her with the desperate alternatives to it. What would the future hold for an unmarried girl turned out in her circumstances? It would be easier to force a farmhand to be responsible in such a situation than a man in Clarington's position. She took the only way she thought open to her. I've seen Lizzie Saxton's daughter with my own eyes, little older I imagine than the girl we've just had before us, rotting of the pox acquired after Clarington threw her out.'

'That poor soul is now with her Maker,' said Sir Edward. 'I was told before we met again that she was found dead in her bed.'

'Then I will put up a modest sum for her to be buried decently,' said Hugh, 'and not in a pauper's grave. Whatever her mother may or may not be, she should have a Christian burial. As for Winnifred, for the time being Jessica is willing for her to lodge at her house, if you are agreeable, Sir Edward. Jessica is no fool and she likes the young woman and considers she is telling the truth.'

'I hope you'll think the girl has been punished enough, sir,' said Simon. 'Hers is not an enviable situation. Forced by her employer to deceive her husband, she is then abandoned and delivers the child almost at the cost of her own life. After which she goes in search of her husband only to find he has contracted a bigamous marriage to another woman. All this will become public knowledge when Harry Thornton stands trial for murder as he surely must, and it will go hard with her with the people here, whatever the outcome.'

Sir Edward heard him out. 'Very well. We will leave matters as they are for now. Meanwhile I will issue a warrant for the arrest of Harry Thornton, first on the charge of having entered into a bigamous marriage with Susan Carter then secondly for having murdered her. I fear this will have heavy consequences for the whole town.'

At the Manor those consequences were beginning to sink in. At first Harry continued to say nothing in answer to his father's demands then, suddenly aware that the proceedings were taking place in front of half a dozen gawping servants, Adam Thornton turned and peremptorily dismissed them.

'I suggest we adjourn to a more private place,' said Clarington.

'What do you mean by "we"?' queried Adam. 'I've already told you to leave my house.'

'This concerns me almost as nearly as it does you,' Clarington returned unperturbed, 'as you will no doubt learn for yourself shortly.'

The three men went into the parlour and, after carefully shutting the door, Adam again demanded of his son if he were responsible for Susan's death. Harry's head had been a seething mass of contradictory emotions ever since the arrival of Clarington. Now, under his father's questioning, he found himself in the position of a drowning man as scenes from the past flashed before his eyes: his first setting eyes on Winnifred and his immediate desire for her; his hasty marriage when he was almost as good as promised to another woman; his cowardice in avoiding telling his father of the match; followed by his giving way to his father's desperate pleas for him to marry Susan Carter and so save the family house and what remained of its lands.

Then more recently his shock at the arrival of the disguised Winnifred; his desperate seeking for a way out of the coil in which he had entangled himself; that last ride through the woods . . . The ride through the woods. He saw as if on the stage of a playhouse the picture of himself lifting Susan down from the pillion, heard again the words that had passed between them, the witch's black dog sitting watching events. The black dog! Why hadn't he thought of it before? He began to breathe more easily. For the first time he saw a possible way out.

'Well?' demanded his father. 'Do you ever intend to speak? I give you fair warning that we will stay here all day and all night until you do. First, is it true what he says? Is this Wynfred fellow really a woman and, if so, are you married to her?'

Harry nodded. 'Yes, Father.'

'You married her knowing you were already as good as betrothed to Susan Carter?'

'She was with child. I could do no other.'

Thornton banged the table. 'No other? In spite of your solemn promises not only to Susan but to myself and her father as well? Then to go through this so-called marriage here as if nothing had happened. What did you expect would be the outcome?'

Harry stared back at him. 'I don't know. I thought . . . I don't know what I thought.'

His father came over and jerked Harry's head up. 'Look me in the eye now and tell me. Did you kill Susan?'

'It's not as you think,' he replied with difficulty.

'It never is,' broke in Clarington. 'So say all murderers.'

Thornton turned on him. 'Be quiet, sir. I can still have you thrown out if I so wish.'

'I don't advise it,' said Clarington maliciously. 'Think of the tales I'll tell as soon as I leave your gate!'

'How was it then, Harry?' continued Thornton.

Harry straightened his shoulders and faced his father. Yes, that was it. The black dog. He suddenly became confident. 'I was bewitched, Father,' he announced, 'and I can prove it.'

Both men stared at him. 'What do you mean?' his father demanded.

'What I say. All that happened that day in the woods can be laid at the door of Mother Saxton, for she sent out her familiar, the black dog, to make me do it.' He noted with satisfaction that he had finally captured his audience. 'We were riding through the woods when I admit there were some words between Susan and me, at which I stopped, we dismounted and I told her that perhaps it would be best in the circumstances if we returned home and went to London another day.

'No sooner did Winnifred hear this than she began to rail at me too, threatening to tell all, brandishing her dagger for greater effect, and so it was that Susan learned not only that she was *not* my wife but that her child would be born a bastard. She was beside herself. There I was between the two angry women considering what I should do next, when suddenly the witch's black dog appeared from nowhere and gave me a most terrible look, like no mortal animal I've ever seen.

'At first, all went dark, then I felt as if I'd been taken over by a power not my own, as if my will had drained away. Then Susan took hold of Winnifred's dagger and I, fearing harm, sought to wrench it from her, whereupon she turned and ran and I after her, still as one in a dream or under the influence of a spell, and when I caught up with her a voice inside my head ordered me to kill her. I was determined to withstand it,' he declared in a ringing voice, 'but even as I tried to pray and seek God's help, I found my arm gripped by an invisible force which forced me to thrust the weapon into Susan's breast.' He rose to his feet. 'Susan's murderer is the witch, not I. It was her Black Arts that forced me to do it and all that came after, for the same voice told me to wound myself and be tied up to avoid suspicion. I would never have thought of such an idea myself,' he added, in as ingenuous a tone as he could manage.

There followed a few moments of silence then Adam spoke. 'I don't know what to make of this. What do you think, Clarington?'

'The old woman certainly has a vile reputation,' he

replied, having his own reasons now for going along with the tale, 'and not only here for she lived near to my estate in Hertfordshire before this. Indeed, she cursed me once herself.' He did not offer an explanation for this and Thornton was too distracted to ask for one.

'Obviously I must go at once to Sir Edward Ratcliffe and tell him that she must be closely examined on the matter. My son's life is at stake and he must send for an expert witchfinder.'

'What about me?' cried Harry. 'If you tell them all this, I'll be put in gaol as well.'

'You surely can't imagine this business can be kept secret,' asked his father, 'after half a dozen servants heard as much as they did?' He went over and flung the door open. No one was immediately behind it but one of the maids was furiously dusting a ledge near by and the chatter of raised voices could be heard from the kitchen. 'No, it's preferable if Sir Edward learns it from me; it will reflect better on all of us. It's as well he's still in town.'

But before he could even call for his horse, there came the sound of horsemen outside in the yard and a loud banging on the door, followed shortly afterwards by an agitated serving wench bursting into the room to inform Master Thornton that the Justice was outside with four men, demanding to see him.

'It seems you're too late, Thornton,' remarked Clarington, settling back once more in his seat.

Sir Edward came swiftly into the room and wasted little time. He explained his business, produced his warrant and informed Thornton that he had come for Harry who would have to answer to charges of both bigamy and murder. Adam heard him out.

'That my son entered into a bigamous marriage, I cannot deny,' he replied. 'He was weak and foolish and had no business to marry this other young woman when he was already promised to another. But he tells me he was seized by passion for the girl, that he had bedded her and that she had fallen with child by him. Stupid, disgraceful and against the law, I agree, but there was no criminal intent. As to the other more serious matter, I would beg you to hear what he has to say. Tell him about the evil witch and her familiar, Harry.'

So Harry once again recounted his version of events, this time ensuring that the black dog played an even bigger part in the story. 'I wonder now,' he added at the end of it, 'if Mother Saxton had already started to bewitch me before I ever set eyes on Winnifred, for why else should I have taken her to my bed when it was already proposed that I should marry Susan? Yes, it's all clear to me now. I was bewitched into lust by the witch, who then put it into my mind to deceive my father and everyone else as I did. Bring me the Bible and I will swear on it that I am telling you the truth, that I was not truly responsible for my actions.'

Sir Edward waved the offer aside, looking decidedly unconvinced. 'Then that will need looking into,' he replied in a brusque tone. 'In the meantime, I must take you into town and have you charged with these offences. You will have to make your plea to a higher authority than mine.' He looked with some surprise at Clarington. 'May I ask what your part is in all this, Sir Arthur? Though your presence here saves me having to send for you, for there are matters to be discussed that concern you nearly.'

Clarington made no effort to ask what these were, merely replying that he had heard that Harry's wife had been killed, that Winnifred had once been a servant of his and that he had been sufficiently alarmed to ride over to discover what had happened. 'I was obviously under the impression that it was she who had been murdered, knowing nothing of the false marriage.'

'You seemed mighty concerned at the fate of a mere servant,' remarked Adam, seizing on this point. A thought struck him. 'Is it possible she was more to you than that?' Clarington did not reply. It was then that a further explanation suggested itself to Thornton. 'I see,' he said slowly. 'That's it – the child! You ranted and raved over the fate of this woman's child. Why should you do that? What was it to you, if one of your wenches got herself with child by your secretary? He made an honest woman of her. Why did you care whether the infant was born dead or alive?'

'Because,' replied Clarington wearily, 'as you have obviously guessed, the child was mine.'

'No!' yelled Harry. 'No, it can't be true!'

'It is all too true,' Sir Edward concurred, 'for Winnifred has herself confessed to it.'

'The scheming trull,' spat Harry, 'the shallow whore! I thought she loved me, or so she told me over and over again, and all the time she was Clarington's stale! God's Blood, she tricked me into marriage and so brought all this upon my head – and now, I suppose, she has betrayed me.'

'Winnifred swears her love to you is steadfast,' Sir Edward responded, 'and that it was ever as strong for you as yours was to her.' He turned to Clarington. 'I must say to you, Sir Arthur, that you are greatly at fault in this matter. You used your position of authority over her to dishonour the girl, as you have done many others, before then, having driven the girl to despair and distraction over the situation she found herself in, you put every pressure on her to resolve the matter by marrying young Thornton.

'I also know from what she has told us that you importuned her continually afterwards to resume her position as your mistress and that she steadfastly refused. As to betraying you, Harry, your marriage to her was already known to me, for Dr Forman had found the entry in the parish record in Condicote. It did not take a great leap of the imagination to suggest that it was you who rid yourself of one of these inconvenient women when the opportunity arose. Now you must come with us. As for you, Sir Arthur, having had your acknowledgement of your part in this, I have no further need to detain you, although I shall do what I can to bring you to an understanding of what you have done. But no doubt, though you were the prime instigator of these events, given your position all you will suffer is a fine.'

As Adam had foreseen, the Manor servants had wasted no time in spreading the news that the master had accused his son of murdering his own wife. By the time Sir Edward and his men rode back into Pinner, word was spreading rapidly all round the town and the sight of Harry in the middle of them caused an enormous stir. They paused for a moment outside the town gaol whereupon Harry turned in the saddle and faced the growing crowd of onlookers.

'Hear what I have to say,' he shouted out to them. 'I am brought here on a grave charge because I have been bewitched! Old Mother Saxton sent her familiar to me and it urged me on; a power greater than mine, that of Satan himself, took my hand and did the deed. As a mere mortal I could not withstand it.'

'See?' came a voice from the crowd. 'Have I not been warning you against this desperate evil in our midst?' Parson Wytherley pushed his way forward. 'What do you say now, Justice, to my fetching in this evil woman to face punishment?' There was a roar of approval.

'It will be seen to in due time,' said Sir Edward.

'Due time?' repeated Wytherley. 'Man's time? It will be settled now in God's time.' He turned and ushered forward a tall, thin man wearing the sober clothing of the Puritan tendency. 'This is Master Arthur Robinson, the witchfinder sent here by the Bishop in answer to my request.'

The door of the town gaol was already open. Blind in one eye she might be, as well as having a crippled arm, but Lizzie Saxton's hearing was acute and she had heard everything. Her legs gave way beneath her and she sat down heavily on the floor, knowing there was no hope for her any more.

Harry was bundled into his cell. Sir Edward dismissed the men who had accompanied him and curtly ordered Wytherley and the witchfinder to follow him back to the Crown. 'I will have Harry Thornton brought before me tomorrow morning, after which he will be sent for trial before one of the Queen's Judges of the Common Law for, as you know, it is not within my powers to try a man for murder. It is then up to the Judge to decide whether or not his defence is acceptable. My personal opinion is that it is not, but that he is a foolish and wicked young man who sought to rid himself of the young woman who thought she was his wife, and is now seeking to save his own skin.

'Nor am I convinced that Elizabeth Saxton is a witch. Whether or not it should be put to the test was to have rested with me and, once again, Wytherley, you've exceeded your brief. If Elizabeth Saxton is to be tried for witchcraft under the statute of 1542 then she too will have benefit of trial under the Common Law.'

The parson ignored this, waving a piece of paper excitedly before the Justice. 'I have here a letter from the Bishop in which he says that Master Robinson must be given every assistance to ascertain whether or not this woman is indeed a witch, and that he will take all necessary steps to ensure that the secular powers do nothing to hinder this.'

Sir Edward sighed. While it was true that the old woman's alleged offence should be tried in a court of law, there was a grey area between what the Church could legitimately seek in the way of proof beforehand and the role of the secular authorities. Meanwhile matters were rapidly getting out of hand. A growing roar was coming from the street outside and Sir Edward went over to the window, opened it, and looked out. 'Then at least I suggest you leave it until tomorrow morning, my good man, unless you want to risk your life pushing through the mob which is even now ensconced outside the town gaol and growing by the minute.'

The townsfolk were becoming increasingly belligerent and inflamed. 'Kill the witch!' 'Burn the witch!' they shrieked. 'Kill her, kill her, kill her!' Cuddy Banks, now feeling fully vindicated, was well to the forefront.

'Didn't I tell you all how I'd seen her capering before Satan in the woods?' he shouted above the racket. 'And you laughed at me! Now see what this witch has brought on us – murder!'

'Aye,' called out another, 'for why else should a decent young man like Harry Thornton be brought to kill his own wife?'

Sir Edward, watching from the open window, shook his head. 'This is the second time within days we have had a witchhunt,' he said, 'and this time I fear I may not be able to prevent mayhem. Therefore I intend sending for aid to keep the peace, if necessary by the use of Troopers.'

Inside her cell, Lizzie Saxton cowered against the back wall, thankful for the stout bars designed to prevent prisoners from getting out, though she knew full well that they would be little protection if the mob succeeded in getting into the gaol; the constable could hardly prevent them carrying her away. In their present mood she would be torn to pieces.

In his next-door cell Harry listened to the sound and fury outside and pondered how he would fare, should the gaol be overrun. Not everyone would believe his story, and it would not be difficult for either Susan's father or Guy Somerton to administer rough justice during the mêlée of a full-scale riot in which people were bound to die. One corpse more could easily be counted as another unfortunate victim of the mob.

Once again Sir Edward faced the townsfolk, flanked by the handful of people such as Hugh Brett and Andrew Page who refused to be swept away by the hysteria. This time he had even more trouble making himself heard, and when he finally succeeded it was some time before the crowd stopped howling him down every time he opened his mouth. Eventually he had his way, telling them to go home at once, that both Harry Thornton and Elizabeth Saxton would be sent for trial and that the witchfinder was to question the latter the following morning.

When he saw this still had little effect, he advised them in no uncertain terms that he had sent for help from the Troopers and that he would not hesitate to have any riot put down by force and its ringleaders arrested and sent to Newgate gaol to stand trial in London. He then had another thought, which was to prove even more effective, reminding them it was now All Hallows Night when folk should be safely behind doors in their own homes well before night fell. Very gradually the crowd began to disperse, hurried on their way by another bout of heavy rain until it was considered that the constable, assisted by the stoutest members of the Town Watch, should now be sufficient to guard the gaol overnight.

Simon had watched the swift-moving events with dismay. He had already told Hugh he intended to leave in the morning, for there was nothing more he could do here and he was desperate to go home to the Bankside and some sanity. Winnifred's fate was still officially in the balance but he hoped that Sir Edward would prove lenient towards her, not least because Jessica had offered to make herself responsible for her until such time that it was decided she could return to her mother. As for Harry Thornton, he must take his chance and might even persuade a gullible Judge of his relative innocence, but there now seemed little hope for Lizzie Saxton. The town required a scapegoat for the series of increasingly unpleasant events that had beset it, and she fitted the role all too well.

As he and John Bradedge rode thankfully out of Pinner the next morning, Simon having promised Hugh that he would return for the latter's wedding, he was chilled to see the constable letting the witchhunter into the gaol. He could imagine all too well what was to come.

Chapter 18

Another Man's Child

'You look glum,' Tom Pope, Simon's actor friend, remarked as he was ushered into Simon's study. He was having a little trouble with his throat and had come for something to alleviate it.

'Tomorrow I'm going to Tyburn to see a hanging,' Simon replied.

'You surprise me. I didn't think that entertainment held any appeal for you.'

Simon snorted. 'It doesn't. It just happens that I know one of those going to be hanged.'

'This sounds like a fascinating tale,' said Tom. 'May I know what it is?'

It was nearly a month since Simon had returned from Pinner, since when he had found little inclination to discuss the nature of the business that had kept him away, besides which he had been very busy. With the cold and the fog came the wheezy chests and the sharpening rheumatics.

'It might be good to talk it over with someone,' he replied, after a little thought. He put some dried herbs into a small pot. 'Butterwort. It's an old remedy but effective taken with honey and hot water. I'll go and mix it in the kitchen and bring it back to you and you can drink it straight away. I'll also give you some to take home with which to gargle.' He smiled for the first time. 'Hot wine and sugar's good too. I'll ask Anna to bring us some in – that is, if you can spare the time.'

'I have no performance today and Jenny knows that when I come to consult you, I'm often gone for some time. She no longer worries that you've found me racked with some deadly disease.'

Simon returned with the draught and a little later, when Anna had brought in the wine, a jug of hot water and a small dish of sugar, he recounted his recent adventures.

'So which of them is to be hanged tomorrow – the witch or Harry Thornton?' asked Tom.

'Lizzie Saxton. She "confessed".' Simon shuddered. 'Hugh Brett tells me that Robinson, the witchfinder, "wrought with her for many hours". No doubt with pins, spikes, pincers, rope and other unpleasant equipment. He sent me a note of what she is alleged to have said.' He picked it up from his desk and read:

Question In what shape did the Devil come to you?
Answer   Always in the shape of a black dog.
Question Whence did the Devil suck your blood?
Answer   The place where the Devil sucked my blood was a little above my fundament and that place chosen by himself and in that place by continual drawing, there is a thing like a teat at which the Devil would suck me and I asked the Devil why he would suck my blood and he said it was to nourish him.

'Bah!' He threw the document down on the floor. 'And there's much more in the same vein, that he had taught her three Latin words, *Sanctibicetur nomen tuum*, that he had made her sign a pact in her own blood demanding her body and soul or he would tear her to pieces!'

'It makes Mephistophilis's bargain with Faustus sound quite civilised,' Tom commented drily. 'By the by, do *you* think she's a witch?'

'No, I do not,' declared Simon. 'She's an unprepossessing-looking elderly woman with a wall eye and a crooked arm caused by a childhood injury inflicted by a

262

drunken stepfather. She's also unexpectedly intelligent. She's had a lifetime of abuse and she was particularly set upon by a group of youths in Pinner led by a lout of the name of Cuddy Banks who's been responsible for much of the mischief in the area. As I told you, I came across her first when she was being attacked by that bully and his band of morris men, though, when apart from their ringleader, most of them were reasonable enough young fellows. But you know how it is, how lads love to pick on those different from themselves.

'So it was that she became the scapegoat for all the town's ills and eventually decided she might just as well pretend to the role assigned to her and agree she was a witch, for in that way she might be left alone if she threatened to put a curse on her persecutors. As to the black dog, I can vouch that it was a perfectly ordinary animal and a source of much comfort to her.'

'And what of the bigamist, he who killed his wife? Is he not to hang too?'

Simon shrugged. 'There's doubt over that. He made a great plea that he acted under the influence of the witch's familiar, that otherwise he would never have done the deed. Many credulous fools believed him and it seems the Judge was half convinced, for while he sentenced him to the rope, he has allowed time for a possible pardon.'

Tom Pope looked thoughtful. 'I see. And you? What do you believe really happened?'

Simon refilled their wine cups and sat back in his seat. 'I'm not at all certain. His wife Winnifred, his real wife that is, says she doesn't believe he intended to kill Susan, that it was done in the heat of the moment, possibly even by accident. But in spite of all that's happened to her and how badly she's been treated, she remains loyal and might well be prejudiced.' He sighed. 'Only Harry Thornton really knows what was in his mind that day when he rode off into the woods against all advice.

'I've wondered about it a great deal since coming home

263

and was able to look at it from a distance. Did he decide, before he suggested the fateful trip to London, that he would take the opportunity to rid himself of one or the other of the women? If so, it could be that it was Winnifred he had in mind, not Susan, for while he was obviously still very fond of her, as witness his behaviour to the supposed strange young man which caused such a stir, Susan's dowry and settlement had saved the family fortunes. Also Winnifred's child, which he had thought to be his own right up until the last, was dead, while Susan was bearing another, an added incentive to her father to keep the money flowing. So he might well have thought that the realistic choice was to murder his legal wife. She was already estranged from her family and had, apparently, disappeared.

'Difficult to explain, though, when the body was discovered and laid out for burial and the strange young man was found to be a woman after all,' offered Tom.

Simon accepted this. 'I run ahead of myself, but I imagine that if it had been Winnifred, he would somehow have persuaded Susan into silence, then stripped and hidden the body very securely hoping that it might never be found, but that if it was, then enough time would have passed for no one to be able to recognise it. After all, "Francis Wynfred" was not expected back in Pinner.

'However, if it was Susan he intended to kill, then presumably he had already dreamed up the plan he later carried out, the false attack by "robbers", the wound acquired during a struggle, the blow on the head which supposedly laid him out and so rendered him unable to describe properly what happened, the binding of his hands.'

Simon drained his wine cup and called to Anna to bring in another bottle. 'If he had succeeded in carrying it off, what then? Would he have risked producing Winnifred as his wife at some future date, without fear of her being recognised? But of one thing I am sure, witchcraft didn't enter into it, nor did it need to. Here was a good-looking rather weak young man, who could be charming when he so wished, who found himself in a quite impossible situation, caught between his supposed obligations to the girl he had taken to bed and the young woman his family was set on his marrying. Murder has been done for less.'

'Knowing your propensity for handsome young women, what did you make of Winnifred?'

Simon gave a wry smile. 'If you're suggesting I had designs on her myself, then rest easy. You might find this hard to believe but it never even crossed my mind. She's an interesting young woman, though. It would have been easy for her to claim Clarington had seduced her, but she didn't. She saw their relationship as a bargain; she went to bed with him and he gave her a better life and money to send home to her family and I think, in an odd way, she liked him. As, indeed, he did her. He'd seduced and fornicated with many women – and don't laugh at me like that, I've rarely, if ever, *seduced* women. She evidently meant much more to him than the usual run of girls he rolled into bed with, and I believe her when she says he told her that had her station in life been different he might well have married her, though I doubt he would have made her a good husband.

'But he cared enough about her to race over to Pinner when he thought she was dead and, in his opinion the solution to the problem of the coming child was a sensible one. It seems he even cared about that too, whereas poor Lizzie Saxton's girl was left to deliver her bastard in a ditch. I'm told he seemed genuinely anguished when he learned that Winnifred's son hadn't survived. No, none of these folk are quite what they might seem.'

'I doubt though that I would have been happy to discover one day that the child I always believed to be my eldest son was not,' commented Tom, 'though in my case I am certain I was Jenny's first and only lover. It's a desperate matter to deceive a husband into thinking another man's child is his.'

265

'Though hardly unknown,' returned Simon.

'Indeed.' Tom paused. 'And tomorrow?'

Simon looked grim again. 'Tomorrow I must go to Tyburn before the carts arrive, plead to be allowed to say one last word to Lizzie Saxton, thrust half a phial of poppy syrup down her throat and then pay some stout fellow a couple of crowns to hang onto her legs so she dies quickly.'

Together they finished the second bottle of sugared wine then Tom rose to go. 'My throat feels splendid,' he said, 'though whether my head will in the morning is another matter.'

As they reached the door Simon smiled. 'What a reputation you give me, Tom. Am I supposed always to exact a reward for rescuing damsels in distress? Though, I confess, I was sorely tempted when on the Scottish Borders. Even John Bradedge jests about it. He wanted to know if I was planning to hire the Great Bed of Ware when I was in Hertfordshire!'

He closed the door behind Tom and went thoughtfully back to his study. One matter that was giving him concern was that he had heard nothing from Avisa since his return, though he had sent a note round straight away to inform her he was back home. A few days later he had received a letter from her from Kent, where she was again staying with her mother, complaining that she had been a little sick but was now feeling better. He was waiting impatiently to hear more.

The next morning was dark and gloomy, all too fitting for what was to come. He rose early, felt disinclined for breakfast, and so wrapped himself in his cloak and rode his horse over London Bridge then turned west for Tyburn. The weather must have put many folk off, for the crowd gathered at the foot of the great scaffold was not a large one. Simon dismounted and secured his horse. Then he made his way to the place where he thought it most likely he would find those sturdy and unimaginative souls prepared to hurry the executioner's victims into the next world before they slowly strangled to death, a task carried out by the friends or relatives of more popular felons. After a few minutes' chat with a burly young man who worked as a butcher's apprentice, he paid him two crowns and assured him he would be there to make certain he carried out the task for which he had been paid.

A little while later the first of two carts rumbled into view. It seemed it was a thin day for felons too, for that was all there were to be. As it drew near he saw that it contained two men, a boy scarce into his teens, a wild-looking young woman with 'infanticide' scrawled on a paper attached to her dress and, huddled against the back of the cart, Lizzie Saxton. There was then a pause and as the executioner and the priest waited for the second cart to arrive, a balladmonger began to move among the crowd shouting out details of his wares including the newest publication: *The Wonderful Discovery of Elizabeth Saxton, a Witch, late of Pinner in the County of Middlesex* by Henry Wytherley, Minister of the Word of God by whose great Mercy he oversaw her Brought to Justice!

Simon pushed right up to the cart and pulled at Lizzie Saxton's shoulder through the rails. She turned a grey and bleary face towards him, then, recognising who it was, hauled herself into a sitting position. He winced as he saw the missing fingernails.

'Have you come for a spell, doctor?' she whispered with an attempt at her old spirit. 'I fear there's little I can do for you now, nor you for me.'

He pushed the bottle into her hand. 'Drink this.'

She sniffed. 'Poppy syrup?' He nodded and she drained it, dropping it down between the rails.

'I won't ask you what happened,' said Simon. 'I can imagine it all too well.'

She yawned, the medicine already beginning to take effect. 'I'll tell you what I told them, "that I confess to clear my conscience and now, having done so, I am the more quiet and the better prepared and willing thereby to suffer death, for I have no hope at all of my life".' She clutched his hand. 'Though I confess to you that I would live longer if I could.'

By now the second cart had arrived and the executioner and his men were coming to escort the felons to the scaffold. 'God go with you,' whispered Simon, 'and may you rest in peace.'

It was all over in a matter of minutes. Simon forced himself to watch to make sure the butcher's assistant did what was necessary, pulling Lizzie Saxton down by the knees as soon as the rope began to bite. He hoped that the poppy syrup would ensure she knew little about it. He began to shiver. He always tried his best to avoid executions for he had no stomach for them. The last time he had visited Tyburn in such circumstances was with Christopher Marlowe when Emma Ball's brother, Cutting Ball Jack, the famous highwayman, had met his end on that notorious scaffold.

As he made his way to the back of the crowd, his eyes were drawn to a man on horseback, and as he did so, a voice said in his ear: 'Now, if justice was justice, that man too would have paid dearly for his part in this.' It was the Pinner schoolmaster, Andrew Page. They both looked again at Sir Arthur Clarington. 'All *he* got was a small fine for getting a wench with child and not marrying her,' said Page. 'At least this time he was brought to court for it. But had it been an ordinary fellow, he'd have been set in the stocks outside the church of a Sunday for three weeks besides.'

With common consent the two men made their way to the nearest tavern. 'A repellent business,' commented Page, taking a swig of ale. 'I believe I came here on the same business as yourself, but when I saw you talking to that sturdy fellow and money changing hands, I realised the matter was being attended to.'

'You're a good man,' stated Simon.

Page made a deprecating gesture. 'I dislike seeing my

268

fellow human beings persecuted whether for their beliefs, their appearance or because of the superstition of others. The fate of Lizzie Saxton was sealed when she stayed on to nurse her daughter as any mother would have done. So, now she's dead. Yet nothing will have changed, cows will run dry, chickens cease to lay, women will deliver dead children and ordinary folk will suffer runs of both good and bad luck as has been the case since time began. But now they have no witch to blame.

'As to the other players in this farce, Thornton may yet swing. Once the witch is out of the way it might well occur to those in authority that his was a tame tale, and time is running out for him. Clarington is shortly to marry his heiress and will no doubt set about providing himself with a legitimate child without delay. Indeed, the air is full of weddings, for Phillipa Carter and Guy Somerton are to marry after Christmas as are your friend Dr Brett and Mistress Morrell, though, being older, they are taking more time about it.'

'And Winnifred?'

'An interesting young woman, that. No charges have been preferred against her and she has returned home to her mother. One can hardly condone her deceiving Harry as she did, but she's young enough and handsome enough to put all this behind her and make a fresh start.' He looked across at his companion. 'You look uncertain, my friend.'

'I don't know,' said Simon, 'yet again I wonder if my participation in such an affair caused more trouble than if I'd left things alone. My meddling didn't save Lizzie Saxton and may very possibly result in young Thornton's being hanged.'

'All you did was unravel some of the story, Dr Forman,' Page comforted. 'Lizzie Saxton was treated badly, but her fooling of Cuddy Banks was deeply malicious and could have ended far worse than it did. Banks might actually have raped Phillipa Carter before Somerton arrived, convinced that what the old woman had told him was true. Fortunately Somerton saved Phillipa, but in doing so later found himself suspected of murdering her sister, since he could not prove how long he had been in the wood that night. If it hadn't been for you, he might have stood trial instead of Thornton. As for the appalling Cuddy Banks, his humiliation ensured he wouldn't rest until Lizzie Saxton was made to pay for it. Then there's Winnifred; the good Lord alone knows what might have become of her, had you not discovered her secret.

'As it is, matters have come out well for at least some of those involved. Guy Somerton will make Phillipa a good husband and she a lively and practical wife. You may even have ensured that Clarington keeps his lust for the matrimonial bed in future, though I wouldn't throw dice on it! No, Dr Forman, great wrong was done and you uncovered it, and since you have been granted a gift in that direction, I've no doubt it was intended you should.'

The two men parted amicably, Simon accepting Page's invitation to supper when he returned to Pinner for Hugh's wedding. The meeting with the schoolmaster had cheered him somewhat, and by the time he reached home some of the horrors of the morning were beginning to fade. He was greeted at the door by Anna, obviously with something to tell him.

'Mistress Allen is here to see you,' she said, with an arch look. 'I've shown her into the back parlour.'

Simon flung his cloak onto a nearby settle and strode into the room where Avisa was waiting for him. He embraced her warmly then held her at arm's length and looked at her critically. 'You wrote me you'd been sickly but I can see no sign of it,' he told her. 'You look very well indeed – glowing, in fact.'

She did truly look well. She was wearing a gown of her favourite russet shade, its bodice embroidered with pinks, which always suited her. She smiled and looked at him slyly. 'So, master physician, you cannot guess what ails me?'

He shook his head and was about to ask some pertinent question when realisation dawned. 'Of course! Sickness! Are you telling me you're with child?'

She nodded. 'At last. At long, long last.'

His mouth went dry. 'And how far forward are you?'

She smiled again. 'I would guess nearly three months, dating from the time I spent in Kent when I fled London because of the Plague.'

'So the child must be . . .'

'Yours, Simon. Though William must never know. He is, of course, delighted for we had given up all hope.' Her face became suddenly serious. 'Don't think I haven't agonised over the deception, but to tell the truth is impossible. It would destroy William, and I believe it would also destroy us. What kind of a life would we lead together, you and I, for we could never marry and I would rightly be an object of disgust: the woman from a modest home who married an elderly wealthy man then deceived him. This will have to be our secret until we go to our graves, and the true pledge of our love.'

She was right, of course. There was no other way. Later, he saw her safely over the Bridge to her home and her husband. She left him, promising to return within the next few days. This close to the shortest day, it was already getting dark as Simon walked back across the Bridge, but instead of returning to his house he went over to the wall by the watersteps and leaned his arms on it, watching the traffic of the river. It was a cold afternoon, with a hint of frost in the air, and the passengers in the wherryboats were huddled up in thick cloaks and jackets.

He turned his back on the waterfront and saw that the flag which had been flying above the Rose Theatre all afternoon to advertise that a performance was taking place, was now being hauled down; even as he watched, crowds of people made a rush for the empty wherries clustered at the bottom of the steps waiting for trade. From a tavern near by came the sound of voices raised in a popular

271

ballad. His initial euphoria that Avisa was to have his child evaporated, leaving him feeling drained and bleak.

'It's hardly unknown,' he had commented when defending Winnifred as Sir Edward Ratcliffe had pontificated over her deception of Harry Thornton. He had even said something very similar to Tom Pope only the night before. But suddenly being faced with the same dilemma was quite different. Now Master William Allen, esteemed silk merchant of the City of London, would be father to another man's child. *His* child. He was about to find a tavern in which to drink himself into oblivion when he was hailed by Tom Pope, remnants of his actor's make-up still clinging to his skin.

'Jenny says you're to come to supper,' he said firmly. 'I told her about Tyburn and she said I mustn't let you brood alone this evening.'

'That's very thoughtful of her,' replied Simon, accepting the invitation.

Tom smiled. 'Come on then, you old bachelor, let's go home where you can enjoy an evening with a proper family. It's more than time you settled down with a good wife and children of your own.'

Author's Note

THE REAL DOCTOR SIMON FORMAN

Almost the only knowledge we had of him for a long time was the note in the *National Dictionary of Biography*, written by Sir Sydney Lee in the late 1870s, which is full of inaccuracies and described him as a charlatan and a quack, a view presumably he had taken after reading of the clashes Simon Forman had over a period of years with the Royal College of Physicians. Later research, for much of which we are indebted to Dr A. L. Rowse, shows he was very far from that and indeed that he had many new ideas gleaned from the Continent which were in advance of those prevailing in the England of his day. As an example, he did not believe in wholesale blood-letting, a common practice then and for centuries afterwards, as he considered it merely weakened the patient. Nor did the fact that he practised astrology, cast horoscopes and also used them for diagnoses make him a quack; most doctors did so then, including one of the earliest respected presidents of the Royal College of Physicians.

Simon Forman was born in Quidhampton, Wiltshire, probably in 1558, the youngest of five children. His father, who worked on the land, died when he was very young, leaving the family far from well off. After going to the village Dame school, he achieved a place at the local grammar school where he was considered a bright scholar.

He was fascinated by the New Science and wanted to study medicine, and his teachers were eager that he should go to Oxford University, but, hardly surprising in her circumstances, his mother was unsympathetic towards his ambitions. The best he could manage was, when possible, to act as servant to a local parson's son who was a student at Oxford and attend some lectures, but he was not allowed to become a student himself as he had no funds and had not been offered a scholarship.

After a year he returned to Wiltshire to find work locally. He soon upset the local landowner, Giles Estcourt, as a result of which he spent nearly a year in prison. There is then a great blank after which we find him working as a medical practitioner in Salisbury (during which time he fathered an illegitimate child) before moving on to London where he set up as a qualified physician formally recognised by the University of Cambridge. He may or may not have studied in Italy, or elsewhere on the Continent.

When he first set up in practice in London he was endlessly hauled up before the College of Physicians who refused to recognise him as a doctor, even when his status was confirmed by Cambridge. They disliked his attitude, considered him an upstart who had risen from the ranks of the poor, and were the most likely source for the rumour that he was a necromancer who practised the Black Arts.

Dr Rowse dates his setting up in London as around 1593–94, and it has been suggested that on one occasion Queen Elizabeth's great Spymaster, Sir Francis Walsingham, intervened on his behalf to prevent his being sent to prison by the Royal College of Physicians. If this is indeed the case, then he must have been practising in London as early as 1590 for Walsingham died in the spring of that year.

Certainly by the early 1590s Simon Forman was living in a good house near to the Bankside (outside the jurisdiction of the City of London) with a garden in which he grew herbs and flowers for his medicines. He treated patients both at his own home and by visiting them, and he almost uniquely crossed the entire social spectrum from the publicans, actors, writers and whores of the Bankside, through the City merchants to the aristocracy and the Court. He enjoyed the theatre, leaving us the first accounts of seeing Shakespeare's plays, and Shakespeare's Bankside landlady was one of his patients as was the wife of Richard Burbage. He had a tremendous weakness for women and was candid about sex. He had a code word (*halek*) for those ladies who paid him in kind rather than in cash. He also had a brief, if stormy, affair with the strongest contender for the role of Shakespeare's Dark Lady, Emilia Lanier, née Bassano.

The long-term love of his life was, however, Avisa Allen who was married to a merchant older than she was and who also 'distilled', that is made medicines from herbs. Since he outlived her and divorce was out of the question there was no possibility of marriage. She became his mistress and their relationship continued until she died. Many years later he married Jane Baker, the daughter of a Kentish Knight. He was an expert on poisons and death, and would have been a witness in the trial of Lady Howard for the murder of Sir Thomas Overbury, but he died suddenly just before the trial, from what might well have been appendicitis.

Simon Forman, like many doctors of his age including Shakespeare's son-in-law, John Hall, kept a meticulous Casebook of his patients and their maladies, and also of the horoscopes he cast. Forman also wrote books both on medicine and astrology. While my portrayal of Simon Forman owes much to poetic licence it is clear that the original was lively, clever and energetic and never ceased to have an enquiring mind.

OTHER PEOPLE IN THIS STORY

The character of **Lizzie Saxton** is based on the real-life Elizabeth Sawyer, 'The Witch of Edmonton', who was hanged a few years later than the year in which this story is set. Pamphlets detailing her 'confession' were sold at her execution and within a relatively short time she featured in the play *The Witch of Edmonton*, attributed jointly to Dekker, Ford and Rowley. Real-life stories, especially murders, were the stuff of a genre of plays I personally think of as 'drama documentaries', one example of which is *The Yorkshire Tragedy*, which seems very much of today, wherein a husband, wrongly jealous of his wife and suffering from what we would call clinical depression, kills their three children and attempts to kill himself. Others include *Arden of Faversham* and *A Woman Killed with Kindness*.

Under torture Elizabeth Sawyer confessed she had a familiar in the shape of a black dog, and it was this same familiar that the young man who murdered his bigamous wife claimed was sent by her to force him to do the deed. Even in the consequent play it is made clear that the Justice of the Peace involved in the case is deeply sceptical about Elizabeth Sawyer's supposed powers, and indeed the writers also point the finger at the wealthy landowner who, having made a young woman in his employ pregnant, persuaded her into marrying '**Harry**' and so led to the domestic tragedy. There are few clues as to the backgrounds or personalities of anyone else involved so these are entirely fictional, and there are no clues even in the play as to the outcome of **Winnifred's** pregnancy. As it did not seem possible to recognise where in Edmonton the original events took place, I moved the action to Pinner which still has its sixteenth-century heart including the Crown Inn which is now known as the Queen's Head.

WITCHCRAFT

Compared with the atrocities committed in Europe, the English seemed almost relaxed about witchcraft, which did not even become a crime under the Common Law until 1542. There was a brief upsurge of witchhunting during the 1590s though only a handful of people (mostly women) faced the extreme penalty. Things changed somewhat when James I, who was paranoid about witches, came to the throne (he wrote a treatise on the subject himself), but executions were still in scores rather than in thousands as on the Continent. Unfortunately, Elizabeth Sawyer's was one of them. But it was all too easy for some poor, and either ugly or deformed old woman to be branded a witch and everything that went wrong locally to be attributed to her; nor was it difficult to extract a 'confession' under torture. The witchhunt, however, was real enough and some never lived to reach prison or the scaffold.

THE MORRIS DANCE

Troops of morris dancers are still very popular though the dancers in this story would never have countenanced women taking part: it was a male mystery. One source of it is said to be from the Moors of North Africa – the 'Moriscos' – though this seems open to argument. Certainly in the sixteenth century it did not only mean a set of dances but included elements also found in the old Mummers' plays such as the hobby horse and Maid Marian, and there has always been a whiff of the pagan about it. The dancers gave performances privately for the rich and also outside taverns and in the street, particularly at the great festivals. Overtones of this can still be found today in the May Day hobby-horse festivities in Padstow in Cornwall and the 'Hal-an-Tow' which makes up part of the Helston Flora.

There was also a good deal of competition between rival teams.

MARRIAGE AND THE RESPONSIBILITIES OF FATHERHOOD

While it was usual for couples to have the banns called in their own parish, or respective parishes, it was also possible to marry on a special Diocesan Licence for reasons of extreme haste, or if it was necessary for the marriage to take place during Advent when 'ordinary' marriages were not allowed by the Church. In fact, Shakespeare married on such a Licence – his wife, née Anne Hathaway, giving birth to their first child six months later. For those with property, the formal betrothal and contract of marriage was binding on both parties even before the religious ceremony, though it does not seem that matters had got that far between **Susan** and **Harry** before he married **Winnifred**. Single men were expected to marry the mother or, at the very least, support any child of a relation-ship, and those who administered parish relief did their best to see that this happened. Refusal could mean sitting in the stocks outside the church on Sunday mornings to encourage a change of mind, but if this still did not work, then the father was supposed to pay a weekly sum towards the child's support until it was at least seven. If the couple did marry, a pregnant bride caused no opprobrium; a study of this in *The Penguin Social History of 16th-Century England* gives statistics that show that one in five of all brides married in York between 1550 and 1590 were pregnant, and in a small town in Lincolnshire, one in three. If a couple married after a child's birth it was automatically legitimised.

Married men who acted in a similar way, however, came into a different category. Shakespeare's rackety daughter Judith married Thomas Quinney even though he was involved at the time in a liaison with another girl who was carrying his child. Shortly after his marriage, a case was brought against him by the girl's family and he was fined and had to stand in the church as a penitent for three Sundays dressed in a sheet and holding a candle.